ARIA

ARIA

Book 3 of The Happily Never After Series

By

HP Mallory

10 Chosen Ones:
When a pall is cast upon the land,
Despair not, mortals,
For come forth heroes ten.
One in oceans deep,
One the flame shall keep,
One a fae,
One a cheat,
One shall poison grow,
One for death,
One for chaos,
One for control,
One shall pay a magic toll.

The Little Mermaid:
In the deeps where no light pierces,
A hero lies
And rises to do battle
Blotting out the fire of the skies.

ONE
ARIA

The kraken's tentacles scythe the inky water and grip Bastion around the middle, sending him sailing a thousand feet downward, spiraling out of sight into the fathomless oblivion of the deep. The water foams, obscuring everything in my field of vision for a distressingly long moment, and the action displaces the sea enough, I can't get nearer, no matter how hard I pump my tail.

"Bastion!"

The cry falls uselessly from my lips, bubbles into the blackness to be heard by almost no one.

This can't be the end! Not the end of my dearest friend in all the world! Especially when he was protecting me...

The deep bellow of the behemoth vibrates every molecule of water for miles around. I'll be shocked if the humans above can't hear it.

Every muscle in my body burns with the effort to keep propelling myself downward, after Bastion. But there are just too many of them—too many krakens. Hopefully Aunt Opeia's spells won't lead us astray...

The krakens keep emerging in droves from the leagues-deep Rheaic Trench. They come filing out of the narrow gorge in numbers I've never seen before.

1

The rumors have to be true, then. My father must have lifted the edict that kept the grotesquerie contained, allowing them to wander free in an effort to isolate the land-dwelling kingdoms above.

The tentacle of a kraken lashes down toward me — each sucker bears down on my position, as large as boulders, as deadly to the touch as a manta's sting. I'm saved from being knocked into the abyss by a muscled arm that brackets my waist and paddles upward with surprising strength. I glance down to find the teal luster of my aunt's shimmering skin. I needn't have looked, though; I've been counting on the strength of these arms for many, many years — since my banishment from Aspamia when I was a mere girl.

"Foolish child," Aunt Opeia scolds me. "You know better! Never rush in!"

Yes, of course, I know better. I've been navigating the frigid depths for over fifteen years. Stealth and caution are the only things that keep one alive when the grotesquerie roam the black waters. But this is Bastion we're talking about. My steadfast friend. The only companion who followed me from the Aspamian reef to this remote wasteland. If he dies, I'll never forgive myself.

Opeia's face softens just a mite as she takes in my panicked expression. "Bastion's strong. He'll emerge, you'll see."

But that brief exchange is all we have time for. Because the kraken has spied us again. It's in motion, and we only escape its crushing weight and the deadly poison of its suckers by a margin of inches. The one advantage we have over the beast is speed. Krakens are fifty feet long, on average, and at least five hundred pounds. It makes their movements clumsy, and their reaction time dismal. We'd be swimming circles around this one — an unusually large specimen that's closer to sixty feet long — if we hadn't been at this for hours already.

I'm more concerned about the flocks of anglerfish swarming up toward us. The bluntnose, frilled, and goblin sharks move as quickly as any barracuda, as quick as or quicker than a merperson. The barreleye and the monkfish are terrifying and they can swim even faster after they've had a taste of merflesh, which they have. Three of Opeia's finest warriors have already lost their lives to stop the grotesquerie.

It wasn't enough.

In my periphery, I can see one of the kraken — a small one, probably an adolescent, given how stubby the tentacles are — break away from the horde and begin swimming for the surface. The glimmer of light above is like the pinprick of a distant star, wavering and far beyond my reach. If I'm spotted outside the trenches, news will get back to my father. And there will be a reckoning for it.

But I can't risk letting the kraken reach the shore. Even the smallest of kraken are able to destroy port towns and lay waste to human fleets. And that's exactly what my father wants — destruction and devastation. I've committed the last decade and a half to defying my father's will.

"I'm taking the small one," I say to Opeia, wriggling free of her arms as we come to a spinning stop yards away from the enormous beast before us.

"It can't be allowed to reach Delorood. Tell Bastion to come after me if he..."

I trail off, refusing to conclude the thought.

Bastion will live!

He has to. I can't live without my unwavering and fiercely protective friend.

There's a flinching around Opeia's eyes. She knows what I'm risking by going to the surface. She knows I'll be in danger — and it's not retribution from the krakens she's worried about. The worst thing I can fear from the grotesquerie is death. At my father's hands, however, I'll face imprisonment and torture, at the very least. Perhaps he'll set his flesh-eaters on me slowly, allowing them to devour me from the tail up. It's one of the more gruesome punishments I've seen — the victim left to propel themselves away from the devouring teeth of some hideous creature with only their human-like arms until they inevitably die either of exhaustion or their eaten to death.

Or my father, Triton, could have me raped, the way he'd done with the captured princess from the glacial southern waters, Princess Avicia. The princess was chained and used by any male who cared to, until her belly grew great with child. Then Triton killed the babe before her eyes, causing her eventual decline into madness.

Yes, my father is a monster.

And Bastion, Opeia and I are risking a lot for the humans who've traditionally hunted us. Sold us as curious sideshow attractions. Mounted our stuffed bodies on the prows of their ships like macabre war trophies. In other circumstances, Opeia would tell me not to go.

But we don't have a choice. The grotesquerie can't be allowed to prevail, they can't be allowed to populate the waters any more than they already have. We must stop them here and now.

I won't give my father his way.

Opeia must be thinking along the same lines, because she inclines her head just a fraction in that way that means she's considering something. I know she loves me, in her way. Me, her brother's eldest child, her first niece. Opeia was exiled for having an opinion that differed from the King's, just as I had been.

That's about all we have in common.

"Go, child. I will hold off the rest," she says.

She claps her hands together quickly and when she spreads them again, golden energy undulates between her palms, seething like agitated gulper eels.

I break away from her then, pumping my tail as hard as I can and slice a path upward through the dark, sailing past the spiny and blackened merfolk that abide in the deeps.

Triton has never liked them, has always shunned them for their ugliness. He banned any of them from setting tail in Aspamian territory. Until Opeia arrived, the dark mer were nomadic, constantly living in fear of the giant squids, the kraken, the sharks, and the other monstrous deep-dwellers. Opeia had given them protection with her sorcery, promised them prosperity if they followed her.

And she'd kept her promises, for the most part. It isn't her fault Triton had the gall to sever the spells that bound these monsters, the grotesquerie, to the depths.

My muscles ache and my eyes begin to burn furiously as I ascend, lagging behind the adolescent kraken by a few miles. I'm not going to reach it before it crests the waves. The color of the water shifts from black to navy, from navy to sapphire, and finally a lovely teal as the light of the moon above filters through the water, illuminating the field of open sea that drapes the gulf. At any other time, I might sing at the sight.

It's been so long since I've seen the skies and the celestial spheres that light it. Burning sunlight or placid moonlight, I don't care. Being beneath the wavering illumination is a bliss all its own.

I don't have long to enjoy it, however. To my horror, I see the kraken propelling itself ever nearer to a large and dark shape that bobs along the surface. A ship. A merchant vessel, most likely, and a prime target for Triton's new attack beasts. I have to slow the kraken, reroute its attention. Perhaps doing so will give the sailors time to abandon their ship. The kraken's eyes aren't adapted for the surface, so smaller vessels might go unnoticed.

I'm not a sorceress. Not like Aunt Opeia. My magic comes in stops and starts, and spells rarely ever turn out the way I plan them. She's tried to teach me, but there's only one spell I'm truly good at—and now I rely on that exact spell.

Drawing in as much air as I can through my gills, I puff up like a blowfish until the magic thrums like a drumbeat in my chest. Then, I release it in a protracted wail of sound.

The water around us vibrates, the trailing bubbles left in the kraken's wake jumping in time to the sound. As I hoped, my magic stops the kraken dead in the water for a second as the noise scrambles conscious thought. Siren's song is a potent weapon when wielded competently, and a ticket to instant madness if done incorrectly.

The kraken immediately pauses and then just simply floats there, immobile from the tones of my song, just as I intended. But, mere seconds later, the kraken shakes off my song as I blink at it in shock. Siren's song should have immobilized it for at least eight or so minutes—at the very least! Enough time for me to alert the men in the ship. But how is it moving now? After only a few seconds…

I swim as close as I dare while its enormous squid-like head begins to breach the surface, sending churning foam across the tops of the waves. It's rising half a mile away from the ship.

I surface closer to the side of the ship, noting its size and beautiful construction. When my tailfin brushes the sealed wooden siding, a jolt runs up my spine and tingles at the base of my neck.

Sorcery.

The ship has been enchanted. Heavily enchanted, judging by my body's reaction—my skin hasn't buzzed so much since I had the misfortune to fall into a deep cave network teeming with electric eels.

My body recoils on principle, though curiosity niggles in the back of my mind. Human magic is rare, most practitioners having been driven from their homes by their foolish rulers many moons ago. This enchantment must be by fae design. But the last Opeia had heard, Septimus of the Unseelie court had either banished or killed most of the fae. So who enchanted this vessel?

Again, I don't have much time to ponder the mystery. The kraken is almost wholly above water now. To my relief, I see a man leaning over the side of the ship, helping mortals into small dinghies. The boats should escape the kraken's notice. I hope so anyway.

But it's not the dinghies that keep my attention for long.

No, I can't stop staring at the captain.

I'm fascinated by his face, which is quite clear in the moonlight. I have no concept of what humans consider beautiful—for all I know, he's as homely as they come. But to me? He's fascinating. An exotic beauty, skin as tan as I've ever seen on a human. Most of them look pale, almost sickly, with their veins standing out like stringy blue lines underneath their skin. And the skin itself usually appears too thin, like it might tear open such as kelp does under the slightest pressure.

But not this man. His skin is tanned almost brown, like he's been kissed by Sol himself. He radiates good health. His long, dark hair is pushed into a tail at the nape of his neck, beneath one of those ridiculous floppy things humans wear on their heads. He's got scrubby growth on his chin and cheeks, something I've never seen on a merman. Is it some sort of moss?

8

Algae? A growth he tolerates? I can't imagine it's comfortable.

His upper body reminds me of Bastion's. Large biceps that appear through a fairly thin covering, which is rolled up around his arms. *Clothing*, I believe it's called? His chest is broad and his shoulders broader. His neck reveals thick, corded muscle and I can see the swell of his large thighs through the covering of fabric he wears above them. He is strong, capable.

I can't see his eyes or read his expression, but it must be something to behold. The white-haired youth in the boat looks stricken when the man casually draws a long blade and severs the ties that keep the boats tethered to the ship. The boat falls, without fanfare, into the water close to me. There is another boat soon to follow.

None of the occupants take note of me when I paddle nearer, trying to get a better look at the man. I notice, with interest, that the captain doesn't find his place within the row boats, but he cuts the ropes that hold them to the side of the ship and then gives the inhabitants a brief wave as they clearly reject his decision, calling out to him.

The captain of the ship is clearly sacrificing himself. Staying to steer the enchanted ship away from the crew he's released into the ocean. And the kraken continues to follow the ship, paying no attention to the small dinghies that float away.

Then, to my astonishment, the ship begins to lift from the water, trailing drizzles of icy spray from its sides as it takes to the air. At first I wonder if the kraken has somehow taken ahold of it? Maybe it's airborne owing to the fact that the Kraken's tentacles have held it aloft? But, no, the ship appears to be lifting of its own accord—no doubt owing to the fae magic surrounding it. The magical sigils shine as the magic ripples over the wood.

I spy a name etched into the craft and I squint at it, trying to make out the meaning.

The *Jolly Roger*. Is it perhaps named for the captain? Could his name be Roger?

The ship rises rapidly from the sea, ascending like a gull, with only half the sound. It spins agilely in the air to face the rising kraken. The shape of the man aboard is hard to make out now. I can really only see a black speck moving against the moon. Then, one of the knobbly black growths that juts from the side of the boat belches out a tongue of flame, sending a projectile toward the kraken with thunderous sound.

The speeding black thing hits its mark, burrowing deep into the creature's large eye and utterly destroying its orbital socket.

The kraken lets out an unearthly scream that vibrates the water all around me. I don't want to feel bad for the beast, but I do. There are more painless ways to finish them.

The kraken lashes one long tentacle into the air, aiming as well as it can with its injury and already limited eyesight. It's lucky to even be alive. The tentacle hooks the ship in the middle and drags it seaward again at an astonishing speed. The man aboard doesn't even have time to move before the kraken brings the entire vessel crashing down against the waves.

The ship breaks apart with a sound like cracking ice and a spray of multi-colored sparks as the enchantments break. The man is hurled like a stone from the deck and lands in the water. He's far from the boats he released earlier. In fact, I can no longer see them and I assume the inhabitants must have begun rowing for the shore.

My thoughts return to the captain. Now stranded in the ocean, he will certainly perish. If the kraken doesn't find him first, some other unsavory sea creature will. Or perhaps it will be the cold that takes him first.

Something has to be done for him. Even if the air up here is comparatively warm, he won't be able to maintain his warm, human temperature when soaked to the skin. Worse, if the blow has rendered him unconscious, he'll drown long before the cold takes him.

I dive below again, narrowly dodging bits of debris as I go. The enchantments on the ship continue to flicker faintly, like the glow of an angler, before they die out completely, leaving only the moon to guide my way.

I reach the man just in time, but then one of the poisoned tentacles of the kraken comes down beside him, thrusting him away from me. While the tentacle doesn't land on him, it creates a huge wave and a vacuum beneath that pulls the man under. I dive beneath the wave and watch as the man dives downward. It's then that I realize his eyes are closed, his head askew and flopping with the current of the water as his long hair furls like seagrass. Bubbles stream from his nose, expelling the last of his precious air.

We're too deep. He won't make it to the surface.

There's only one thing I can think to do, though it will no doubt annoy Opeia and Bastion. I propel myself downward as fast as I can until I reach out and grip the man around the arm, pulling him to me. Then, leaning forward, I press my lips very gently to his throat. I trace my tongue along the point where his blood pulses weakly beneath his skin, and expel the barest hint of my magic. My power hums warm and ready beneath my lips, and when I draw away, there's a perfect imprint of my lips on his neck.

The beginnings of a mate mark, a mate mark that will stop the human from drowning.

My heart jumps wildly at the implication of what I've done, but I don't have time to examine my feelings too closely. I scoop him up and into my arms and pump my tail as fast as I can, angling north toward Delorood, leaving the kraken behind to be dealt with later.

For now, there's a sailor to save.

TWO
ARIA

Cassio Island is a dot rising above an otherwise unblemished stretch of sea — a tiny beauty mark on the landscape.

At high tide, the island is barely more than a sandbar with sparse vegetation, just a smattering of palms hunched against the wind. Between the palms are a few wooden shacks that, quite frankly, I'm surprised are still here. Humans built them many years ago and owing to the elements, I never imagined they would last as long as they have.

The palms have been kicked up into a hearty gale now that the kraken's flailing has beaten the four winds. Eurus, the unlucky east wind, has obviously been riled, and rain will come soon to pelt the place into submission. I need to get the human inside one of the rundown shacks that line Cassio's shore before that happens.

Easier said than done.

Neither half-form I possess — fish nor bird — is well suited to this place. My talons would cut the poor man to ribbons, and the doorways of the shacks are too narrow to allow my wings to pass easily. While my tail is awkward, it's the only way I can ensure to reach the island and deliver the man to safety. I'm afraid jostling him might lead to worse injury. Still, what other choice do I have?

Maneuvering him into a half-embrace, I wriggle him away from the tide that licks at his toes. I seat him on my lap and face away as I feel the rear of my tail meet the sand. The cresting waves curl around us as I balance him on my lap and use my hands to pull myself backwards and up the embankment of sand. My hands claw through the sand, barely finding purchase as I drag us forward inch by awkward inch. And it is indeed awkward. More so, because every time he moves in my lap, one of his booted feet strokes along the glans of my tail. It's erotic in the extreme. New and intense sensations climb up my body. My nipples harden to sharp little peaks and slickness coats me in preparation.

It's my own fault, really. The mate mark primes my body for copulation, though I can't ever do such a thing with this human. Wrong parts, for one. And his seed could never fertilize my eggs. I'm not sure how the humans copulate, but it's probably nothing like our ways.

Still, everything in me throbs with need, even as I drag him through the narrow entrance to the corrugated tin shed nearest the shore. The shack smells strongly of fish and brine. A soft coating of moss drapes the walls, now that the fisherman is no longer in residence. Probably scared away by the increasing number of attacks lately.

There's a rectangular object in the middle of a pile of refuse that appears large enough on which to lay the man. When I touch it, I find it covered in a soft heap of something—perhaps collected palm fronds and coconut fibers? I have to clear off buckets, nets, and wickedly curved implements that make me shudder when I imagine them piercing my scales. Ignoring the beastly implements, I reach the soft object below. I believe the humans would call it a bed?

I pull the man to the bed and lay him down gently. It's then that I notice his face. It's striking—his jaw is quite defined and square and his nose is almost large but masculine. His pitch black eyebrows are heavy and match the shade of his hair and the growth of dark algae on his face. He wears something shiny and hooped in his ears and when I tug on the strange baubles, I find them joined to his earlobes. His eyelids are closed and I attempt to pry them apart. But when I do, only the whites of his eyes meet me. He looks quite unappealing without eyeballs so I quickly close his eyelids.

My eyes move down to his mouth. His lips are quite full for a man and they are a pretty pinkish color. I pull the top lip up and find his teeth are large, white and surprisingly straight.

It's then that I encounter another problem. The man's clothing is sodden, soaked to his skin. Protected by the elements as he is now, the wetness of his clothing isn't likely to kill him, but it might make him ill. Human health is fragile, or so Opeia tells me. She used to be our healer, so I trust her words.

I'm momentarily stymied by the complexity of his garb. I've never quite understood clothing and the clothing he wears appears quite elaborate.

I'm not quite certain when he managed to don his coat, when previously I'd only seen him in a thin layer that covered his chest and stomach but he wears a coat now. My fingers tremble on the brass fastenings, and it's an effort to slide the heavy thing down his arms. Maybe because his arms are corded with muscle, crisscrossed with scars beneath the see-through fabric of his shirt. There's also an obscene number of fastenings on the coat, this time done in mother-of-pearl, harvested from a clam. My respect for the sailor dims a little. So much cruelty to create something so silly and useless.

But eventually, I'm able to remove his coat. The thin fabric beneath is next and I find that a bit easier to peel off his body. There's more of that strange algae growth on his chest. Dark, springy curls of it smatter his pectorals and trail down, in a narrowing line, to his waist. I run my fingers through it curiously. It has a different texture than the stuff on his head and face. Wiry and coarse, even while wet.

He stirs a little, mouth parting to let out a soft moan. My body throbs still harder with need. Absurd as it is, I want him to touch me. Ease some of the hunger with his long fingers.

Oh. That's strange. One of his hands appears normal, calloused and human. The other, though, is anything but. It gleams in the low light, obviously fashioned of metal and it's shaped like a hook. I'll need to clean it before I go, lest it rust.

The fitted clothing that covers his legs and waist is the hardest thing of all to remove. The fabric is plastered to him like a second skin. I have to tug and wrestle with it, but the fabric finally loses the battle and slides off in a wet heap of fabric. And when it's off,

I find myself transfixed by the odd shape that's snuggled between his strong thighs.

It's long, slightly curved, and veined, quite round and thick in its circumference. At the base, where it meets the rest of his body, there's still more of that dark, wiry… algae. I run my fingers through it and find it even coarser than the algae on his chest.

But, it's the strange cylindrical anomaly that hangs from his body that keeps my attention. I wonder if somehow an innkeeper fish has attached itself to him for the thing looks quite tubular and… perhaps it's an overlarge worm? Where the wiry hair grows from its base, there are two sacs. The worm is half-engorged, ruddy with blood. I brush the mushroom-like tip of it, wondering if the thing is alive or dead. It's velvety, soft to the touch. I pick it up and try to separate it from his body but the worm-fish doesn't appear to want to go. When I push apart the dark algae, I realize the strange thing is attached to him! It must be some sort of growth or perhaps he's playing host to a parasite? I want to explore it more, but I have the sense doing so wouldn't be welcome.

If he wakes and discovers I'm aware of his parasite, he might be quite embarrassed.

The human makes another soft sound. I need to leave this place before he sees me. Sailors don't care for sirens. My sisters prey almost exclusively on these humans, using their enchanting voices to enthrall their minds and lead them to watery graves.

I shuffle back to the water's edge, feeling the heat of the sand as it burns my tail. I sigh gratefully when I've submerged in the ocean once again. The cool water is a shock to my system, and my glans shies away from the temperature. The urge to toy with my flesh recedes.

I've done what I can for the brave sailor. If possible, I will come to him again by night and give him kelp, chlorella, or spirulina to eat, and I'll direct him to the small pool of rainwater that he can drink.

Until then, I have to make myself scarce. I am tempting the gods' wrath by saving him, as I have. Safety awaits me in Opeia's kingdom and I need to return as quickly as I can. I risk death by being spotted in Triton's waters.

So I swim into the depths and then dive down, shoving thoughts of the sailor's strange appendage away. He's no longer my concern and I hope that overlong parasite nestled between his thighs won't kill him.

**

I've almost reached the trench when a spiny dart whizzes by my ear.

I twist in mid-stroke, my heart lurching against my ribs as the dart narrowly misses me, clattering harmlessly off the rock ledge of the trench. Toxopneuste darts, coated with the most virulent poison available. One brush from those spines and I'd die, choking on my own vomit.

Desperately, I crane my neck to spot my attackers, and spy them a league away, readying another volley. I recognize three of the soldiers in the lead. Sen is easily the largest man in Aspamia, aside from my father. Wide shoulders, rippling with muscle that makes Bastion or the unknown sailor look puny in comparison. Broad chest, dusky nipples showing against the white-gray of his skin. I've seen him hurl a Tiger Shark a mile away, winding up and tossing it like it was a game of ball. It hadn't returned to fight him.

Sen's thick, muscular tail pounds the water as he closes in on me. His glans is showing, obviously aroused at the thought of hunting me. He can probably smell my desire, leftover from when I touched the human.

I was once promised to Sen, before my banishment from my father's kingdom. The few times we've crossed paths since, he's attempted to mate me forcefully. Triton has no doubt promised him the chance to rape me if I'm captured. Perhaps Sen means to copulate with my dead body once the darts have finished me? I hope never to find out.

He's flanked by Kendosk and Cei, his ever-loyal lieutenants, who are equally aroused. Has Sen offered them a turn, as well?

But it's the line of women behind them, bearing the dart guns, that punch me in the chest with sorrow. My sisters: Piper, Viola, Cadence, Sonata, and Melody. Each wears an identical expression of distaste. I've long known Piper hates me. But the others? Has Triton turned them all against me? It would appear so.

My father's second wife, Andromeda, heads their line. She's grinning, relishing the chance to end me. She started out life as my father's concubine, gifted as a slave to him by another kingdom. She likely sees this situation now as a chance to eliminate Triton's only trueborn heir. My half-sisters are her brood, and they will become my father's successors, should I die.

"Arianwen," Sen croons, stroking his glans with apparent delight. The large rounded nub pulses grotesquely. If he catches me, he'll push it against my slit until I open and then he'll rub against me until he comes, spewing seed inside to coat my eggs. I shudder and feel the need to be violently sick. I'd rather be dead than allow his glans to touch me.

"Surrender now, my sweet," he continues. "Your father promises leniency if you come quietly. You need only be chained to my bed until Morningstar rises. And Morningstar will be along soon, I'm sure. The seals are already breaking."

I gape at them. Gods above, I'd known those seals were a bad idea! I'd told my father as much, when the devil, Morningstar, had been packed away into the nether realms. Evil can't be contained by something as corrupt as blood magic. The sentiment had gotten me banished.

Sen grins. "Yes, I like that. Keep your mouth open, love. I'd love to feel that little pink tongue on my glans."

"I'd rather feel a fishhook in my cheek than suck your glans," I spit back at him, enraged and disgusted. "You revolt me."

This scuppers my plans. There's no way to return to the sailor now, not if my sisters and their guard know I've emerged from the trenches. Worry clenches in my gut. Cassio Island is not far from Delorood. But what chance does the sailor have of making it to shore with the adolescent kraken prowling the water? And without a boat or ship? Even if, by some miracle, he avoids the kraken, there's still my father's guard to worry about. I can't leave the poor man to starve to death on the island, even if he's already dying from that tumorous growth or parasite I spotted between his thighs. Leaving him to die is… unjust.

I have to escape and consult Opeia. Which means I have to evade Sen, who's nearly on me now. A little closer and I can…

I suck in air, let the power build, and then let out another wail. Siren's song rarely works on other merfolk, but I know Sen is vulnerable to mine. Sure enough, he halts, shuddering from head to tail when the sound scrambles his thoughts. I dive, counting on Andromeda not to shoot me through Sen's back. She'd receive an earful from my father if she killed his favorite bruiser.

I descend as quickly as my aching body will allow. Cold and dark embrace me and, for once, I'm grateful to retreat from the light. The depths are safety. Bleak as they may be, they're home.

There's no sign of the grotesquerie when I finally reach the proper depth. Opeia's spells must be working, then. The grid of yellow magic lasts only a matter of days, especially now that she's had to spread the grid wider and wider to contain more of the beasts. I swear they're spawning at an accelerated pace. Perhaps something to do with the breakdown of the seals. Morningstar's presence fuels the darkness within all things.

Opeia is waiting for me when I arrive, flanked by Bastion. Relief washes through me, a cleansing tide that erases most of my guilt. Both are battered, but they're alive. It's more than I expect, most days.

Their expressions are grim, though, even as they move to embrace me. Bastion stiffens as he gets a whiff of my scent.

"Aria…" he starts, eyeing me suspiciously.

"Sen was waiting. He tried to…"

I let my voice trail off, hoping he'll buy the lie that Sen tried to force my pleasure. Bastion is not my mate, but he could be. He's not the worst choice I have — golden haired, with lovely azure markings that dot his brow ridge, cheekbones, and appear as freckles across his nose. I wish my own markings were so pleasing. But sage is a bland color. I'm perhaps the least attractive of Triton's daughters. And Bastion has always been known as one of the most attractive mermen, that was before he was labeled a renegade and an enemy to my father's court.

Bastion nods, accepting my explanation without question. He scowls. "I'm going to cut off Sen's glans and feed it to him!"

I'm not sure which I like more — the words, or the lilting baritone of his voice.

"No time for that," Opeia interjects. "Come, child. We must counsel. Something has to change, and drastically. And I think I have just the plan."

Bastion and I exchange a glance, probably thinking the same thing.

Opeia's grand plans always result in trouble, which we already have in spades. Whatever she's scheming, I don't particularly want to be part of it, even if I love my auntie beyond the bounds of rationality.

But we've essentially been backed into a corner and we have little options left to us.

Bastion shrugs. I sigh.

Then, we follow in her wake.

THREE
ARIA

Opeia's home isn't palatial, like the one I grew up in, but it's cozy and makes up for the lack of space with charm.

The network of caves stretches for miles, heated by an underwater volcano that lies smoldering and mostly tame. A layer of bioluminescent algae carpets the floor, gently pulsing blue and green. A dozen of Opeia's scrying orbs litter stone shelves, providing further illumination. She has a horde of human treasures here, salvaged from sunken ships. She particularly values the gilt-backed chair she retrieved from the wreckage of a royal envoy's vessel. She lounges on it now, violet tail draping over one side as she rests her back against the other arm and regards us both with interest.

Bastion and I sit tensed on a stone shelf across from her, waiting. Bastion sits close to me and I relish his strength and friendship. Without him, I don't know what I'd do...

"We lost twenty-six soldiers today," Opeia says, voice tight and pained.

The news draws a gasp from me, and involuntary tremors rack my body. Twenty-six? That was over half our fighting force! We were too few in number already. How will we be able to face the rest of the grotesquerie when it inevitably surfaces again? Opeia's spells can't contain them for long. "How?" I ask as my stomach falls.

She nods. "When the leviathan surfaced, it snapped them all up in its jaws and ground them between its teeth before anyone knew what had happened."

Bastion's eyes are downcast, his face a rictus of sorrow. He knew more of the dead than I did. As a general, he was trusted to lead them — they were his men. And he'd been elsewhere when they died. I reach out a hand to him, trying to offer him some comfort, but he draws it back, shaking his head.

"Don't, Aria," he mumbles.

"Bastion?" I ask, surprised he won't let me touch him. Usually he loves my touch.

But he shakes his head. "I'm disgusted with myself already. I don't want your pity on top of it."

I let my hand drop, oddly hurt by the rebuff. There's little Bastion and I don't share. But he's been cold lately, and I can't fathom why.

My throat closes around a keening sound. What are we going to do? For ten years, this has been my only home. The thought of seeing it destroyed threatens to break me.

No. Never!

I refuse to let Triton steal this home away from me and from Bastion and Opeia! My father's already stolen so much from us as it is.

Opeia continues, in tune with my thoughts.

"We need help. I've got enough magic left in me to hold the grotesquerie off for perhaps another month before I'll need to rejuvenate. And in that time, something has to change. That's why I'd like to send you both to the surface."

I blink at her in surprise.

"What?" Bastion starts.

I nod, seconding his shock. This was the last thing I expected to hear! "The surface? Auntie, you know that's a death sentence?"

"We most likely would not survive the surface," Bastion says in agreement.

"You know Andromeda and her guards are waiting for us to do something just like that!" I continue, shaking my head because I'm amazed she would even consider it, let alone voice it. "It's too dangerous!"

Opeia slams a fist against the arm of her chair. "It's too dangerous to stay here, child."

"I understand it's dangerous here," I argue. "But up there... it's suicide!"

She shakes her head. "Listen to me. I have a plan."

I fall silent, grimacing. I hate being treated like an errant child. Opeia does it so rarely that it's easy to forget she's been more of a mother to me than Andromeda ever was, even when Andromeda was playing simpering caretaker. It was probably a relief for her to drop the act when I was banished.

Opeia's expression softens, her translucent hair fanning lazily around her head. It's tinted lightly blue, the light of the algae floor reflecting back up to her, giving her a royal appearance. "That was rude," she says with a little smile aimed in my direction. "I'm sorry, Aria."

"It's okay," I say with a smile. Then my attention returns to the problem at hand. "Why are we going to the surface, Auntie?"

A small smile graces her full mouth. "Always straight and to the point. I love that about you, dear."

"Opeia?" Bastion says, clearly trying to keep her on topic.

"Yes, I intend to send you to the surface," she says. "And I'm fully aware it sounds ludicrous and I'm aware it might appear to be a suicide mission. But, the truth of the matter is, if you stay here, it's simply a matter of time until your father's forces come for us. And when that happens, we will all be killed. We've lost too many of our soldiers and our numbers are too small. We need aid. Combatting the grotesquerie is a fruitless effort at this point, unless we have more people to back us. To that end, I want you to approach the King of Delorood. Make a deal with him."

"A deal?" I ask. I know nothing of the King of Delorood.

She nods. "If he sends worthy warriors to help us stage a coup against Triton, we can guarantee him safe tides."

Once again, I'm left blinking at her in shock. Of all the things I expected to fly out of her mouth... Has she lost her mind?

"They're mortal, Auntie," I say, frowning. She does realize the king and his soldiers are human? "And they're land bound. They can't help us with our battle beneath the waves. They'd all drown."

"The Kingdom of Delorood is more advanced than the rest of Fantasia," Opeia insists, her lips tight. "They have aquatic suits and artificial lungs which means they would be equipped to fight alongside us, beneath the water."

"But they're human," I return to my original point. "And humans hate our kind."

"Just as we hate them," Bastion adds. I can tell by his expression that he's angry and doesn't agree with Opeia's plan but he's too polite to say so.

"I want you to at least petition the king," Opeia continues. "If such fails, all we've lost is a little time. If you succeed, though, the benefits to us are vast. If we have the benefit of the king's men backing us, that means our position will be incredibly bolstered and we would actually be given the opportunity to throw your father off the throne." She pauses. "This is the only way we have of seeing someone new take Triton's throne."

"You," I say quickly. "You should take his throne."

Bastion nods.

The throne should have been Opeia's by birthright. She's older than my father by over a decade. But Poseidon hadn't wanted a woman on the throne. An inevitability at this point, because Triton's fucked Andromeda until her tail chaffed for years and still she's only produced daughters.

Opeia's smile is weary. "No. I'm needed here. It has to be you, Aria."

But I don't want it—I don't want the throne. And she knows that. I've seen the corruption of absolute power. I don't trust myself not to become drunk with it, just like my father. I don't want to rule the seven seas. I hate the thought.

Bastion sighs, scoots closer to me, and shoves his hand into mine, squeezing gently. He misinterprets the anguish on my face.

"I'm here for you, Princess. However it turns out. I'm here for you."

He's always been there for me so this isn't a surprise. I just wish I had the same faith in myself that he does. Bastion has always been consummately loyal, even when I don't deserve it.

"It will be difficult for both of you on land," Opeia warns. "Human forms are awkward, but you'll need legs to navigate and to fit in." She faces me then and worry seeps into her features. "Things may be... requested of you, Aria."

"Things?" I repeat.

She nods. "From the King. The sorts of things Sen wishes of you. It's how humans often seal alliances. If you aren't willing..."

"I'll do it," I say softly.

What choice do I have? Taking Triton on now is suicide. And if he doesn't kill us, the grotesquerie will finish us off soon enough. We're running out of options. If I must lay my body on the line, so be it.

Bastion's hand slides out of mine. His eyes, blue as cobalt, seem to ice over. His expression twists once before going completely blank. I can't understand why, but I sense I'm being rebuffed. The rejection stings all the more in light of what we're facing. I can't do this alone. I need him with me, supporting me the way he always has.

"So," I say, clearing my throat as I face my aunt again. I can't focus on Bastion's changing moods. Not when the future facing us is as bleak as it is. "How will this work?"

"I will bespell you both," Opeia explains. "When you emerge from the water, the transformation will begin. After that, you have precisely two weeks before you need to return to the water or your legs will return to tails."

"Two weeks?" I say, shaking my head. "That's not nearly enough time!"

She nods. "I know it seems rushed but I can't conceivably stretch the spell any longer and keep the grotesquerie in check at the same time."

Bastion's voice comes out terse when he finally speaks. He's been rather laconic through the discussion. "So, what's the plan to get us to the surface, Opeia?" His lips are tight and his posture is rigid. I don't understand why he appears irritated. Have I done something? Said something?

My aunt grins. And then she explains. I feel my heart drop down to my stomach and Bastion looks like he wants to throw up.

"You're insane," I say as Bastion merely nods beside me.

"I know," she says with a delighted laugh. "Now, let's get you going."

***

I have to agree with my previous thought. This is insane.

We're poised above one of the cracks that lead to the fathomless parts of the deep. The part that usually spills forth monsters. The part that is currently trying to disgorge yet another kraken.

Aunt Opeia lifts a small section of the spell to allow one through. This one is barely out of its infancy, smaller than the one that attacked the ship that bore the name *Jolly Roger*. I normally wouldn't be afraid to face it, especially because we're counting on the kraken to shock and frighten Andromeda's brood long enough to allow us pass... except, Opeia's plan is so much worse!

"I can't believe she wants us to ride it," Bastion mutters, shaking his head in bewilderment. "Even kraken babies are deadly. If I didn't know better, I'd say she was trying to get us killed."

"But you do know better," I answer.

He nods. "But I do know better."

The red luminescence that edges the kraken's tentacles and suckers is meant to draw in prey. Now the glow just looks like a death omen as the thing finally wriggles free of the spell. As promised, Opeia's magic snaps the crack shut after this last kraken escapes, preventing anything else from emerging.

Thank the gods.

The kraken's sense of smell is fantastic, and I expect it to come hurtling at us. But Opeia's cloaking spell is too thorough to allow for that.

"Get ready," I advise Bastion tersely, hoping my voice doesn't betray my screaming panic. This had better work...

The kraken passes by, tentacles trailing in a gentle locomotion, unhurried as it pulses its way toward the surface. I take a deep breath, reach out, and anchor myself against its squid-like head. Bastion attaches himself on the other side. The tentacles would be easier for us to keep hold of, but one brush against the poisonous suckers could be fatal. Better not to risk it. Besides, the kraken's skin gives easily beneath the pressure of our fingers, allowing us to hold on. It's intensely warm for a creature so used to the depths.

It would be pathetically easy to kill this thing, if I had a mind to do such a thing. A spear to the eye, driving fast and hard into its brain, and it would crumple to the ocean floor like a flimsy bag. But I won't. Opeia's plan is the only one we have to reach the surface unmolested. The enchantment allows us to appear as innocent barnacles attached to the thing's skin. It'll ignore us, for the most part.

But it won't ignore the merfolk waiting above the trench, hoping for me to reemerge. They scatter quickly with panicked shouts and curses. Sen has to pull Piper out of the way before she's crushed in the grip of the baby kraken's tentacles. They disperse, but not quite fast enough. Kendosk is snatched mid-stroke and dragged screaming toward the underside of the kraken, where its mouth lies.

The scream cuts off abruptly and is followed by a series of horrific snapping and slurping sounds as the beast devours its meal. Only a hand escapes consumption, floating languidly toward the surface with the fingers splayed open, caught in that last moment of agony.

I shudder. Even if Kendosk was despicable, he didn't deserve such an ignoble end.

Sen and the others are woefully underprepared to deal with the sea monsters, after so many long years of not facing them. Their spears and darts do little against the kraken. And so we ascend, higher and higher, toward the wavering light of the surface.

Hours have passed. The sun is shining weakly through the water, casting brilliant beams down on us. Even in our grim hour, I can still find some joy in that.

If Opeia's plan works, I may never have to descend to the dark again. Wouldn't it be glorious to live in a world awash with light—to never have to worry about my father and his evil plans again...

We release our grip on the kraken as it surfaces and then we swim away from it as quickly as possible, going in opposite directions just in case it picks up the scent of our trail. The baby kraken can't follow both of us. We agree to meet near the tide pools on Cassio Island.

***

I hesitate for the briefest of moments when I approach the island. The pools are on the opposite end of the island from the fisherman's shack. I feel the need to stop and check on the captain of the ship—just to make sure he's still alive.

It will only be a brief delay. Bastion will forgive me, right?

I change direction, gliding instead for the north end of the island.

33

Time to check on my sailor.

FOUR
HOOK

My head aches.

My mouth tastes like I've licked a Beluga's asshole, and the inside feels like gritty rock when I run my tongue over my teeth.

I must have swallowed saltwater after...

I sit upright, realizing seconds too late, doing so is a bad idea. Pressure and immense pain harpoon the side of my head. Black spots dance a reel before my eyes, and dizziness threatens to drag me down to the mattress again. I'm more fucked up than I first assumed. I must have drunk in more than just the saltwater. Perhaps a little bit of that sea bugger's venom has gotten into me, too.

By sheer, unadulterated stubbornness, I manage to keep myself upright, digging the fingers of my good hand into the windowsill nearby for support. I squeeze my eyes shut, count to ten, and take deep breaths, working to swallow. The sides of my throat rub together like sandpaper. Water will help clear the worst of the aches, if I can find any. A tricky proposition, when surrounded by the sea. I don't know which of the small islands near Delorood I've washed up on.

"You ought to be careful," warns a softly lilting voice from the corner of wherever the fuck I am. "Move too quickly and you'll be sick."

The voice is quiet and lovely, but not familiar. Not Kassidy's. That brassy lass would never be so softly spoken.

My eyes wheel, looking for the source. Fuck, I've been so discombobulated, I haven't even considered the fact someone might be here with me.

Then, I see her. At first glance, she almost blends in with the metal walls of the fisherman's shack I find myself in. But as I blink the film and black spots from my eyes, I see she's a different shade than the rusty tin siding. Her opal skin has a soft, almost pearlescent glow, like a betta fish. And her hair… when she moves, it ripples, changing colors as I view it. It's utterly breathtaking all on its own.

But that's not what has my mouth hanging in the sea breeze. When she steps into the light filtering through one of the many holes in the shack, I see her full silhouette.

She's completely naked and she's goddamn beautiful, in an alien, ethereal sort of way.

Because there's no doubt in my mind — she s not human. No human has eyes that large and that shape. The lashes are thick and brush her cheekbones when she glances down sheepishly at her feet. Those cheekbones. Intricate patterns in sage green sweep from the outer corner of each eye and drop down to dust along her cheeks, moving inward and stopping shy of her pert little nose. She has a lovely rosebud mouth, just full enough that a man might imagine what it's like to kiss those lips.

Like I am now.

And her hair... It seems translucent, reflecting the color of the light around her. Now, it's the palest blue, the shade of the sky outside.

I lose the battle with my good conscience and let my eyes sweep over the rest of her. Every. Bare. Inch. She's completely starkers.

She's lean and well-muscled, like one of the lasses back home in Neverland. Ah Neverland…

Home has never been a kind place, and does not produce kind people. No rest or repose for any of us. My first lovely lass had been cut from similar cloth. If, in fact, this lass hails from such a rough place.

She's got scars that crisscross her shoulders and trail down her back. She's seen battle. I'm not certain why but this realization surprises me. Perhaps it's owing to the fact that she's as strikingly lovely as she is.

Her breasts are bare, nipples pointing forward, the taut peaks absolutely mouthwatering. I want to feel the skin beneath my tongue. Or maybe I'd rather be fixed between those pale, sinuous legs. The vee between her thighs is bare and her quim glints prettily. She touches it with a frown, bringing her glistening juices to the light as she examines them curiously. My cock goes rigid, straining toward her.

I finally snap myself from the stupor for long enough to put the pieces together and I inch away from her a little.

Siren. A fucking siren.

I'm not sure how she's managed to grow legs, but it's the only manner of creature she can possibly be. Her skin reminds me of a fish because she *is* part fish.

She seems unabashed by her nudity, because she's probably never worn clothes in her life. Aye, she's probably never been in possession of a quim, in all likelihood.

I clear my throat with difficulty. It hurts like bloody fuck to do so.

"Who are ye?"

She tilts her head a fraction, popping those glistening fingers in her mouth curiously. She screws her face up a little at the taste.

"Call me Aria," she says, speaking again in that lilting voice. It's so damn pleasant.

I bet she's drowned a thousand sailors like me with that voice. No doubt I'd be tempted to jump off the side of the *Jolly Roger* for this lass if she'd come at me with desire flashing in her eyes, her tits just visible above the foaming waves and her song rippling through the air.

She looks at me pointedly. "Who are you?"

"I'm Hook."

Her lips purse and her brows pucker. The look of childlike confusion is pretty damn arresting. I try to remind myself she's dangerous — even as she continues to touch her quim as if she wonders why it's wet or, even perhaps, what the bloody thing is.

"Did ye rescue me?" I ask.

She nods and I find this information of interest. What the bloody hell would she have rescued me for? Most her kind desire nothing more than to watch sailors take their last breath of ocean water as they die a cold and miserable death.

No telling what she's after by bringing me here.

"You speak with a strange accent," she says. "I've never heard it before."

I nod. Not many people outside of Neverland have. "Aye, 'tis a piratin' accent, lass," I explain.

"Is Hook a common name among your people?"

I chuckle humorlessly. "Depends on what ye mean. 'Round Delorood, nae. But there are stranger names in the land from which I hail."

My brother, Quinn, ran with a group of men with names like Riddle, Nibbles, and Mayhaps. We'd been born Theoden and Quinn Teach. But Neverland was and is about the name you earn, not the one you were given.

"And where is this land?" she asks.

"I hail from the clan o' the Scottish in the Neverland island o' Alba."

She stoops, retrieving something from her feet. It looks like a conch shell. She shuffles closer, as unsure as a colt on her new legs, and offers me the shell when she's near enough.

"Water," she explains. "From the pools on the island. My aunt says the sea is poisonous to humans. Drink."

I take the shell from her, tipping it back to dribble the sweet liquid into my mouth.

"Why do ye care if the sea is poisonous to humans," I start.

"I won't have you die after I risked so much to rescue you."

Questions begin to spin in my mind again. Why rescue me? It runs contrary to a siren's nature, doesn't it? And what is she risking by doing so? Is there some unspoken rule that dictates merpeople must kill humans, and she's defying it?

"I'm obliged to ye, lass," I say with a nod. She returns it.

I drink the water down in a few greedy swallows and already, I want more. Aria smiles and takes the conch from me, dipping it dutifully into a tin bucket at the foot of the bed before she offers it to me again. The next few minutes are spent guzzling water, until my stomach sloshes like a wave onto the surf. The stuff is a little stagnant and probably not clean, but at the moment it's like fucking nectar.

She watches me curiously, toying with the edge of the heavy sail that covers my lap. She must have draped it over me at some point after we arrived. I'm glad of it. It keeps her from seeing the very obvious reaction I'm having to her exquisite body being so near mine.

For the sake of the fucking Blue Faerie, why am I reacting like this? I've seen a siren before, but her draw wasn't half so potent as Aria's. It's a struggle not to take her to the bed, roll her beneath me so I can explore every inch of her beautiful body. And that would be a horrible idea. She's probably never seen a human man nude before, much less had the desire to fuck one. I'd scare her. And once scared, she'd probably kill me.

"You should remain still," she advises, stretching her body in a perfect arch to work out the kinks in her back. It has the added benefit of showing off those tits that are both heavy yet pert. "Moving might make things worse."

My balls are beginning to ache. It's been so long since I've been inside a woman. Since things with the Guild have picked up, making me almost exclusively a ferryman for their agents, I've not had much of a chance to solicit the services of a working girl or barmaid.

"How do ye figure?"

My voice comes out a croak, and it has nothing to do with swallowing sea water. The pain in my throat has dulled to a barely noticeable ache. Instead of feeling like a bit of jerky left in the sun, I now feel only marginally shaky. I'll recover within the hour, if I can keep the fresh water down.

"I fear you might have gotten some of the kraken's venom in your system," she explains. "Moving might cause it to circulate. The mark I put on you should speed your healing though."

"What mark?"

She shrugs and nearly trips over her own feet as she approaches me. Clearly she isn't used to them. "The mark attaches your life force to mine."

What's the girl done to me? I begin searching my body for sucker marks or scales. But it's the same as usual, aside from the rust forming on my mechanical hand. I can see the bulge of my hook in one of the inside pockets of my frock coat from here, so I'll at least have a replacement.

Aria extends a hand, frowning when I draw back.

"I'm not going to hurt you."

"Sirens dinnae have a reputation for bein' merciful to men like meself, Popsy."

Her expression clouds over with anger and her pupils go to slits, like a sea snake's, for a moment. It's damn eerie, and I shy still further away from her.

"I am not like most sirens, Hook."

"Clearly. Nary have I met one with legs. Seen one with bloody great wings before, but never legs."

"And my name isn't Popsy," she finishes.

"Aye, 'tis a nickname, lass."

She smooths her hands over her lovely stems for a moment, seemingly fascinated by the smooth texture. So am I, frankly. I've never seen a woman's legs so smooth. Her skin is like the back of a dolphin, and I long to touch her and see if the comparison stands up.

"They aren't permanent," she says with a wee bit of sadness in her tone.

"Nae permanent?"

She looks up at me then and shakes her head. "I need to travel to Delorood, I was sent with a proposition for the King. A cessation of hostilities."

"An' I factored into that how?"

Her cheeks tinge lightly lilac, and I realize with a start that she's blushing. It's so fucking beautiful. I reach out without thinking, run my hand over the heated arch of one cheekbone. Her skin is silky smooth, and yes, it does have some similarities to dolphin skin. Most of her feels cool to the touch, except where her blood bubbles to the surface. I've always wondered if sirens ran hot or cold. Did they lean more to their human half? Now I know the answer.

She nuzzles into my touch with a small, kitten-like sound of pleasure. I can't help myself. "I want to kiss ye," I murmur.

She stares at me blankly. "Kiss?"

"Aye, kiss."

She shakes her head. "I... don't know... what that means."

Morningstar's reeking balls!

Merpeople don't kiss? How impersonal is their fucking?

"I can show ye," I coax, sliding two fingers beneath her chin and tipping her face up.

"Is it pleasant?" she asks, while studying me suspiciously.

"Aye, verra pleasant."

She seems to think about it. "Very well. It seems fair, since I've put a mark on you."

She lifts a hand, running her fingers lightly over the side of her neck. Now that she's touching it, I can feel the rough outlines of a lip print seared into my own skin.

"I would like you to kiss me, Hook."

I've never been so happy to oblige. I close the distance between us and press my lips to hers gently. She trembles beneath my touch. Her breasts move in time, drawing a small groan from me. She's so lovely. I'm doomed to be under her thrall. At this point, I don't even care if she intends to drown me. So long as I can feel that tight quim around my cock once, I'll die a happy man.

Her lips part, and a wee pink tongue darts out to taste my lips. My cock hardens to the point of pain.

She shimmies her body closer, so she's straddling my thigh. Her slick heat is maddening. She's so fucking wet! Does she even know what it means when her quim throbs with need? I want to show her what the little pearl at the apex of her sex does. I want her to scream my name as she loses herself to the ecstasy of orgasm.

I'm poised to ask. I don't touch women without permission, and she could say no. But I hope against hope she wants this as much as I do.

Before I'm able, the door of the shack bursts open, the frame wrenched loose by incredible force. The structure groans and threatens to buckle around us. Aria and I jerk apart, necks craning to see the intruder.

It's a man, easily my size. Perhaps a wee bit bigger. He's broad-shouldered, rippling with muscle, and also completely nude. He's as striking as Aria, in his way — luminescent silver skin, hair as long as Aria's, though his is of a yellow shade. The markings on his face are blue, instead of green, and contrast strongly with his skin.

Fuck me. Are they all so beautiful?

"Good morrow, mate," I start.

The man's eyes narrow as he focuses them on Aria, then on me, and his lips pull back from his teeth. I'm taken aback by the needle-like incisors. Like a bloodsuckers, they are.

He lets out a primal sound before he lunges, fist flying toward my face.

FIVE
BASTION

I don't know where the damn human came from. Cassio Island has been abandoned for many months, ever since Triton failed to keep a handle on the grotesquerie. Too risky. Delorood kept its barbaric peoples near the shoreline, instead of sending them out to sea. So why is this thing here?

He's a shade I've not seen before, skin so tanned it looks like fresh soil. He's as muscled as I, and probably more sturdy on his feet. These damn things don't want to cooperate. They stumble often, so my gait is staggering and clumsy. I dislike them intensely. I'll be grateful when we can return to the depths, miserable as they are. At least there, I'm sleek and quick.

But, no matter. The human has his hands on Aria! Close to her throat!

When I first opened the door to this shanty, I noticed the man's mouth mashed against hers. He was trying to eat her face!

So I blasted through the door as my lips pulled away from my teeth in a snarl. None of us are flesh-eaters, but I wish to make an exception for this land dweller.

No one will harm the princess! Not when I am here to defend her!

I lunge forward, almost tripping over the debris that litters the floor, but I somehow keep my balance. I seize the front of his outer covering and pull it clear off him. Then I reach for his shoulder and yank him off her.

"Bloody hell, mate, that's no way to greet a stranger!" he yells as he comes off the mattress with a cry of surprise, mud-colored eyes flying wide open. He doesn't have time to raise his hands in defense or surrender before I've driven my fist into his stomach. He doubles over, landing on the ground, the air leaving him in a rush. Puny humans, with their limited lungs. It's so easy to paralyze their diaphragms. I despise having that weakness myself for the next two weeks. I want my gills back. This mouth-breathing is undignified.

The human barely turns his head in time to avoid my fist again. I aim to break that squarish jaw before he can use those blunt teeth to rip my dear Aria's lips off. She'd regrow them eventually, but to see her maimed? The thought is unbearable.

My fist collides painfully with a water pail, instead, and it tips, spilling stagnant water from one of the island's pools onto the floor. Through the thudding pulse in my ears, I can hear Aria screeching something, but can't make out the words.

Then I see it, and I go cold. My arm stops mid-swing as it sinks in.

On the human's throat, in the hollow below his ear, is a perfect blackened imprint of Aria's lips. I would recognize the shape and texture anywhere. I have stared at her face for too many hours not to know the contours by heart.

A mate mark!

Not completed, because it isn't edged with the shade of her markings. But it's clearly a mate mark, all the same.

But, why? Why would she mark a human? This human?

Betrayal spikes through my veins, the taste of kelp and bitter bile rising in my throat. I shoot a glance over my shoulder, and she recoils from the accusation in my eyes. She chose this... this vagabond? This barbarian, over one of us, one of her own?

I have never asked. It's not my place to court the princess. A lowly servant will never be able to touch a goddess.

But this? He isn't even her same species!

How would he mate her to seal the union? How would he give her children?

Why would she do this? She can't have known him long, a mere hour at the most, yet I've been steadfast for years. It's unjust.

The human uses the opportunity to pull to up to his feet, then once he's standing, he draws up his knee and shoves it into the space between my legs, where a jutting appendage dangles. I had thought it a growth or perhaps a worm.

The agony is instantaneous.

It steals the breath from my fragile human lungs and causes me topple sideways, clutching myself. My vision flashes white. A rushing fills my ears. It's pain as I've never experienced before, and I've been gutted by a swordfish. I still bear the scar above my tail line to prove it.

The human looms over me, as naked as I am, raising a glinting metallic hook, ready to drive it into my nose. Then, a soft hand with tapered fingers catches his wrist, holding it firmly above his head with strength that belies her svelte and comely frame.

"Enough," she commands, spearing us both with a glare. "Is this how all males are? What's wrong with both of you?"

"He attacked me, nae the other way 'round," the human grumbles as he takes a seat on the large rectangular mass in the center of the room.

"The human was trying to eat you!" I defend myself. I can hear the churlish note in my voice, even as I speak.

"Eat the lass?" the human chuckles, shaking his head. "Yer off yer bloody rocker, mate!"

Aria's eyes narrow on me, her scowl all for me now. The injustice rankles. Why am I being punished? I'm merely acting on my duty to protect her! At least, partly. I do want to take a bite of the human for daring to bear her mark. Unworthy mouth breather.

Then her eyes drop to the place between my legs and she studies the bizarre attachment with interest. I pull myself up to standing, though the pain still lingers and I find myself bending over slightly.

"You've got one too," she says as she leans over and reaches for it, batting it playfully. The creature moves from one side to the other and then begins to increase in girth and length as she touches it.

"Aye, enough o' that or the lad's gonna do somethin' I dinnae wish to see," the human says, purposely turning his head from us both.

"Is it a worm?" Aria asks as she looks at him. "Or a growth of some sort? A parasite?"

"A worm?" the human blasts out, chuckling as he slaps his thigh. "Nae! 'Tis a todger!"

"A todger?" Aria repeats, testing the word out on her tongue. "Is it… part of you? I mean, is it one of your… appendages?"

"Aye, 'tis a todger an' each man has one."

"Oh," Aria says as she glances down at herself. "I don't have one." She reaches her fingers between her legs and rubs the strange slit there, pulling her hand away as she studies the glistening wetness left on her fingers. "This must be a clam between my legs?"

Perhaps it is a clam as it looks quite like one.

"Oh, bloody hell," the human says as he takes a deep breath and rolls to his feet in a graceful movement, adroit and confident. I envy him for more reasons than one.

As soon as he's upright, his chuckle rings through the air—a rich, throaty sound, and Aria shivers. Her nipples pucker. I wonder at her body's reaction to him. It's not cold in here as it is in the deep.

The human notices, too. He can't seem to keep his eyes off her breasts. I feel as if I'm missing something crucial. They're just breasts. Why does he stare at them so hungrily? Does he wish to eat those, too?

"Why were you attempting to eat Aria's face?" I demand, wanting to stick to the subject.

"Ye dinnae know what a blimy kiss is either, do ye?"

"Kiss?" I repeat.

"Old, hairy balls!" the human roars with laughter, smacking his hand on his thigh once more. He seems quite daft. As I watch, his *todger*, as he termed it, seems to echo his chuckles and moves accordingly.

"Balls?" I repeat, glaring at him.

"Humans touch their mouths together as a form of pleasant greeting," Aria informs me primly. "Which I would have told you if you'd spoken with me, instead of charging our... human friend... like a bull shark!"

"He's not *my* human friend," I groan and then duck my head, chagrin seizing me. She's right, of course. The humans' customs are sure to be strange. I stand upright even though the pain still lingers. It's not quite as bad now though.

"My apologies," I say, trying to keep the seething envy from my voice. It isn't my place to question the princess' decisions. Completely baffling as they may be.

Then I lean forward, seize a fistful of the human's black hair, and mash my mouth to his. Aria is right. A kiss is pleasant, in its way. It makes my lips tingle. The human is feverishly warm to my touch, and his mouth sears mine.

The human pulls away from me with a chuckle and wipes his mouth.

"Feck me! Months o' celibacy, an' now I've got a comely lad an' lass. 'Tis almost worth losin' the *Jolly Roger*." His face darkens. "Almost." Then he clears his throat and the mirth slips from his expression. "Ye'll want to be careful there, mate. Ye're pretty enough, but most the menfolk on land object to bein' greeted as such. They prefer women."

"But Aria just said kissing was a way of making pleasant greetings?" I ask, flummoxed.

"Aye, well, 'tis a bit different." Then he looks at Aria. "An' ye, lass, shouldnae be goin' aboot offerin' kisses to every scallywag ye meet. They might well try to take more from ye than ye be willin' to offer."

I notice as his eyes travel to the center of her thighs and stay there. My eyes follow the same path and I find myself studying the strange clam between her thighs. Yet, it doesn't quite resemble a clam, truly. It's not the same color and I have yet to see it spit out sea water. Aria's species of clam appears more like an opening, similar to a wound, but it does not reveal bloodied flesh. And there are bizarre lips that surround it. I should like to inspect it later.

"Then kissing is not meant for greeting?" I ask the strange human.

The man rolls his eyes skyward. "Nae, mate. Ye'll learn soon enough, I'd wager." Then he pauses and runs his eyes over my chest and arms. "Are all mermen as solid as ye?"

"Yes."

He lets out another of those bleak chuckles and rolls his shoulders forward, stretching. "Good to know." He turns to face Aria. "Now, what do ye say we make our egress from this depressin' wee sandbar an' find shore? Ye're nae gonna be able to speak to the King of Delorood from here."

"If only we could," I mutter. Unable to help myself, I throw a vexed glance at the princess. "Opeia's enchantment was activated the moment we stepped foot on land. If you'd waited until we reached

Delorood before coming on land, we wouldn't face this problem." I take a breath and continue to glare at her, for this is her fault. And now I see why she didn't wait for Delorood. The human is the reason we're landlocked here. "We are, for the most part, human now."

"What does that mean?" the human demands.

"It means we're stranded on this island," Aria answers. "No tails, and my wings are next to useless this far out to sea. They'd be sodden before we could even reach the thermals above."

She's shamefaced, shoulders curled forward, hands clasped before her in contrition. Instantly, my anger evaporates. It is not my place to question her. It is only my own bullheadedness and sense of entitlement that causes the rift between us. I am valued by her, clearly, if she reacts this badly to my censure. I want to comfort her. But what can be said? I've spoken nothing but truth. How are we to make it to shore without drowning ourselves or the human?

Hook just stares at us both. "Ye're both pullin' me leg, right?"

"Pulling your leg?" Aria asks as she glances down at his legs with a frown.

I admit, I am quite confused as well. "We are standing opposite you," I point out. Does she find his foolishness charming, as well? It would annoy me. It already is. "Neither one of us is near enough to pull your leg."

"Bloody hell, that's nae what I..." He rubs a spot between his eyes and appears quite chagrined.

"Travelin' with the pair of ye is gonna be a right nightmare."

He shakes his head and mutters darkly for a few more seconds before standing up straighter.

"Explain to us, please, Hook," Aria says, smiling at him encouragingly.

He faces her and his eyes drop to her breasts again and the worm growth attached to the inside of his legs begins to stir and grow. I wonder if it's eating him from the inside out? I wonder if the same will happen to me? I should hope not.

"There's an option ye're both clearly missin'," he says. "I 'spose it makes sense, since ye're used to swimmin' everywhere. But there be boats on this island, Popsy. At least one o' them has to be in good enough condition to ferry us to the shallows outside Delorood, at the verra least."

I exchange a glance with the princess. She looks as uncertain as I feel. A boat? One of the human death traps that fails as often as not, tossing sailors into the sea to drown?

"It doesn't sound safe," she hedges.

"Safe or nae, it seems yer only option. Unless ye'd like to try yer hand at swimmin'? Swimmin' with a human body…"

He has a point. I dislike that idea immensely.

Aria straightens and then nods warily. "I suppose you're right—we would not get very far swimming without tails or fins. Let's find those boats."

"First things first," the human says, glancing between us and then himself. "We're gonna need to… cover up."

I make a face. Human outerwear. Ridiculous and cumbersome.

"I have a plan," he says as he reaches for the pile of his own clothing.

"What is it?" Aria asks.

He tells us and I don't like it. Aria doesn't appear to like it either, which mollifies me.

"All right," she agrees with a sigh at last. "Let's put some *clothes* on and go. But I'm removing them the instant I'm allowed."

Hook grins. "There's naethin' I'd enjoy more, Popsy."

SIX

ARIA

Human lives are a misery. No wonder Triton forbids excursions onto land. This day has been possibly the worst in my recent memory. The sun, which ripples and shines like a lovely golden disc from beneath the water, beats down on the land with a burning fury. My skin begins to bake after only a half-hour beneath its rays. And the color is already turning into an angry shade of red.

There's some relief where the fabric of the clothing Hook fashioned me covers me. I heartily disliked the clothing Hook provided us, at first. It was already difficult to walk on these wobbly sticks that pass for appendages without being encumbered by portions of the heavy sails, tied around me as though I'm a mast. Now, I'm grateful for them.

Hook wrapped the sail around my chest and secured it in place so my arms, upper chest and back are uncovered, as are the majority of my legs, beneath my upper thighs. The skin beneath dews with sticky and slightly odorous liquid, but at least I don't feel like a beached whale.

My arms burn with more than the heat though. Every muscle fiber is screaming for mercy as we paddle our way toward the shores of Delorood. Without the easy glide of water to buoy me, it feels like gravity has settled weights at my shoulders and elbows. Humans must constantly be aching from their daily toil. Thankfully, we're nearing shore, so the tortuous journey is almost over.

We've been traveling most of the night and into the next day, taking shifts, with two of us rowing and the third sleeping. It's Hook and I awake at the moment. How Bastion can sleep through the scorching day, I can't fathom, but I'm grateful he can.

I'm not sure if the human nose can scent well, the way a merman's can, but my clam, that odd place between my legs, grows sticky when I look at the human man. And the scent is quite different than the beads of liquid at my brow and beneath my arms. It's muskier.

And I'm not certain, but I believe the clam might be responsible for the strange sensations that seem to blossom from it. It's akin to a deep sense of yearning, a need that makes little sense to me. And the yearning need as well as the musky scent seems to increase whenever I catch a glimpse of Hook's muscled arms or the way he stares at my body with unabashed hunger.

Part of me wants to cross over to his side of the boat and press my mouth to his again. He's kissed me, as he calls it, once more since we left Cassio Island. It makes my lips tingle and it makes my clam grow quite wet. It was perhaps a few minutes okay that Hook greeted me again. And I greeted him back, enthusiastically.

Hook's eyes twinkle knowingly as he catches me looking at him.

"A pence for yer thoughts, lass?"

"I hate being human," I gripe. "It's miserable. You're all so dry."

Hook tilts his head and lets out one of those appealing laughs of his. "Guess I never thought o' it that way. I 'spose this place must seem like a desert to ye, after the way ye've lived. Awful moist where ye're from."

"And it's hot on land," I continue, a whine creeping into my voice. "I've lived in the deeps for over half my life. It's frigid, and the pressure is immense. Yet, here I sometimes feel like I might fly away and then other moments I feel like I'm bearing a heavy weight upon my shoulders."

"I'll keep ye grounded, Popsy. Want me to hold ye?"

Yes.

"It would probably tip the boat if I were to stand up and move to your side," I answer on a sigh.

He grins at that and inclines his head. "Aye, I 'spose 'twould. But 'tis a pretty thought."

Yes. A pretty thought indeed.

***

We reach the port shy of sundown. By that time, I've been able to sleep for a two-hour stretch and rest my aching muscles. The rest, while it helps my muscles, does little to help my baked flesh. My skin has begun to peel in places and it's now a deep red. Do humans shed their skin like snakes? I don't know but dislike this immensely.

Hook ties our small craft to the dock and swings a leg up and onto the wooden platform. He extends a hand to me, and I take it. It takes me a few miserable seconds of effort before I can clamber out of the boat. It sways, trying to tip Bastion and I into the sea. Eventually, with both men doing their best to steady me, I am able to make a somewhat graceful exit from the craft.

The wood grain is almost unbearably rough beneath my peeling flesh, and my eyes prick strangely. Still more uncomfortable wetness emerges from my human body, but this time it's pouring from my eyes. Will this body ever stop producing water from strange places?

My breath hitches strangely and water continues to pour down my cheeks, salty and warm. It tastes a little like the sea.

Hook glances over his shoulder at me after helping Bastion from the boat. His expression twists in concern.

"What's wrong, lass? Why are ye cryin'?"

Crying? Is that what humans call this outpouring of water? I struggle to form words around the hiccupping sound caught in my throat.

"It h-hurts... My skin hurts everywhere."

"Morningstar's balls!" Hook swears as he takes in the redness of my shoulders and arms for the first time. "O' course! Ye've never had a sunburn. Come, Popsy. Let's get ye inside. I'll find somethin' that will help soothe yer pain."

Hook shepherds us toward the end of the dock, scowling at the night guards who patrol the edge of the port. There are three, all of them shorter than Hook and a great deal flabbier. One has a gut so large, it strains the buttons on his clothing, threatening to tear them off completely. It's this corpulent, balding man who steps forward, holding a device with some sort of dart pointed at Hook.

"State your business. There ain't meant to be another ship arrivin' until next week. Last one we had on the record was 'sposed to arrive two days ago."

"Aye, 'twas meant to be me," Hook says testily. "The *Jolly Roger*, check yer bloody records instead o' pointin' a crossbow at me."

"Name?"

"Ye know my feckin' name, Jones," Hook says and eyes the man angrily.

"Name?" the man repeats, glaring back.

"Cap'n Hook for feck's sake!"

"What business do ye have in Bridgeport?" the man continues.

"I was meant to be carryin' a delegation."

"A delegation?"

"Aye. I was bringin' provisions for the Prince's army. Instead, we was forced to abandon ship when a beastie rose out o' the sea. I've been delayed over a day. Now, if ye'd please excuse me, the bonny lass needs medical attention."

The man narrows his eyes, examining me next. His attention is focused curiously on my breasts. What's visible of them, in any case. Hook arranged the heavy sail around me into a flowing shape he termed a "frock," leaving my shoulders, neck, and most of my legs bare.

Sometime on the journey over, he'd requested we do something about our hair. I hadn't understood what he'd meant at first. It took some doing, but we were able to halt the ongoing colors that wave through our hair, in favor of just one. Bastion had chosen a light yellow. I rather fancied the color of Hook's coat, and adopted a deep magenta color, though he told me to settle on something less colorful. When I told him I fancied the color of his garb, he relented and allowed me the magenta. Though I'm beginning to think it an unwise choice now, given how strangely the portly man regards me.

"She fae?" the man asks, with a thick edge of dislike in his voice. "Ye know there be laws 'bout fae comin' to the shores of Bridgeport."

"O' course she ain't fae, ye bloody tosser," Hook replies hotly. I've never seen him so undone.

"Only ever seen fae with hair like that."

"Only Unseelie fae left, isn't there?" Hook responds to which the man nods, but never takes his eyes off me. "See any horns, bat wings, or strange appendages on her?" Hook continues. "Nae? Damn bloody right! 'Cause she ain't a bleedin' fae!"

"I heard there was Seelie fae left," the man argues stubbornly. "One o' their princesses. An' that blue woman, right?"

"The Blue Faerie is dead an' Tinkerbell is naethin' more than a bloody myth," Hook says dismissively.

"Then what the bloody hell is she?"

Hook motions to me with a wave of his hand. "She's one o' them werebears. They're all strange lookin'." Then he leans into the man and whispers loudly. "Dinnae disrupt her temper though, 'tis an ugly thing."

The man's eyes widen slightly but he motions for the others to point the crossbow away from Hook.

"What's wrong with her? Plague?" the one in front asks, pointing to my peeling skin.

"A sunburn, ye bleedin' imbecile," Hook drawls. "Her home's situated in an old-growth forest with lots o' snow most the time. She's nae used to the heat an' the sun o' this climate. I need a balm or grease mix or she's gonna hurt worse come morn."

Worse? There's worse pain than this in store for me? The very thought draws a whimper from me.

Hook's expression tightens and he clenches the one good hand he has, brandishing the hooked appendage attached to the other wrist at them.

"I dunno," the man starts as he looks all three of us over again.

Hook huffs out his indignation and appears frustrated. "Did ye nay hear who I am, lads?" he insists.

"Cap'n Hook," the man answers with a yawn.

"Aye an' have ye heard the tales o' mean Cap'n Hook? How I lost me a game o' cards owin' to a cheatin' rapscallion?"

"No."

"Aye, I took his feckin' eye with a scrape o' me hook in return for his lyin', cheatin' ways. Ye dinnae want to find out what I'll do when I'm truly angered."

This does draw a reaction. The guard takes a step back from him, but Hook isn't finished.

"Aye, that's right. Ye've ignited me temper now, ye have. An' ye've got thirty seconds to clear out before I start fishin' for yer gizzards. I'm a wee bit rusty, so it might take me a bit to find what I'm lookin' for."

"Welcome to Bridgeport," the portly man says through clenched teeth. "Take yer furry friends an' go before we stop feelin' so peaceful."

Hook sneers and bows at the waist with a flourish that somehow conveys mockery. "How magnanimous o' ye, bloody fecker."

It looks like it might devolve into a brawl, but Bastion pushes past me, coming to stand shoulder to shoulder with Hook, staring the men down.

"She's hurting," Bastion grits out. "And I am *not* rusty. I will rip your innards out without hesitation."

"Go," the man orders, jabbing his weapon toward the shadowy port town beyond.

Hook takes me very gingerly by the shoulder and leads me away, his posture not relaxing until we've left the guards a hundred feet behind us.

"It hurts," I groan again. The stone underfoot is worse against my baked skin than the wood.

"All right, Popsy. Up ye go."

Hook braces one arm against my back and uses the other to sweep my legs out from under me, lifting me easily from the ground. I let out another soft cry when the material of his coat rubs against my skin. It's not as coarse as the stone or the wood, but any touch hurts.

"Shh. 'Twill be over soon, lass."

"My entire body burns," I say as I lean against him, feeling bitterly sorry for myself.

"I'm sorry. I wasnae thinkin'. I willnae let this happen again."

I'm acting like a wretched little fingerling. Bastion has to be as badly burned as I am where the material doesn't cover his skin. Granted, he wears more fabric than I do, as we'd managed to find a few articles of clothing in the shack. Hook also fashioned a cloak made of the sail for Bastion and it's done a fine job of keeping his upper body covered. I hadn't been able to stand wearing mine in the heat. Now, I'm paying the price for that choice.

As to the city of Bridgeport, it exists on top of the sea, on a long and narrow slip of wooden pier that teeters over the water. The streets are incredibly narrow, compared to the wide open avenues I grew up swimming along in Aspamia. They remind me unpleasantly of the tunnel in the deeps I'd gotten myself wedged into when I was a mere girl, new to the cold, dark place. No matter how hard I'd tried, I couldn't wriggle free of the space. How much worse would it be to be stuck between one of the buildings here, with the miniscule spaces between the houses. The thin, spindly legs I sport would certainly not be up to the task of kicking my way free.

The human buildings aren't half so beautiful as the ones in my former home. Triton's castle was all sweeping architecture; its halls, vaulted ceilings, and towering spires were fashioned from layers of polished antigorite, peridotite, and olivine. Even Aunt Opeia's kingdom was more beautiful than this wretched place.

Cold, minimalistic, austere beauty, to be sure. But still beautiful.

In comparison, these buildings are stumpy, blunt, and unattractive, with the same color as basalt. And just beneath the smell of brine is a rancid odor. I've not smelled anything quite so foul before. It's somehow worse than the sulfurous gasses that vent from the underwater volcanos.

Yes, I definitely won't miss the human experience. I belong in the sea.

Hook stops before one of the taller of the gray buildings and pounds furiously on the door until another human arrives to open it. The door swings inward, spilling a soft amber glow onto the street. The doorway is filled by a woman wearing a dress with a different cut to mine and in a light coral color. She has ample curves, black hair, and a sour expression screwed onto her round face.

"We ain't open, sailor. Be gone with ye."

Are all humans so surly?

Hook makes a sound of frustration in the back of his throat and draws out a pouch from his pocket. I spied it when I'd dragged the coat off him. He brandishes it at the woman and shakes it, and something rattles in the interior.

"Fifteen gold. Thirty, if ye can provide a balm for the poor lad an' lass. They're burned by the sun somethin' fierce."

The woman squints at Hook suspiciously. "Forty, an' ye can earn yerself a meal in the mornin'."

"Fine," Hook says impatiently. "Let us in."

The woman steps aside and allows Hook to sweep into the building. I only get a blurry impression of the main floor. There's a rack of some sort, holding more coats. I see a wide bench-like thing with a bell on its surface, along with a wall of shelves behind it and a series of hooks holding keys. She snags one of them and tosses it to Bastion.

"Second floor, third room on the right. I'll be up with the balm in a minute."

Bastion stares at the keys in bewilderment. Keys are something of a curiosity in the sea. Doors, as well. Triton has only the one, to block the entrance to the castle. Generally, there is no need for such a thing. But humans seem to love them. There was a door on every building we passed.

Hook sweeps up the staircase, to the second floor. He sets me gently on my feet when we reach the door indicated, and takes the keys from Bastion, slotting the larger into the door. He unlocks it and pushes the door in.

The room beyond is small. My chest tightens and the sense of claustrophobia creeps in again. I hate this. How am I supposed to escape quickly from a cramped space such as this one? How do humans live like this?

"Is this safe?" I ask as I eye each length of the narrow hallway. "It seems so... difficult to escape. So small and narrow."

"Calm down, lass," Hook says, stepping into the room and tugging me gently along. "The mistress will be up with the balm soon."

I shake my head. It's useless to explain the insidious fear to the human, who's probably used to such small spaces.

Bastion steps in after us, eyes darting over the surfaces in the room. There aren't many. There's a pair of beds, a chest at the foot of the nearest, and another door in the room. Does it lead to another, smaller room? Who could possibly live in such a tiny space?

Bastion looks as anxious as I feel, with slightly green cast beneath his silvery skin. Like me, he's probably wishing we were back in the streets. At least there are places to run if we are attacked.

The landlady arrives quickly, as promised, and slaps a container of something into Hook's palm. He thanks her and then offers it to Bastion.

"Strip down an' rub it on yer skin, mate. Then try to get some sleep."

Bastion gives Hook a grudging nod of thanks and pries the lid off the container. He cautiously dips a hand into the stuff and comes away with a glob, which he smears experimentally on his face and neck. The relief in his expression is immediate. He wastes no time stripping off the heavy layers of clothing, standing completely nude only a minute later, as he rubs the glistening stuff on his skin.

Once again, I stare in fascination at the strange part between his legs. It's a similar size as Hook's, though it's not half-engorged the way the sailor's was upon my first viewing it. I want to touch it again, to see if the tip feels as velvety and warm as Hook's did.

Bastion heaves a sigh and gratefully sinks onto the bed, eyes fluttering closed as he hands the balm back to Hook. The sailor uses the remaining key to unlock the trunk at the foot of the bed and pulls out a thin cloth, which he drapes over Bastion. It seems light enough that it doesn't chafe.

"Yer turn," Hook says after a moment, turning to face me. "Off with the frock, Popsy. Let's get the balm on ye."

I tug eagerly at the strings that keep the frock in place. It comes apart almost at once, the coarse fabric of the sail sliding off my tortured body at once. It's a measure of relief to be nude again. I don't understand why humans enjoy their clothing so much. It's so binding.

Hook stares at me for a long moment, and the ache in my clam returns. Hunger flickers across his face. Muscles in that strange and demanding place between my legs flex and a strong pang of want seizes me. Once again, my nipples pucker with the exposure to the air and to his gaze.

"Mayhap ye ought to lay on yer stomach, lass," he suggests after a long moment. His voice is strained, quiet. "We can start with yer back first."

I lay down on the bed, gritting my teeth to contain another whimper as my burned skin sends up prickles of protest. Then Hook is there, leaning over me, hands slicked with the greasy balm.

A sound of pure pleasure escapes my lips as the cool gel sinks into the skin of my calves. It's like being doused in cool ocean water, easing the pain away by degrees. I wriggle a little as he spreads the stuff over my arms, my neck, the top of my back, and then down my legs again. It's incredibly pleasant.

"Is my clam burned too?" I ask.

"Yer clam?" he asks with a chuckle.

"Yes, it feels… as if it burns."

He takes a deep breath. "Nae, 'tis nae burned, Popsy."

"Then why…"

"I dinnae have the… patience to explain it to ye, lass," he barks out, surprising me.

My body aches in an entirely new fashion by the time he bids me roll onto my back.

"Do ye want to do this yerself, lass?" he asks. "Mayhap I ought not touch…" He gestures broadly down my body and focuses on my breasts. I'm not sure what he's prattling on about.

"They're just breasts. They're not even necessary."

"Nae necessary?" Hook replies with a frown.

I shrug. "We don't feed our young that way."

"Then why do sirens have them?"

"They're just leftover from Poseidon's mating with a human woman all those thousands of years ago. Some sirens cut them off."

Hook blanches. "They cut them off? Why?"

"Easier to swim and fight. I've thought about doing the same as I'm forced to do battle often."

"Nae, lass, dinnae ever touch yer breasts!" he says, shaking his head. "They're quite lovely."

"Well, lovely or not, they're unnecessary and they get in my way in a fight. And fighting is most important as the grotesquerie is getting out of hand."

"The what?" he asks.

"The grotesquerie. The krakens are only one of the creatures that make up the horde of monsters trying to escape the deeps. The one that attacked the *Jolly Roger* was an adolescent kraken that escaped our dragnet."

Hook just boggles at me for a few seconds. "That... that *thing*, was still growin'? 'Twas enormous!"

I laugh humorlessly. "They get much, *much* larger."

He hesitates, then reaches out, fingers skimming the swell of one of my breasts. He cups a hand around it. The blood in my veins warms, bubbling in a furious stream to my face, odd heat suffusing the skin there. When he rubs his thumb along the taut peak, he makes a soft, hungry sound.

"Dinnae cut them," he says, finally. "They're beautiful. Every part o' ye is lovely. I'd hate to see ye mutilate yerself."

"You like them?"

He nods. "Aye, love them. Most human men do. So ye might want to keep them covered. 'Tis nae yer fault, but some men will see yer nudity as an invitation to do things they shouldnae."

"I hate human clothing," I gripe. "It's so cumbersome. It makes my body sticky — as if it's not sticky enough as it is."

"Where are ye sticky, Popsy?"

"My underarms, under my breasts, in my hair, and down there."

His brow bounces up. "Down where?"

I gesture down at the spindly legs I've been given. "There. That... thing down there. My clam, I suppose. It gets sticky every time you touch me."

A slow, almost smug grin curls his lips. "Oh."

"Oh?"

His smile broadens and he appears quite pleased with himself. "That's... erm... arousal, Popsy."

"Arousal?"

"Aye, it means ye desire me."

"Desire you to do what?"

I know I want him to press his mouth to mine again. I've never felt anything quite like it. I want to explore this curiosity further.

Hook tugs his lip between his teeth, chewing it thoughtfully as he stares at me. I note idly that the thing between his legs has changed again. It's pressing hard against the front of his trousers, straining against the buttons that keep it clasped.

"I can show ye, if ye like. But I'd have to touch ye there." He says and motions to the strange, burning place between my legs. At the thought of him touching me there, it seems to grow even wetter and I have the distinct feeling it would like that very much.

"Is it pleasant? Like the mouth kissing?"

"'Tis... more than that. 'Tis what humans call foreplay. What we do before matin'. If I do it right, it should stop the discomfort ye're probably experiencin'."

Humans have a pre-mating ritual? That sounds absurd.

But I can't deny I'm curious. And if Hook can stop the ache of the demanding clam, I'm interested. "How do we do it?"

Hook's breathing hitches, the bulge in his trousers growing larger. I can see the outline of him against the fabric.

"Spread yer legs for me, lass," he instructs, tone husky and commanding. I oblige him, spreading my legs apart so he can see the newly formed part of me. He approaches, leans his weight onto the bed, and then climbs over me, bringing his mouth down on mine in another tender press of lips.

The fingers of his good hand skim the swell of my breast, explore the contours of my stomach, and trail down the curve of my hip. My hips perform a slow rolling motion as he caresses my thigh and then his fingers slide to the folds between my legs, gingerly touching the clam.

And the creature living there most certainly approves. A shock of pure pleasure dances through my insides and forces a sound from my throat. The sound only seems to spur him on. He runs his finger past the top of my clam and focuses on a little button there and something that feels like bliss begins to rain down on me. He leaves that spot and pushes two fingers into the clam, and the muscles clench tight in response, trying to pull him further inside.

"Gods," he breathes. "Ye're so tight, Popsy."

"Is that good?"

"Ye bet yer fine arse."

"What's an arse?" I ask as he pulls his fingers out and pushes them back in again and I groan out because the feeling is... spectacular.

He grins, white teeth bright against his tanned face. His dark eyes twinkle with mirth, like the question amuses him.

"Ye're so naïve, lass. I shouldnae be doin' this."

At the thought he might stop, I grow desperate. "Don't stop, please," I pant. The feeling of him inside me is exciting. Pleasurable in the extreme.

I was told by my stepmother that females can only find this pleasure while mating, with a man's glans pulsing against ours. But Hook doesn't have a glans. So I'm not sure how he's doing this. But, I don't want him to stop. Neither does the clam. It's most eager.

"Ye sure?"

"Yes."

He withdraws the fingers and I start to protest before he thrusts them back in again. In and out, a steady pulsing rhythm that has my back arching off the mattress. His thumb slides between the folds, finds the little pearl-like shape at the apex and circles the edges with just enough pressure that my vision pulses white. A moan escapes my mouth. My hips continue to roll without conscious thought, following the pressure of his thumb, the thrust of his fingers, trying to meet some unknown need.

"Gods, ye're beautiful," Hook breathes, wonder playing out on his face as he gazes down at me. "No wonder men drown themselves for a chance at ye lot. Most captivatin' thing I've ever seen—an' I've met fae lasses."

He curls his fingers inside me, dragging them along a spot that makes my toes curl. My back comes off the bed, every part of me trembles, and more of the sticky wetness gathers between my thighs. I can't find it in myself to be bothered by it. Hook was right. The ache between my legs is gone, replaced by a sense of deep satisfaction.

What sorcery does he possess to do this? We aren't a mated pair, and I'm not attempting to have a child with him. And yet he can make me feel almost boneless with pleasure.

My eyes are half-lidded, heavy with the need to sleep as the pleasure finally abates. Hook chuckles.

"Sleep, Popsy. I'll take the floor."

"No," I murmur. "Sleep next to me."

Hook looks like he might argue, but at my pleading expression, he capitulates. He strips off most of his clothing, leaving him in only a short length of cloth that covers the bits between his legs. The long protuberance is still straining against the cloth. He scoots me gently to the edge of the bed and turns me onto my side so he can curve my body against his. The hardness presses against my... what did he call it? My arse?

I'm facing Bastion's bed, and notice something Hook has overlooked. Bastion's eyes are open, observing us as a look of mild interest crosses his face. Then, he closes them and rolls onto his other side before I can attempt some sort of explanation.

Guilt slides like a piece of bad kelp into my stomach, erasing the satisfaction that comes from Hook's touch. But Bastion has clearly dismissed me by his actions of turning the opposite direction. That means I can't speak to him until morning.

So, I close my eyes as well, hoping that when I wake, things won't be half so confusing.

SEVEN
HOOK

It's another two days before I'm confident the pair are well enough to travel. By the second day, the worst of the peeling has passed, and the balm seems to be doing its job well.

Aria protests the sojourn, insisting we travel straight to the castle. I remind her she's going to impress no one by showing up injured. She doesn't like my response, but can't fault my logic. She's quite a feisty one. So we stay, and the pair grudgingly eat the bread and cheese they've been given.

Aria, in particular, seems to like the meals I provide her, though they're relatively plain. I've had better fare on the *Jolly Roger*, and there've been times when all we had were crusty biscuits and grog. I'm not sure how the rough bread and barely-edible cheese can settle in her stomach. When we leave Bridgeport, I'm going to make sure she's treated to a proper supper. Possibly in The Hollows. Or perhaps I'll take her to the Tiddly Tigress. Layla owes me a favor after I smuggled her out of Neverland, all those years back.

I use the remainder of my gold to buy the pair proper clothing. It'd been a poor choice to fashion Aria a dress from one of the smaller sails. Too much exposed skin. She's burned worse than Bastion. As lovely as I think she'd look in one of those fancy ball gowns, I'm not going to put her at risk. Now, she's wearing the same linen shirt, jerkin, and trouser combination as Bastion, her lurid magenta hair twisted into a braid at my insistence and tucked beneath a hat.

Presumably she can turn it any color she likes. It'd be more convenient if she turned it a golden color, like Bastion's. It would save us more confrontations like the one on the docks. But the lass seems awfully fond of the color, and I have to admit it's a little flattering she's modeled it after my coat! It's almost like having a tangible claim to her, a sign to anyone who looks at her that she cares for me, in some fashion anyway.

We're walking the main drag through Bridgeport. The castle is situated on a large rock at the far end of the massive pier. The rock was brought here by means of fae magic, before such magic was outlawed. And the castle sits atop the rock, with an equally good view of the ocean and the land.

The city itself isn't the picturesque kingdom one would think. It used to be, once upon a time, before the beasties started crawling out of the ocean, stripping the plant life, churning the pristine beaches into silty ruin, and utterly gutting the navy. I can't blame the guards for their defensive posture, given how badly things have gone for Bridgeport of late.

And it's going to get worse before it gets any better. The King of Delorood has remained adamant in his position against Morningstar. With Triton allowing the beasties to roam free and attack any ships with goods bound for Bridgeport, they're going to be isolated—and starved within a few months, when their stores run low and they're incapable of fishing. It's fortunate Aria has come with a message from her ruler.

Without safe tides, there's no supply lines to anyone. The war will be over before it even begins.

I feel a pang for the *Jolly Roger*. If we had a fleet of flying ships, maybe...

But it's impossible. The Blue Faerie, who enchanted the *Jolly Roger* to give it the ability to fly, is dead, her niece Tinkerbell murdered or missing. There's only Unseelie fae now, and they've already thrown their lot in with Morningstar in exchange for the destruction of the Seelie Court. There's no help to be had from that avenue, either.

If Aria's people can't deliver what she's promising, we're well and truly buggered.

"Are all human cities this... plain?" Aria asks, staring around at the disheveled remains of the port town.

It's clear she's trying to keep the disdain from her voice. I'm irrationally defensive, hailing from a port town myself. Granted, nothing in Neverland is ever peaceful or pretty. Bloodstained and wild, Neverland is second only to Wonderland in terms of sheer fucking insanity. Bridgeport might not be pretty, but it's still safer than Neverland.

"Ye're nae seein' Bridgeport at its best, lass. Triton's beasties have done a feckin' number on the place. They'll be lucky to survive the comin' season. Keepin' things pristine is a low priority at the moment."

Aria's cheeks flush again, that lovely and unique shade that I'm coming to love. She's turned that color every time she's come to me in the evenings, asking me to touch her.

Just the thought of her spread out on the bed, quim wet and glistening for me, makes me uncomfortably hard. I'm not sure how much longer I can go without asking her for more. But there's so much she still has to learn about humans and human bodies. Like the fact that kisses aren't always greetings and that clothing isn't optional.

"She didn't know," Bastion interjects hotly. "Don't you condescend to her, human."

"Blimey! Keep yer feckin' voice down," I hiss back. "Ye want another brawl? Because that's what we'll get if they find out what ye are."

"I care little," he growls. "Don't think I won't bash your skull open. She is our lady, and you will treat her with respect."

"Cap'n Hook?"

I half-turn in surprise when I hear the familiar voice. It's not as musical as Aria's, but still holds its charm. There's a note of strength that bolsters every syllable.

Sure enough, when I turn, she's standing not ten feet away, bartering with a merchant. Her three husbands are clustered around her, taking a position to her right, left, and back—silent, dangerous slabs of muscle that can turn into enormous bears at the slightest provocation.

"Kassidy?" I ask.

A bright, sunny smile touches her mouth. She's a short thing, barely coming up to my sternum. Narrow but muscled, though not unattractively so. She's a thief, built for speed and combat, unlike the willowy woman at my side. Aria looks like a stiff breeze will knock her off her newly acquired legs. Kassidy's hair is golden and grows in as thick as a hedge, spiraling in wild curlicues. It's no surprise she's long been known as Goldilocks.

She looks more disheveled than usual, bedraggled in a way that's not sexy. I'm just glad she's alive and appears mostly intact.

Kassidy disentangles herself from her pack of menfolk and rushes me, arms outstretched. I step forward with a laugh, catching her when she launches herself into my arms. We've never been bosom friends, but I like her. She's beautiful, intelligent, and in possession of the largest set of brass balls I've seen this side of Neverland. It seems she's as happy to see me as I am to see her.

"Oh, Hook!" she exclaims, pulling back to plant a wet kiss on my cheek. "Oh, thank the Gods! You're alive! We saw the *Jolly Roger* go down. We thought…"

I pull away and grin, buffing my hook against my frock coat in a casual manner. "I'm made o' sturdier stuff than that, Miss Aurelian, an' ye right well know it!"

"Who is this?" Aria demands.

Aria's musical voice holds a sour note. It's a tone like nothing I've heard from her before, and when I tilt my head to look at her, I find her staring at Kassidy, blue-green eyes narrowed to slits.

Ah, shite. I've made the lass jealous. Not polite, to be embracing other women while I've been finger-fucking her to explosive orgasm every night since we reached land.

I gently take Kassidy's hands and disentangle myself, stepping back about three paces until Aria's expression eases from murderous to merely hostile. Her slim shoulders are rigid, her hands clenched into fists at her sides. It's hard to forget, beautiful as she is, that she can assume another, deadlier form with talons, wings, and a ripping beak.

"Aria, Bastion, this is Kassidy Aurelian. She an' her *husbands* were aboard the *Jolly Roger* when we were attacked by the kraken."

The adolescent kraken. Fuck. I *still* can't believe that thing was a child.

Aria's tense shoulders ease down a wee bit when she hears the word 'husbands.'

"I didn't know that was possible," she murmurs.

"What?" Kassidy asks.

Aria studies her with interest. "You have more than one mate?"

Kassidy takes my silent cue and retreats toward her husbands. They're all fucking massive, seven feet tall, at least. Nash and Leith favor one another, one with dark hair and the other with slate gray. Sorren is the outlier, pale and chocolate haired. The four of them then return together, each of the men nodding to me in greeting as I return it.

Kassidy casts Aria a curious glance. "What do you mean?"

Aria's gaze, meanwhile, is plastered on each of Kassidy's husbands but not in a desirous way, as she sometimes looks at me. Instead, she appears to be inspecting them. "Do you hail from giants?" she asks them.

"Giants?" Nash says with a smile as he faces Leith, who only smiles.

"She's nae from 'round here," I offer, dropping my voice so the crowds streaming around us don't overhear.

Kassidy gives me a frown. "I knew that the moment I set eyes on her, Hook," she says with a laugh.

I nod. "Aye. She... she's the one who rescued me when the *Jolly Roger* went down. She's one o' the..." I cast another nervous glance around. Fuck, there's so many people here. I look at Kassidy again and whisper, "She's one o' the... ladies o' the water."

Kassidy's eyes light with understanding and grow round as she swivels them toward Aria once more. I've been trying to hide the glaringly obvious markers of Aria and Bastion's inhumanity, keeping Aria's hair out of sight, coating their skin in a layer of mild filth to keep the markings from showing and to dull the luminous sheen. Still, the markings are there. The skin that shows through is still very obviously not human. If people looked up from their own feet once in a while, they'd notice such things. Good thing they don't.

Sharp as she is, Kassidy can't fail to note them.

"Oh. Uh... wow."

"I'm Leith," one of Kassidy's husbands says and offers Aria his hand. She just looks at it and then looks back at him before she holds her hand out as well, though doesn't make any motion to take his.

"She doesnae understand our customs," I try to explain.

"I am Aria and this is Bastion," she says and motions to Bastion who stands behind us as though he wants nothing to do with anyone. Which is most likely the truth. Surly bastard he is.

"These are my cousins, Nash and Sorren," Leith continues as both nod to Aria and she nods back to them.

"She's here to talk to the King, Popsy," I continue, speaking to Kassidy. I keep my voice pitched low, though I haven't technically said anything incriminating. "About a cessation of hostilities."

Aria turns her murderous glare to me. "*Popsy*?" she repeats and I immediately recognize my mistake. "That was the strange title you gave me... and me alone... or so I thought?"

"Aye, well, 'tis... aye, I made a mistake, that's all," I say as Kassidy's eyes go for the sky and a smile teases her lips.

"Then I am *Popsy* and I alone?" Aria tests.

I nod. "O' course, Popsy, o'course."

Kassidy arches one golden brow skeptically. "Returning to this cessation of hostilities you mentioned, Hook," she starts as she turns her attention from me to Aria. "You can do that?"

Aria's gaze is still unfriendly, and she just responds with a curt nod.

"She's chatty," Kassidy drawls, a dry, almost mirthless smile replacing her earlier delight. "I like her."

"Ah, dinnae fight, please," I say, barely holding back a groan. "I'm takin' ye all to the same place. Cannae we just get along?"

"This... woman," Aria says, tone clipped. "She's your ally?"

"Yes," Kassidy starts, but I take a step in front of her to let it be known I should answer Aria's questions.

"Aye, a friend. An' me passenger. I'd appreciate it if ye could both learn to talk to each other civilly."

Aria saunters forward in a glide of hips that's pretty damn mesmerizing to watch. I'm not the only one who thinks so. Bastion watches in fascination as well, as do about a half a dozen men in my periphery.

She looks down at Kassidy who looks right back up at her, fire burning in her emerald eyes.

"If you are a friend of Hook's, I can consider you my ally as well," Aria says finally, deigning to grace Kassidy with a tight smile at last. "Welcome."

And then, before I can stop her, she leans forward to take Kassidy's face in her long-fingered hands and gives her a long, rather wet kiss right on the lips. I do believe there is tongue involved, as well. It's almost more interesting to watch than the sinuous roll of her hips and ass as she releases Kassidy's face and walks away from us. Bastion follows her.

Kassidy blinks, following Aria's retreating figure for a few seconds before she faces me. She appears a little dazed. Good. I'm glad I'm not the only one who finds Aria's kisses drugging.

"Wow," Nash says as his eyes travel from Kassidy to Aria and then back again. "Just... wow."

"Uh... what was that?" Kassidy manages to croak a minute later.

"Whatever it was, can we see it again?" Sorren asks.

"Aria's a wee bit... confused aboot what kissin' is for," I hedge, shrugging as I exhale and wonder how much and for how long I shall suffer from Kassidy on this subject. "She believes kissin' is a greetin'."

"And I'm sure you have nothing to do with her confusion, Hook?" Kassidy asks me and I can feel her suspicious stare boring a hole into the side of my face. I don't meet her eyes. I know I was being a scoundrel, stealing kisses from the enchanting siren before she even knew what a kiss was. I have no doubt Kassidy is going to give me a dressing-down later. And truth be known, I deserve it.

"I don't know about the rest of you," Nash says with a rich, rolling laugh, "but I'd love to see that welcome again."

Agreed. But aloud I say, "C'mon, ye bloody louts. If we want to make it to the castle before the witchin' hour, we have to move our arses."

Aria returns and takes up a position near my elbow, still casting glances at Kassidy. The expression vacillates from irritated to intrigued, as she watches Kassidy interact easily with her men.

"Humans can have more than one mate?" she murmurs, almost to herself.

"Perhaps there's something useful about being human after all," Bastion says, almost seeming to continue her line of thought.

I know the lad wants her. Can see it so plainly on his face, it's painful to watch. Aria clearly has no idea what she's doing to any of us. I smile thinly. If the lad has the courage to tell her, I won't stand in his way.

I'm a pirate, but I'm not prone to that sort of greed. If the lass is inclined, I can share.

The question is, can Bastion?

EIGHT
ARIA

It's shockingly easy to bypass the castle gates.

Not so long after we arrive, Hook reunites with his crew — four men, which brings our number up to ten. My emotions totter back and forth. I feel a little safer, moving in a school like this one — a much bigger school. At the same time, I dislike the fact that Hook's attention is so thoroughly diverted by other people. In particular, he's most excited to see his first mate, Sam.

Unreasonable hurt flashed through me when Hook announced his bond with Sam, calling Sam his 'first mate'. I was immediately confused, as Sam was most decidedly male, and therefore I wondered how it was Hook hoped to mate with him? Was Hook confused? Did he not understand that Sam had no eggs to fertilize? I wondered if perhaps humans were as ignorant as Bastion believed them to be?

But then Hook patiently explained that to humans, the term 'mate' means friend, not lover. Usually. I find the whole subject of greetings and words with multiple meanings quite frustrating to say the least.

And then there is the subject of the female, Kassidy. I was quite irate when Hook called her by my name, Popsy. But then he explained it was a mere mistake and I felt infinitely better. Well, perhaps not infinitely. She is quite a comely creature and there was a level of friendliness between the two of them that caused me some chagrin.

Until I realized Kassidy possesses three husbands! I quite approve of her situation and I wonder how difficult it would be to duplicate. As I am more than certain I'll have to offer my hand in marriage to the King of Delorood, I should also like to retain Hook, and marry him as well. Perhaps having two husbands will prove possible?

The werebears with whom Kassidy travels have a very reasonable view on the subject of mating, I believe. They would provide wonderful examples to all men! Kassidy is their mate, and they bristle any time someone new comes too near her. It's still strange to learn that other species have more than one mate, although I quite approve of the practice, even if it is quite foreign to those who live beneath the sea.

Yes, it's possible to mark more than one merman as my mate, but ultimately, both must do battle for the privilege of having me. Once my mate is chosen and the act consummated, any other marks I have put on others will disappear. It's why I was not unduly worried about marking Hook. My mark will keep him alive, in the short term, until I can find a merman to mate. And when I do, the mark on Hook will disappear.

But... what if I never chose another?

I've never felt so... drawn to another being before, as I am to Hook. There's something of a practiced charm about him, something he seems to direct at most people. But when we're alone, some of that pretense slips away. He's a sober man, beneath the smiles and japes. I think he might be just as serious as Bastion, when it comes down to it.

Hook steeps in deep melancholy. He doesn't speak much about the place he comes from, this Neverland, but what tidbits I have been able to glean point toward a childhood as fraught as mine. Perhaps more so. He hasn't said so, but Hook has had nothing and no one most of his life, from what I can tell. No one to take him in and offer comfort, the way Aunt Opeia has done for me. He's happiest with his crew, it seems. So it's selfish for me to horde him away like sunken treasure, even if I want to. And I do.

I blow a breath out of my mouth, flapping my lips. It's something I've seen Hook do when he's frustrated. It's strangely satisfying. But then I grow disappointed and quite unhappy when I think of this… attachment I've formed for this strange human.

This dalliance is doomed to failure, I'm afraid, much as my imagination runs away with me. Hook is human. And I have less than two weeks to enjoy this new shape before Opeia's magic gives out and I'm forced to return to the sea once more. Entertaining dreams of a future with Hook is absurd. He's land bound. I'm tied irrevocably to the sea. It can't happen.

Hook grins at me. "What's that sound for, lass?"

Too embarrassed to admit my thoughts to him, I settle on a half-truth. "This journey is taking too long. Did we need to bring the cargo with us? Couldn't the King send for it?"

Hook's men drag a load of crates in a cart behind us. Apparently, all but one of them were recovered and hauled to shore in their small craft after Hook's ship

87

sunk. Perhaps the Kraken ate the remaining crate? Or maybe it's sitting at the bottom of the ocean. I care not.

"The cargo got us through the gates, aye?" He traces a thumb across my bottom lip, and tingles spread anywhere his fingers touch. My entire body yearns toward him. I wonder how he'd react if I shimmied out of the trousers I wear and guided his fingers toward my clam. As to that subject, Hook tells me it's actually not a clam, but just a "sex organ" that is wholly my own. And he says I should not refer to it as a clam because doing so is quite… crude and *slang*, I believe the word was.

Hook calls this bizarre thing between my legs my *quim*. I've heard other words for it, since we left the hostel. Pussy. Cunt. Slit. Box. Minge. I think I like Hook's name for it best.

"Yes," I admit grudgingly. "I am glad the situation at the gates didn't result in a fight. But I still hate being sticky."

"Sweaty," he corrects with another chuckle as he looks at the golden-haired woman and her husbands with a shrug and a smile. "Sweat is the liquid on yer forehead, Popsy," he whispers to me.

"And what's the stuff between my legs, then? The stuff that gets stickier whenever you touch it?"

The inquiry makes almost every head in the vicinity turn. Hook's cheeks flame red, and it's fascinating to watch. I was told humans bleed red. I've only ever seen the purple-black stuff that runs through my body. If I pricked myself now, would I also bleed red?

"That's… different.' He sounds embarrassed.

"It's strange," Bastion chimes in, nodding. "My todger does the same thing — it leaks. But only on the tip."

"It leaks?" I ask as I turn to face him, thoroughly interested by the information.

Bastion nods. "Yes. A strange, sticky substance comes out. And I've noticed my todger quite has a mind of its own, in general, sometimes growing longer and stiffer. Especially each morning. Why is that, Hook?"

Everyone is paying attention now — the crew, Kassidy, and her husbands. And Kassidy and her very handsome husbands all appear to be hiding smirks. I am not certain why.

The one called Sorren has a darkly amused smile on his face. "Oh, this is going to be good."

"Blimey! Nae time for explanations!" Hook snaps, flushing still further when the others laugh. "We need to get this cargo inside before somethin' worse turns up to stop us."

"Oh, come on, Cap'n" Kassidy says with a broad grin. "We'd all like to know your answer to Aria and Bastion's questions."

But Hook promptly shakes his head. "Nae time, nae time! 'Tis more than just bad luck that's been impedin' us, an' ye know it. Do ye want to risk this shipment after everythin' we've gone through?"

"No," Kassidy says, and her grin fades a little around the edges. "You're right. We have to get the cargo of Ambrosia inside."

The matter is laid to rest, though I can't fathom why Hook appears so flustered. Bastion's question is a pertinent one, isn't it? I've wondered about his and Hook's todgers myself. Hook's protuberance is stiff and long every time he gives me pleasure. I want to touch it again, but haven't had the courage to ask him for the privilege. I resolve to ask him later.

I'm quickly sidetracked as we enter the courtyard, and a pang of longing twists my insides as I get a good look at the castle's interior. It's not as striking as Triton's palace. Most of the walls are still made of rough basalt, but they're at least decorated with colorful swaths of cloth in shades of blue, green, and white, mimicking the cresting pattern of a wave.

The floors are fashioned from smooth, reflective obsidian. Every now and then there's a pillar composed of speckled gabbro, twined with a climbing green plant. With the exception of the vegetation, the place has a monochromatic feel. The furnishings are slightly different, the people milling about all human. But, for an instant, it reminds me of my days in the palace. I never had the chance to explore every shining corridor of my home, preferring to stay in my room, learning everything I could about the politics of the world above. At least, what stories I could glean from others. Those stories seem wholly inaccurate now that I've gotten a chance to interact with humans personally.

We're gawked at as we're led through the halls by a tall, thin man. He's got knobbly arms and legs, and a hooked nose. With the graying hair, he reminds me a little of the long-legged water fowl that pick off fish near the ocean's edge. I stand straight-backed, chin up.

I have to appear assertive. Regal. Imposing. How else will the King take my proposal seriously?

"The King is currently deliberating with his counsel," the man informs us politely. "But he has been apprised of your arrival. He'll meet with you in the throne room in a few hours. In the meantime, we'll have baths drawn for you and clothing provided. What style and color would the ladies prefer?"

Kassidy barks a laugh. "Do I look like the dress sort to you? Men's clothing will do just fine."

"Agreed," I second. The garb human women wear exposes too much of my skin to the blistering sunlight. "I would like to wear something like Hook's clothing."

I run my fingers idly along the velvet surface of his frock coat, admiring the texture. It's one of the softest things I've touched since climbing on land. I'd like one for myself. A petty request, to be sure. But it makes Hook smile.

"In blue, I think," he says. "To match your eyes."

The man mumbles something under his breath, but he doesn't argue. He leads us to our rooms and seems even more put out when I refuse a solitary chamber. Yes, the chamber is larger than the one in the hostel, but I'm irrationally afraid of parting with Hook. He's been my anchor, protector and guide since my arrival. And I need him to help me navigate the tricky human politics that are so foreign to me.

"I've got her, mate," Hook says, placing a bracing hand on the small of my back. The man looks scandalized, and splutters when Hook swings the door shut, cutting off his protest.

"Time to sponge ye off, Popsy," he says when the servants clear out the side door. "Cannae go before the King with dirt on ye, unfortunately." I believe he's worried about revealing the marks that feather my face. Marks that belie my kind.

There's a small chamber attached to the room where a basin rests, full of foamy water. It smells sweet, a floral scent I don't recognize. When I dip an experimental finger into the stuff, I find it's tepid, which is promising. It won't scald my skin.

I begin stripping off layers at once, grateful to be nude. I will never get used to the clothing humans wear, nor the sheer number of garments they insist on piling on. As always, Hook's eyes stray to me and flicker with want. His appendage strains the front of his trousers again.

"You never did tell me what the protuberance does," I say.

Hook closes his eyes briefly. "Why do ye need to know? 'Tis naethin' ye have to worry aboot. An' I've got nae business teachin' it to ye."

"Teaching me what?"

"Ye gods," he says and expels a frustrated breath. "First of all, it's nae called a feckin' *protuberance*, lass."

"That's right. It's called a todger."

"Aye, among other things."

"It has more than one name?" I ask and then nod. "Just like my clam."

"Blimey," he says and shakes his head. "Aye, like yer clam."

"My quim," I correct myself with a shy smile.

"Aye, Popsy."

"What else is your todger called?"

"'Tis called a cock."

"A cock? Like that rooster bird you pointed out? Didn't you call that a cock?"

"Aye." He breathes out a frustrated sigh.

"What is a cock, exactly?"

"I dinnae know what yer males have, but a cock is the sex organ humans have."

He just looks at me and we both grow quiet. Then he takes a step closer to me, his fingers trailing from my navel down to the curve of one hip. My body quivers in response to his touch, my quim squeezing tight in anticipation of his fingers.

"Will you touch me again, Hook? I've been wanting to feel your fingers."

He chuckles deeply. "Ye play upon me conscience, Popsy."

"Your what?"

"Ye make me feel guilty."

"Why? You've done nothing but protect me and help me and you make my quim feel... so good."

"Aye," he says and nods with a sad smile. "Ye dinnae know anythin' aboot our world or our ways. 'Tis like... Gods, 'tis like I'm takin' advantage o' ye."

I shake my head. I don't like this guilt he feels. "I want your fingers there," I point to the place I want them. "I like it when you touch me there. I like your kisses. I like it when you make me... *cum*, as you call it."

He groans. "Aria, dinnae say things like that."

"Why not?" I counter. "It's the truth. And I'm only ignorant because you refuse to share your knowledge. What does your cock do?"

He struggles not to let his laugh become another groan. He trails his fingers lower, to quim between my legs. He slides one finger through my folds, and it comes away wet.

"Me cock goes in here, ye sweet, lovely lass. A man puts his cock here an' thrusts inside ye over an' over again."

"Like you do with your fingers?"

"Aye. An' when he's finished with his thrustin', he spills his seed inside."

"His seed?"

"Aye," he says again and nods. "'Tis similar to the liquid Bastion mentioned at the tip of his todger. Only, when a man cums, there's much more that shoots out." Then he stops talking and rubs his scrubby chin. "Well, some men are dribblers an' nary anythin' much comes out at all really. Nae me, I'm quite the shooter an' me load is quite heavy, if I do say so meself. 'Tis quite legendary 'round these parts."

I don't understand what he's talking about. "Why does this seed come out of you? Is it meant to grow trees?"

He chuckles. "Nae.'Tis meant to make children, Popsy. Though a man can pull out o' a woman's quim to stop from makin' wee ones, if there's enough time." He clears his throat. "I'm quite good at me timin'."

My body thrums with need. I can feel my pulse in every part of me. "I want your cock, Hook." I decide. "I want to feel you inside me, making your seed."

Hook's eyes smolder, sending fire searing into me. It only spurs my desire, makes the ache between my legs almost painful.

"Dinnae say that, lass." He takes a deep breath. "I'm on the edge o' holdin' meself back as it is."

"But I want it," I insist. "Please."

This is a perfect time to learn. Opeia told me I may have to trade my body for the favors I seek. How am I to do that if I don't know how humans mate? I'm still at least partially a siren. There's no way Hook can give me children, even if he spills his seed in my body.

"Ye dinnae know what ye're askin', for feck's sake!"

I reach for his trousers, slide my fingers into the waistband and find his hardness. I grasp it firmly, trace the underside. There's a vein pulsing blood into his cock. I slide my thumb across the tip, and slickness coats my fingers.

His head actually falls back and he lets out another curse, drawing the word out in a moan.

"Put your cock in me," I coax. "Please, Hook. I want so desperately to feel it."

Hook lunges for me then, shrugging off his jacket almost violently. My bare back hits the wall a few seconds later, and I'm only saved from a knock on the head by his hand, which quickly flies up to cup the back of my neck. His mouth presses urgently against mine, and I pull at the shirt he's still wearing. The buttons pop off, hit the obsidian floor with soft clinks and go spinning off toward the corners of the room.

His mouth is demanding, his tongue sliding against mine, and I open my mouth obligingly. He caresses my tongue with his, coaxing me into a rhythm that draws a moan from me. Slickness coats my thighs. He rocks his hips against mine, and delicious friction brings me close to that edge his fingers tip me over every night.

Hook shoves his trousers down and his cock springs free. It's ruddy, fully erect, and a little intimidating. That's intended to go inside me? It doesn't seem possible. It's just so…. so large! Merfolk have a more sensible approach, I think. But there's no time to worry about it.

Hook hoists me higher up the wall, slings my legs around his waist, and then lines himself up with my quim. The head slides past my folds, giving me a sense of how thick and hard he is. Then he thrusts his entire length inside me, latching onto my neck and pressing just the edge of his teeth into my skin.

"Ouch!" I say as I feel a quick pain from deep inside me.

Hook stills immediately and the pleasure bleeds from his expression. "I'm sorry, Popsy, I forgot ye are a maid," he says as he shakes his head and stills within me.

"A maid?"

He nods. "Yer body has never had a man inside it. An' there's a piece of flesh that was ripped away when I pushed inside ye."

"It hurt."

"Aye, but the pain fades… if I continue."

"Then continue."

He pushes forward and is much more careful this time. It's almost too much. As he pulls out and pushes in again, a gasp escapes me, and he stills. His bite turns into a series of soft kisses on my throat. He's so thick and long, and he fills me completely. He's right—there's no longer any pain. The sense of intense satisfaction ripples through me. My nipples are painful little peaks, rubbing against his chest.

"Are ye all right?" he whispers, voice husky.

"Your cock… it's so big," I pant. "So much of it. Oh Gods, Hook. Please…"

His fingers can't hold a candle to this. It feels right to have him holding me to his chest, his cock wedged between my legs, so deep inside my quim that I'm half afraid he'll come out my mouth.

His fingers curl, nails biting into my hips, and then he draws almost completely out of me before slamming his cock into me again and again. His hips slap against mine, a motion that might be painful in any other circumstance. Not here. Not now.

I moan and I cry out and I've never made such sounds before. I curl my legs tighter, ankles digging into his back. I meet him on his next stroke, sliding down his length, quim clenching tight.

"Feck, Aria…"

Once he's started, my human body knows what to do. I move in an undulating motion, as easy and inevitable as the tides, with Hook as my anchor to keep from being dragged under. He tangles his hand into my hair and it's enough to have my vision flashing white, the hair going incandescent as I find release. There's much Hook doesn't know as well, like the fact that a siren's hair is just as alive as the rest of her body, with nerve endings that react to touch. The sensation of his hands coiled tightly in my hair is so intense, I actually have to muffle a scream into his shoulder.

Hook's strokes stutter for a moment as his eyes go wide, his teeth clenched against whatever he's feeling.

"If ye keep doin' that, I'm goin' to shoot early, lass." He rolls a strand of my hair between his fingers. I shudder, buck against him again, let out a soft, mewling cry. That's when he notices it. "Yer hair... 'tis never done this before when I..."

"It's alive," I tell him when I can finally suck in a breath. "As much as my skin, bones, and blood."

Hook twirls the strand around his finger, and an answering curlicue of pleasure twirls down my spine to settle between my legs. I moan again.

"That's gonna be interestin'," he says with a sly grin. "Another time, though."

He releases his grip on my hair, instead petting the nape of my neck and trailing kisses across my jaw as he thrusts into me, slower than before, drawing out the pleasurable torment. I feel like I might burst out of my skin with need if he continues. A fluttering sensation begins between my legs and Hook groans, then speeds up again, dragging his cock along that delicious part of my quim that makes my human toes curl. I clamp my legs around him as tightly as possible and borrow one of his favorite words.

"Oh... feck... Hook... feck… I'm going to..."

His laugh is triumphant. "Cum for me, Aria. Again. I want to see yer face light up an' yer lovely hair glow."

One last thrust and I dive over the edge into perfect bliss. Hook's hips jerk one last time and he stills with a groan. A hot splash of something hits between my legs, and then he's through.

We stay like that for a few minutes, locked together in an intimate embrace. The glow of my hair fades by degrees. It's saddening to realize I'm going to lose this in less than two weeks.

"I want your cock in me every night," I tell him. "For what remains of my time as a human."

He smiles as though he's proud of himself. He should be. "Ye dinnae have to twist me arm, Popsy. I'm yours."

I try to stand, but my legs refuse to support me and I slide to the ground. Hook has to catch me before I fall.

"Careful, lass," he murmurs gently. "Yer legs can be a bit wobbly afterward."

A moment of silence passes, and then Hook clears his throat.

"So, what now?"

"Now we bathe," I say primly, stepping toward the tub. "We're all sticky."

Hook barks a surprised laugh and genuine elation lights his eyes. I shiver again, despite myself. I love this man's smile. Love the ease at which he accepts things. I think I could love *him*, if circumstances were different.

"Aye, that we are, lass."

NINE
ANDRIC

The delegation has finally arrived. Thank the Gods.

We've been waiting on the much-needed Ambrosia for months. When the Guild's representative, Kassidy Aurelian, had suddenly cut off all communication months ago, we'd feared the worst. It had been a blessed relief to realize she'd merely been stymied, not killed.

She's a pretty little thing, flanked by her new husbands, the ruling family of the werebear nation. Each of them looks like they could easily take apart three or four of my men without getting winded. It's a relief to know she's swayed them to our side. If Morningstar had acquired their people... well, I shudder to think what could have resulted.

"Sit, sit," my father greets the party jovially, gesturing broadly to the vacated counsel table. "We'll have a meal prepared shortly to celebrate your arrival, and we can discuss what's to be done from here. You must introduce us to your... fellows. I must admit, we were not expecting quite so... many of you."

I've been wondering about the number of them myself, but I've been too polite to give voice to the question. My father is not a cruel man, but I know better than to speak out of turn. I won't make us appear weak and disorderly in front of our allies when we have so few.

Two of the delegation are clearly not human. Possibly even less so than the bears, who look dangerous but not overtly alien.

In my travels, I've seen women with deep brown skin, and I've seen women so pale, they could be mistaken for vampires. But I've never seen a woman with skin like hers. It's got a subtle silver sheen to it that glimmers in the diffuse light of the throne room. Intricate patterns sweep from the corner of one eye down to her nose. Are they tattoos? I've never seen tattoos in that color before. It's almost a soft green, sage perhaps. Could they be tribal markings? But if so, why does the man not possess them as well?

His are blue, shaped differently from hers.

Both the woman and the man are undeniably beautiful, but it's the woman I'm particularly intrigued by. Built tall and lean, standing straight-backed and confident... from the waist up. She doesn't seem to know where to place her feet and I don't think the blame can be solely placed on the heeled boots she wears. She wobbles every once in a while, and the captain has to steady her. He does it with a patience that suggests he's used to it. Perhaps she has some sort of condition?

Whatever the case, I can't keep my eyes off her for long. She's just too damn beautiful, even wearing men's clothing. Somehow, the crushed blue velvet frock coat (almost a mirror to her captain's, though less worn) suits her better than the layered dresses my father no doubt offered. I can't picture this woman in anything pink and frilly.

"Yes, our number is larger than I assumed, as well," Lady Aurelian says. "I'm afraid I don't know much about the newcomers, my lord," she continues, casting a bemused glance to Captain Hook and the two strangers. "We were attacked by a kraken on the way to your kingdom. We lost one of our crates in transit, but Hook was able to stall long enough to allow the crew and our delegation to escape. These two..."

She gestures at the pair near the Captain.

"Rescued him. I'm told they're, ah..." She gropes for a word.

"Merfolk," the exotic woman supplies as she looks at me straight on, with no worry for my reaction.

Her pronouncement succeeds in stilling all activity in the throne room. My father sits a little straighter on the throne, one hand balling into a fist on the armrest. He doesn't appear happy.

"You brought *merfolk* into my city?" he asks, spearing the captain with his brazen expression.

"No one brought us," the woman says tartly, meeting my father's eyes with a look so impertinent, it would have gotten anyone else whipped. "We came of our own volition. If you do not wish to hear our proposal, we will return from whence we came and you may deal with the grotesquerie on your own when the defenses that hold them back inevitably crumble."

"The what?" my father asks.

"The grotesquerie," she repeats. "Beasts. Monsters of the deep."

My father barks a bitter laugh, shaking his head. I can't help but notice it's grown whiter in the past few years. The burden of war isn't one he should have to bear twice in just a little over a decade. And his health is failing. This is no time for him to be commanding an army. If he'll lay down his pride and retire quietly to the coves, I can keep him safe and happy until he goes.

But my father is hardly the quiet and retiring type.

"Unless you've failed to notice, *girl*, your defenses have accomplished rather little. My fleet is still being destroyed and we can't venture into deeper water. The shallows around Delorood are already depleted."

"What you fail to realize, *senex*," she replies hotly, "is that it could be so much *worse* for your vessels. The kraken that destroyed Hook's *Jolly Roger* was an adolescent that escaped our dragnet. My forces have killed six this month alone. And that's not taking into account the barreleye, monkfish, eels, and large shark species we've prevented from leaving the trenches. We have kept a great deal from your shores already, *your highness*."

The venom in her tone, as well as her words, brings my father up short, and I examine her more critically with this new information. She's unsteady on her feet because she's not used to having them.

"Who are you?" My father finally asks, relaxing back into his chair.

"My name is Princess Arianwen."

Arianwen? That's... that's incredible! If it's true. I've only heard stories about the exiled princess and half-believed them to be a myth. Cast out by Triton for her defense of Delorood and the rest of the land-dwellers, she'd been missing for years. Some thought she was dead.

Clearly, such isn't the case.

"Feck's sake, Aria," the captain mutters under his breath. In the silence of the hall, his words are still audible. "Ye didnae tell me ye were a bloody princess!"

She ignores him, stepping toward us instead, planting one booted foot onto the first stair leading up to the dais.

"Why should I believe you are who you say you are?" my father demands.

"If I were Triton's pawn, do you truly think I'd have come to you for aid? I'd be leading an army against you."

"You've brought a soldier," he points out to the other man of her kind—the one who stands beside her and hasn't left her side. The male stands up straighter and gives us all a flat, unfriendly stare. Arianwen rolls her eyes.

"You can hardly think of Bastion as a threat when you have *dozens* of guards with gutting weapons at the ready," the princess responds.

I wince at the naked flippancy in her tone. The defiance is unexpected and, if I'm honest, very refreshing, but it won't earn my father's favor. It does convince me she's royalty, though. No one, outside of a monarch, speaks to another noble with such disdain. She's never been a serf or a beggar, if there's even such a thing in Triton's city.

"Perhaps you should say what you've come to say, princess Arianwen," I interject, risking my father's

ire. But the round of jabs and accusations benefits no
one.

Arianwen turns her head a fraction to look at me,
and that lovely face softens somewhat. She examines
me, taking my measure. It makes me sit up a little
straighter. I know I'm fit and attractive. But I'm not
built along the lines of Kassidy's men. I'm not even
built like Hook, who looks like life beat him with a
flail, shoved him into the sun to bake, and brought him
back as tough as boot-leather. With the black goatee
and equally dark, flyaway hair, he's got a roguish look
to him. But he's all man and I can understand why
women are drawn to him, as it's always been rumored
they are. I'm definitely not beautiful, the way Bastion,
the princess' guard, is. But she doesn't seem...
displeased by the sight of me.

"I am here to negotiate a cessation of hostilities, on
behalf of my Aunt Cassiopeia," she continues. "We
propose a coup to depose Triton and put my aunt on
the throne. She is in line with your cause. We also wish
to see Morningstar stopped. For so long as the war
wages, we can guarantee safe tides in our waters."

My father sucks in a breath between his teeth and
considers her with less hostility than before. I can't
contain my mounting enthusiasm, and can see a
cautious echo of the same on his face. If the princess'
offer is genuine, it will change everything. Life in
Delorood and all the cities therein can resume as it
once did. More than that, we can begin to recruit and
render aid to the other principalities of Fantasia, as
we've been promising. I know at least some of the
nobles in the north are sympathetic with our cause,

even if Ascor and others have thrown in with
Morningstar's emerging forces.

"And what do you want in return?" I ask, because
my father seems reluctant to address the defiant siren.

Her shoulders straighten still further, pushing her
impressive chest forward. As her coat shifts, I note,
with some embarrassment, that the shirt is thin and the
hard outline of one peaked nipple is showing through
the fabric. It's damn distracting. And dangerous.

Don't fuck or fuck with sirens. It's one of the first
rules young sailors are taught. Being drowned is a
merciful death. More often than not, vengeful sirens
will use their bird form to shred any sailor unfortunate
enough to fall under their thrall.

I have to imagine this one is the same—if driven
and angry enough.

"We require several of your soldiers in their
aquatic gear to stage the coup," she continues. "The
last tangle with the grotesquerie left our forces
depleted. We can't hope to hold them back again. After
Aunt Opeia's spells fail, the monsters of the deep will
begin to rise. We want to stop that from happening. If
Opeia can gain possession of the trident and assume
the throne, she can banish the grotesquerie to the
deeps for good. We are willing to offer much to secure
these troops. Along with the promise of safe tides,
there is also an offer of..." Her eyes drift from my
father to me, giving me that speculative look once
more. "Marriage. To you or your son. A pact, to show
our loyalty to your cause."

While I am quite shocked by her offer, my shock
doesn't compare to the captain's. He inhales so deeply,

the sound echoes through the room. Outrage spasms across his face for an instant before he can hide it. He stares at her with a look of naked betrayal, and I have to wonder just how close the two have grown in the short time since his rescue? If Lady Aurelian is to be believed, and there's no reason she shouldn't be, they've only been on land for a few days, at the most.

Has the captain fucked her? I don't like the thought. Which is absurd, since she's not mine. Furthermore, even if I were to accept her offer of marriage, I hardly think she would remain monogamous. She'd need a consort, at the very least, so she could produce heirs to her own throne. And as regards my throne… Fuck if I know if it's even possible for her to bear my children… human children.

As I study the captain and then the princess' guard, Bastion, I note he too seems quite indignant over this whole subject of betrothal. His eyes are narrowed and his jaw is tight. His hand have turned to fists at his side.

Hmm… this princess certainly has harpooned the hearts of both men. I can only wonder how… is she fucking both of them?

My father turns in his seat to regard me, finally. There's really only one choice if we accept her offer. The healer says my father's heart is weak. He's had to radically alter his diet already, and he's been advised to avoid all physical exercise, other than taking simple walks about the kingdom. As it is, he can barely walk the halls for long stretches. He's not up to the marital duties of a young woman.

"Andric?" He makes my name a question, and I know what he's asking.

I try to consider her offer logically. Try to ignore the promise of sensuality that fairly leaks from her. It's difficult. She's possibly the most beautiful creature I've ever seen, strange hair and markings notwithstanding. And if I marry her, she's tied to our kingdom, sworn to our cause... Truly, we can't afford *not* to have the tides. Without them, no supply line can be established and we'll quickly starve to death. We may as well run the white flag of surrender if that happens.

So, it doesn't really matter what she or I want, in the end. If a loveless, non-monogamous and possibly sexless marriage is what I have to enter into in order to save my people, I will.

I nod. "If the princess is willing, so am I."

Arianwen's expression flickers, and she begins staring at me again as though no one has ever offered her a choice.

With a pang, I realize such is likely the case — exiled at a tender age, sheltered in the deeps where combat wasn't optional, then sent to me to propose a marriage she doesn't want — she's had to carry out the will of others all her life.

I have the urge to step off the dais and cross over to her, cradle her fine-boned face in my hands and brush kisses across those cheeks. Murmur reassurances that I'm not cruel and that she will have agency where I'm concerned. If she wants nothing to do with me after the marriage, so be it. But she will *always* have a choice.

Slowly, she inclines her head. "Yes. I am willing."

My father claps his hands, a smile finally curling the weathered edges of his mouth. I can't help but notice how deep the creases in his face are becoming, like a crumpled piece of parchment.

"Excellent! We'll retire and then reunite for supper, yes? This seems like an occasion to celebrate!"

But Princess Arianwen doesn't look like she wants to celebrate. She's pensive and seems a little worried. She keeps shooting glances at Captain Hook, who stands as rigid and still as a statue. He refuses to meet her eyes. She does nod her head respectfully toward my father after a moment.

"That's agreeable."

Murmurs finally break out in our wake when our group makes its egress. I offer Arianwen a hand after I descend the dais, and she slides her own hand into it cautiously. I marvel at the texture of her skin. As smooth as silk. There's a light silver sheen to it, when candlelight hits it just right.

"I'm Andric," I tell her, offering a smile and hoping for one in return. It doesn't work. If anything, she looks more anxious. "It's a pleasure to meet you, Princess Arianwen."

"Aria," she says quietly. "I prefer people call me Aria."

"Aria," I amend, smoothing a thumb over her knuckles. "It's a pleasure to meet you."

That's apparently all the captain can tolerate, because he turns on one heel and stalks away. Aria slides her hand from mine and starts after him without returning the sentiment.

Hook is a lucky bastard. If he can't understand or forgive her, he's a fool.

But, Aria doesn't seem the sort to suffer a fool. Thus, again, I find myself quite intrigued by the nature of the relationship between the two of them — the legendary Captain Hook, known for his independence, who now acts the part of the spurned lover? And a princess who is no stranger to war, brought low by her lover's jealousy?

Curious, yes, and hopefully remedied when the captain takes his leave of her.

TEN
Aria

I lose track of Hook.

Surer on his feet, he manages to dodge me
effectively and disappears into the castle's interior
before I can catch up to him. I'm irritated at my
infernal human body for betraying me, and I now find
myself tucked into an alcove, salty moisture rolling
down my cheeks yet again. I've been sitting here a
while—until the heaving of my chest starts to slow and
the piteous noises coming from my mouth eventually
cease.

And then I turn and start for the castle, all the
while experiencing a sinking feeling in the depths of
my stomach.

***

My face still feels hot, though I've tried washing it
a few times. Prince Andric is waiting for me just
outside my room, and when I walk out the door, he
smiles and extends his arm so I can place my hand on
his forearm. Hook was the first to show me that
position, and it makes my chest ache to think of him.

Prince Andric is not unattractive, by any measure.
And were I not so head over heels for Hook, I might be
quite delighted by the prospect of making Andric my
land husband. He's different from Hook. Skin pale like

sea foam, though his hair is just as dark as Hook's.
Andric's eyes are an exquisite teal, as though one
could glimpse the sea in his gaze. The color is quite
intriguing. His body is not unpleasant, either —
slimmer than Hook's, though Andric's quite a bit
taller. No ticklish facial growth, just a shadow along
his jaw where it ought to be.

I can definitely do worse for a husband. He's not
the one I want, but he's attractive, I must admit. He
seems kind, if not a little aloof. He doesn't speak much
and when he does, he's somber. He weighs his words.
It's a good quality in a leader, even if he's not a
scintillating conversationalist.

I examine him critically, especially his trousers,
where I can just make out the line of his cock against
the fabric. It seems to be a good size. I will not mind
having it inside me when the time comes. But, still,
he's not Hook. There's no ache between my legs when
I look at Prince Andric. Not yet, anyway.

Thoughts of Hook make me anxious. He'll be at
the dinner, I hope? Perhaps I can corner him and ask
for forgiveness and explain why I made the decision I
did — that there was no other option — that it was the
will of my aunt. Regardless, I should have warned
Hook. I should have told him what I intended to
offer — my hand.

But the moment I step through the doors of the
great hall, my vague, half-formed plans fly out of my
head.

The stink hits me first. The thick, meaty smell
hangs like a fug in the air, and I know I've smelled it
before, in various forms. Beached whales. Sickly

merfolk, in their final weeks before perishing. The corpses of kraken that are too large to force them back into the trenches in their limp state.

This room reeks of death. And a cursory examination shows why.

There are carcasses everywhere! The table is lined with them. Fish of every shape and color, laid out in fillets. Some of them whole, slathered in sauces or rubbed with spices. Clams, painfully pried open. Lobsters with their skin boiled red. And then there are beasts I can't name, land dwellers, I assume, but those too are arrayed in positions I can only assume are unnatural. One appears to have a fruit tucked into its mouth.

Fresh water leaks from my eyes and I wrench my hand free of Andric's grip. I've heard tales of the appetites of humans. But I never expected *this*. They're not just eating these poor, unfortunate creatures. They make art with the corpses!

It's sick.

And I simply cannot and will not watch the humans carve these poor creatures up.

Behind me, Bastion makes a noise of outrage as he, too, witnesses the carnage.

I backpedal, putting as much space between myself and the reeking room as possible. My back hits a wall, head knocking painfully against stone. I get my feet beneath me, still my wobbling knees, and pelt back the way we came. I don't know where the exit is, but I have to find it. I have to get out of this confining slab of carved stone and back to the ocean. I don't belong here with these barbarians. We can find allies elsewhere, surely?

A voice calls after me, but it's drowned by the pulse in my ears and the sounds of horror that escape me, no matter how desperately I try to hold them in.

I bump into walls several times, fall and scuff my hands and stain the knees of my trousers. I send a metal suit clattering to the ground with a noisy bang. I leap over it, roll, and keep going.

When I find the exit, I let out another soft cry — this time, in relief — and sprint through the open doors, past the guards. One tries to stop me. I release a warble of sound, a very weak echo of my siren's song, but it's still enough. It does something... odd, to humans. The guards go slack-jawed and stare at me in wonder. One extends his arms, like he wants to embrace me. They both drop their weapons.

I've never seen this sort of response, because I wasn't old enough to visit the drowning coves before my banishment and too afraid to go after. But I have heard tales of my cousins sunning themselves on rocks, inviting sailors to come to them with their song. And when those sailors got close enough, the sirens would push them under the water and hold them until the thrashing stopped. I hear Orva possesses a necklace of human bones she can loop around her tail twice. Punishment for human cruelty on the ocean, for pouring their waste and their refuse into the sea. Punishment for all the sirens killed and mounted on masts.

Now I understand the need for that vengeance. Now I've seen, firsthand, what humans are capable of—what they do to my kind. Now I understand.

And now I'm going to do the only thing left to do—I'm returning the sea. Damn these humans and their barbarity! Doing so will ruin any chance we have of securing allies. I realize that. And I also realize Aunt Opeia will have my tailfin. But I need to be in the water, need to have some connection to my home. Land is dry. It's painful and barbaric and humans are cruel.

I hesitate when I reach the muddy path that leads down from the castle and into the city of Bridgeport. From here, all I need to do is run to the far end of the pier. Then I simply need to climb up the embankment of dirt that leans against the rock wall separating the city from the sea. Then I just launch myself off the edge of the wall and into the ocean.

I can't leap in human form. My half-form will only take me so far, but perhaps it will be enough. I begin stripping off layers of clothing which I generally can't stand, dropping the finery to the ground. Itchy, confining stuff. I'm grateful to be rid of it.

It's a sweet ache, like stretching sore muscles, as I release my wings. Keeping them folded beneath my skin is like maintaining a clenched fist. It hurts after a time, but I've gotten used to the ache. I've not had an opportunity to reach shore for many, many years, and to unfurl them beneath the water would make them next to useless until they could dry.

I let out a sigh, elation seeping into my veins despite the panic still churning my guts. It's almost worth being sunburnt to have the opportunity to use my wings. If we can successfully overthrow Triton, perhaps Aunt Opeia can brew me a solution to make my wings repel moisture. What I wouldn't give to ride a thermal into the night sky. Even in the evening, Bridgeport is muggy and pleasant. If only they weren't murderers here.

Poised on my tiptoes I stand, arms outstretched, wings pointed toward the sky, ready for flight. I'm about to launch myself off the side of the wall and toward the water when I hear footsteps. I spin, letting my wings fold modestly over my front. I still don't understand why human men are obsessed with breasts, but Hook tells me to be careful. So I cover the damn things as someone sprints up the footpath after me. Maybe it's Bastion. Or Hook... Can I stand to see either the captain now?

The depressing answer is yes. I still want to see him, even if he's a murderous flesh-eater. I'm more disgusted with myself than I am with Hook, knowing I want his mouth on mine and his cock inside me.

But as the shape grows closer, I see it's neither my friend nor my lover. It's Prince Andric.

"Stay back," I warn him, flashing my teeth. These humans only seem to understand aggression, so I'll give it to him. Failing that, I can use my song.

Andric obediently slows, coming to a halt three yards away from me. He raises his hands in a pacifying gesture.

"You're angry," he observes with some surprise.

"Yes, I'm angry!" I yell back at him.

"Why? Is it my father? He's a bit obstinate but I can speak to him about…"

My lip curls in disgust. He doesn't even understand what he's done wrong! "I'm not angry about your father!"

"Then what are you angry about?" he asks and his eyes appear… kind?

"The fish."

He stops speaking abruptly, his brow creasing. He looks more like his father with the mass of lines on his face. My dislike for him intensifies.

"The fish?" he asks, clearly still confused.

"You butchered them! Laid their carcasses out like it was an art form! The lobsters… Gods, and the clams? It's…"

I choke on my own disgust, acid stinging my throat. I'm in danger of bringing up the bread and cheese Hook fed us for breakfast.

Realization dawns on the prince's face, and remorse limps along behind it. "Oh. I didn't think… I'm so sorry, Princess Arianwen. I didn't know. We thought…"

"Thought what?"

"Fish eat other fish all the time, don't they? We just assumed you were the same."

I flare my wings wide in agitation, forgetting momentarily that I need to keep them wrapped tightly around myself for modesty's sake. I gesture broadly toward my body.

"Do I *look* like a fish?"

"Well, no," he starts but I don't allow him to finish.

117

I glare at him instead. "Even in my mermaid form, do I look like a guppy to you?"

Andric's head dips.

"No, you don't. You're right, we should have asked you what you prefer to eat and what you don't. If you were any other land-faring species, we would have thought to inquire but..." He chews on his lip. "You have to understand, Princess. It's been so long since anyone has even *seen* a siren. Even those in the drowning coves have disappeared. Triton keeps all his people beneath the sea and away from us. We haven't opened a dialogue with your people since before Triton reigned."

Some of my anger drains away. My father has reigned for... Gods, has it been a century now? More? He's nearing middle age. So, yes, it has to have been about one century. Human lives are far more fleeting. My father has been on the throne since before Andric was alive. Possibly before his father was even born. Our alliances with the surface-dwellers have always been with the tacit understanding that we avoid each other. So it's entirely possible he's being honest.

"You speak the truth?" I ask. "You're not..." What was it Hook says? "Yankin' my fin?"

A tiny smile quirks Andric's lips—a dimple pops in his right cheek, and it spills light into his eyes. It's surprisingly attractive.

"Well, at the moment, you don't have any fins to yank," he says with a little laugh but when he takes note of the fact that I'm still glaring at him, the laugh dies away. He nods instead. "Yes, I'm being honest, Princess," he says as he faces me with eyes that seem honest enough. "We didn't know the food would offend you and I am so sorry it did. I'll speak to my father and I'll ensure this never happens again." He takes a breath. "You have my word."

A breeze picks up, ruffling my hair and feathers and tickling my skin, bringing my nipples to attention. I expect Andric's eyes to drop to my chest, the way Hook's do, but he keeps his gaze resolutely on my face. He doesn't even appear to notice I'm wearing nothing. It's much like standing with Bastion.

When I say nothing, Andric steps a little closer and stoops to pick up my coat.

"Would you mind coming back? I can and will have the cooks prepare some seaweed wraps and fruit, instead."

I'm troubled he won't look at my naked body. Perhaps he doesn't desire me? How am I to seal the pact with him if he doesn't want to touch me? I step closer and run a hand along his chest. He clears his throat and appears wholly uncomfortable.

"Do you find me unattractive?" I ask, worried such might be the case.

His eyes go wide. "What?" he says and seems quite befuddled.

"You haven't looked at my breasts once," I answer with a shrug. "Hook tells me human males find them pleasing?"

"Yes, they do…"

"Don't you want to touch them? Or at least look at them?"

"Well, I…" he swallows, looks down at the ground, and then brings his attention back to my face. "Yes."

I take one of his hands. It's big and rough, much like Hook's. I didn't expect such. He's a prince. What labor does he do that makes his hands coarse?

I guide his hand to my breast, curling his fingers along the underside and pressing his thumb against my nipple. Andric makes a sound in the back of his throat that makes my body clench hard and an ache begins between my legs.

Andric draws his hand away. My skin feels cold where he no longer touches it. My eyes prick strangely. "You don't want to touch me?"

He chuckles weakly. "Yes, of course I want to! You're the most beautiful woman I've ever seen, Aria. But just because I *can* do a thing doesn't mean I *should*."

"I don't understand."

He seems frustrated and runs a hand through his hair. "I could bring you to the ground right now and take you, and I know you'd let me, Princess."

"Please… call me Aria."

He nods. "You'll do anything to secure the alliance—I understand that and I admire you for your resolve. But you don't *owe* me your body, Aria. If you ever come to my bed, I want it to be because *you want to*—because you want to feel me inside you. Not because you feel duty-bound, owing to this agreement between us." He sighs. "And I don't want you ever to be afraid of me—afraid I might force myself on you."

"I'm not frightened of you."

Frightened of my father, yes. Of losing Hook, who I've become absurdly attached to, yes. Frightened of Bastion's mood swings, and of losing Aunt Opeia, yes. But I'm not frightened of him.

Exasperated by his ignorance, perhaps. Not frightened.

"But you are scared," he insists, as if plucking the thoughts from my head, "of what's coming and that's why you've come here, seeking our favor. And your fear is natural. But it doesn't mean we have to rush into anything."

"Then you're rejecting our alliance?"

He smiles patiently and then sidles closer to me, sinking down so he can dangle his long legs over the side of the wall. He shivers in the light breeze and I sink down as well, curling one wing around his shoulders. He traces one feather idly with a smile. I shiver. More warmth pools between my thighs. Human men and their propensity for touching. My wings are as sensitive as my hair. If he touches them too much, I might climax. Wouldn't that be a spectacle?

Thankfully, he drops his hand. I curl my wing around him to keep the wind off his face.

"No, I'm not rejecting the alliance. I'm amending the terms. You and I can marry, if you still want that. But I'm not going to…"

"To feck me?" I finish for him because he seems to have lost his words.

He swallows again as a smile takes his expression. "Right." Then he looks at me. "The word is 'fuck', Aria."

"But Hook says," I start.

He nods. "It's the same word but his accent makes the pronunciation different."

"Oh," I say and try the new word out on my tongue. "Fuck, fuck, fuck."

He chuckles and holds my chin up so we're looking each other in the eyes again. "I'm not going to fuck you. Not until you want me to."

I raise an eyebrow, a spark of mischief kindling in me. I smirk at him. "And if I told you I wanted it here and now?"

He blinks at me once, then laughs. "Tease."

I shrug easily. "Not a tease. A siren. It's in my nature."

He hums thoughtfully and leans backward, brushing my wing again. It may not be teasing for long. His touches are driving me wild.

I cup his face and press my lips very gently to his. Then, with all of my strength, I roll him beneath me, straddle his waist and kiss him harder. My skin tingles. My quim aches. I want him. But he doesn't want me. Not here and now anyway. I wonder if he has another woman? Someone he loves? Maybe this agreement is as difficult on him as it is on me?

I climb off him after a moment. "Thank you, Andric," I murmur. "For being kind."

And then I saunter toward the castle, with the weighty feel of his stare on my back.

ELEVEN
ARIA

Supper is a quiet affair, and Hook is conspicuously absent, though the rest of the party is seated around a long and rectangular table, the king sitting at one end and Andric sitting at the other. I sit beside Andric and Bastion, the latter who busily glares at the staff, even as he slurps seaweed and enjoys the novel fruits that grow on land. I'm partial to something called a mango, but Bastion seems to prefer a fruit known as an orange. At Andric's prodding, we begin a conversation about our respective customs. The most inane details seem to fascinate him.

I learn new things, as well—news about Morningstar and the efforts made to defeat him, thus far. I'm a bit awestruck when I learn the golden-haired woman, Kassidy, is Chosen. One of *the* chosen. And that another, named Neva, has also been discovered.

At learning Kassidy is Chosen, I also realize how much I need her. "You have to come with us on our mission!" I say at once.

Kassidy leans back in her chair and regards me skeptically. "Why would I do that?"

"Because you may be the only one who can lift the trident!" I insist.

"The trident?" she repeats, clearly confused.

"Yes! Poseidon's trident!"

"And what is that?"

123

"The trident controls the sea. No one has been able to wield it since Poseidon sank into the sands and entered a death-like sleep a century ago."

"Then your father can't wield it?" Kassidy asks.

I shake my head. "No. The trident didn't choose my father. My Aunt Opeia couldn't wield it either, but she can at least maintain control of the sea if we can snatch my father's scepter away. It won't be completely effective, but it should keep the grotesquerie at bay."

"I still don't understand why you think I should come along," Kassidy replies, frowning.

"You're Chosen," I answer with a shrug. The trident has to be wielded by someone of great power. I think you're the only one who could possibly do it!"

She lets out a pealing laugh, but I can hear a note of doubt behind it. "And if I'm able to free the trident, what then?"

"Then you would rule the ocean," I say, not really understanding the question. Isn't it obvious?

"Rule the ocean as in… live in the ocean?" she repeats, frowning.

"Yes, of course," I answer.

She shakes her head. "In case you haven't noticed, I'm not a merperson. Besides, I know my final battle takes place on land, not beneath the sea."

I'm flummoxed. Doesn't she understand how important this is? That in order to defeat Morningstar, she needs an open sea to easily transport troops and cargo?

Bastion leaps to my defense, setting his orange aside at last. "You would only have to remain in the sea long enough to establish order, Lady Kassidy. Lady Cassiopeia and Princess Aria will see to the rest."

Kassidy exchanges pointed glances with her retinue. The three hulking males sit as close to her as they can manage, and each one of them has a hand on her somewhere. Leith is the tallest, I think, and I still marvel over his looks which strike me as a walking contradiction. With hair as gray as shale, it seems he should be much older. But his face belongs to a man in his prime. His eyes are bright but his shoulders stoop a little, even when he's happy, as though weighed down by his title.

Nash has a similar cast to his features, though with an edge of hard cynicism that is absent in either of the others' faces. I've never seen a bear in person before, so I cannot say how fearsome they are, but I do sense his power. It's close to the surface, like the magma running through Aunt Opeia's caves. It's the type of power that simmers beneath the surface, threatening to burst forth at any minute.

Sorren is the outlier. If I hadn't been told, I wouldn't believe he shares blood with the other two. He's as pale as Andric, with eyes as blue and bleak as a winter sky. His hair is brown and he intimidates me the most of the bunch. Even in the short time I've known him, he's shown himself to be sharp in both mind and tongue. I think, of the three, he will be the most vicious if crossed.

Not that I plan on crossing him. No, I need him. I need all of them. If we're going to defeat Morningstar, we need strong and able men such as the three of them. And we need Kassidy the most.

"What do you think?" Kassidy asks, eyes flitting from each handsome face, seeking confirmation.

"I think we'll have to chance it," Leith says soberly. "Andric is right. We can't afford to lose the tides. So, we'll take the fight to Triton."

I'm thrilled.

"We?" Kassidy echoes. "You can't mean…"

Nash snorts. "Yes, we fucking can and do mean to go with you! We almost lost you in Grimm, you thieving little minx. We're not going to risk letting a kraken eat you!"

I smile faintly and don't mention that any kraken would be unlikely to go for prey so small. Humans have so many bones and such little meat. It would simply thrash her and release her corpse, most likely.

Sorren nods. "If you go, Kassidy, we all go."

"We welcome any help you're willing to give," I interject. "And we do need soldiers. You're our best bet of seizing power from Triton. Even if Triton's defeated and killed, my stepmother or half-sisters could wield the scepter and we'd be in no better a position. Promise me you will at least try?"

Kassidy stares down at her plate for a few seconds, contemplating, before her gaze shifts to the window. Like most things on land, it's rather small and cramped. I doubt I could fit my human body in the gap without having to fold in on myself. But it allows in a pleasant sea breeze.

Outside, silvery moonlight traces the waves. They're deceptively placid tonight. I know at least two kraken roam the waters, and possibly more if Opeia's magic hasn't held.

"We need the sea," Kassidy repeats, almost to herself. Then she turns back to face me. I really do smile this time, because determination glints in those sparkling green eyes, as hard as flint.

"All right. I'm in. Who else is coming with me?"

"Thank you," I start before I'm interrupted.

"I am," Andric says, jumping into the conversation at last. He's mostly stared at me through dinner, watching me with the oddest expression on his face. I can't fathom what he's thinking, but I'm too uncomfortable to ask in front of the other guests.

For all I know, he's angry with me for trying to cement our alliance earlier. Perhaps he longs for another love and I overstepped my bounds? Who can say? Humans are so difficult to puzzle out, their reactions and sensibilities strange.

"You can't," the King says at once. "I won't allow it."

"You can and you must allow it, father," Andric argues. "Think how it would look if I agreed to marry Aria and then let her charge into the depths alone! What sort of husband would I be? Do you want the Prince of Delorood to gain a reputation for cowardice?"

"This isn't about our pride, Andric," the King continues stubbornly.

"Then what is it about?" Andric demands.

"Our survival. We're in this state due to your obstinate contention that life beneath Morningstar's reign will be no life at all."

"And you think it would be a life?" Andric demands.

127

The old man sighs. "I'm not entirely sure what I believe. But you are my son, and I've trusted your judgment thus far and look where that's led us! We've lost half our fleet, we have almost no food. We're facing extinction. And now, you want to dunk your head in the sea and hope something doesn't bite it off? It's ludicrous!"

"If it's succession you're worried about, old man," Andric says coolly, "you can always place one of my cousins on the throne. Or perhaps Augustus. Didn't you have a bastard with that little sable-haired witch you liked so much back in the day?"

The temperature in the room sinks, and I'm not the only one who notices. I stare longingly at the door, wishing to be anywhere but here. I need to find Hook and see what I can do to mitigate the damage I've already done. I don't understand why he's so upset. I had thought our dalliance merely that. Was it possible he cared for me more than I thought?

"The princess looks tired," Kassidy says after meeting my beseeching gaze. "I'm going to help her get into some nightclothes and see that she gets to bed. Is that okay, Aria?"

"Yes, please," I say, latching eagerly onto the chance of escape.

She takes me by the hand, and I find hers as rough as the hands of any of the men I've encountered. What must she do that they've become so calloused? I admire her more now that I did before. She's the strongest woman I've ever met and yet she's so small.

She pulls me away from the great hall and the argument rises in volume and tempo as we make our way out the door. I wince. I haven't actually heard a family argument for years, not since leaving Aspamia for the trenches. Aunt Opeia and I have an accord on most things.

Kassidy squeezes my hand gently as we scuttle quickly down the hall, moving as swiftly as possible from the dining hall.

"Don't look so grim," she says. "They'll sort it out."

"I don't know," I start.

Kassidy nods. "The King is being a stubborn old codger, but he'll come around. Andric is one of the best warriors in this kingdom, and he's completely right in the arguments he made. It *will* upset the social order if Andric doesn't stand up for you and assume his place by your side."

"I don't know that it's so simple," I respond as I look down at her hand holding mine and squeeze it a little harder. I've not had a female friend before and I hope Kassidy will become one.

"What do you mean?"

I shrug. "Andric doesn't want me," I admit, feeling a little embarrassed admitting as much to her — a woman who has three men who desire her.

"Um, have you seen yourself?"

"You are kind," I answer but then shake my head.

"What in the world makes you think Andric doesn't want you? He was staring at you all through dinner."

"He won't share my bed, even after we're married. He said so." I sigh. "And he'd be risking very much for someone he just met and doesn't apparently like."

Kassidy's laugh is like a soft peal of bells. It's enchanting and I understand how her men find her fascinating. She's quite attractive, as far as humans go. Her golden hair shimmers in the torchlight that illuminates the corridor, and she's got skin that's slightly tanned with a pinkish hue on her cheeks and a spattering of attractive freckles across the bridge of her nose. Her body is tiny but compact, with enough muscle that she must clearly be a warrior. She's strong. Capable. And she has a dry wit. I can't help but wonder if she weren't taken, would Hook want her?

If I were a human male, I should think I would.

"If Andric won't share your bed, Aria, it's because he's honorable," Kassidy says with a smirk. And this time she tightens her hold on my hand.

"Honorable?"

She nods. "Prince Andric always struck me as the type of man you read about in children's stories. The type of man who rarely exists in reality."

I'm confused. "What do you mean?"

She tilts her head to the side as she considers my question. "I mean, he's one of the rare men who thinks with the brain between his ears, not the one inside his cock. He values the chance at peace too highly to fuck things up by... well, fucking things up."

"There are brains within men's cocks?" I ask, completely baffled.

She immediately begins laughing. "No, no! It's just a turn of speech… never mind."

At my uncomprehending stare, she blows out a breath and the smile slips. "Trust me. I can tell Andric wants you. And if I can see it, then it's plain as the nose on your face, because I'm terrible at navigating relationships and lovey-dovey bullshit."

I'm not sure I believe her, because her comment sounds silly when she has three husbands, but I let the matter drop, moving on to one that's more pressing. To me, at least. "And Hook?"

"What about Hook?"

"What sort of man is he?"

Kassidy's steps stutter and she drops my hand, leaving it feeling empty and cold. "A good one," she answers immediately. "Though not in the same way that Prince Andric is good."

"I believe I've hurt Hook," I say, appreciating the chance to speak about my problems with another woman, one who might understand.

We're not far from the quarters I share with the captain now. She casts a glance at the door and lowers her voice when she speaks.

"Did you make him any promises?" she asks.

"Promises?"

"I can only assume you both are... intimate?"

"Intimate?"

"Fucking?"

"Oh!" I say and then give her a smile. "Yes."

"Well, were you clear about what it was before you started fucking him?" She pauses and then realizes I have no idea what she's going on about. "Were you clear that you didn't expect anything other than sex from him?"

I shuffle guiltily. The mango aftertaste goes sour in my mouth. "We didn't talk about it. We mostly just..."

"I get it," Kassidy finishes with a hint of wry amusement. "That may be the problem." Then she motions to his door. "Talk to him, if he's still awake. We'll leave by morning, assuming the prince can sort things out with his father."

Kassidy doesn't give me time to respond. She gives me a little smile and walks away before I can make the cowardly request that she enter the room first to smooth things over with him.

I hesitate before the door, almost too frightened to knock. This fear is entirely brainless, isn't it? I've faced scarier things than the rugged sailor in the room before me. The grotesquerie is more fearsome, more dangerous, and much more likely to kill me.

But facing Hook's disappointment hurts more than being stabbed in the tail by my father's pronged scepter. I really do hate this human propensity to leak out of the eyes. It's starting again, the damned annoying phenomenon that Hook refers to as *crying*.

That's how Hook finds me. Dithering outside his door, tears streaming down my face, looking about as composed as a child. He takes one look at me, sighs, and then steps aside.

"Come in, Popsy. Stop cryin'."

"Hook..." I croak, angry these tears are interfering with my ability to speak.

What do I say? I'm sorry? I'm not quite sure what my crime is. I regret his pain, but how to mitigate it? It's absolutely crucial I secure the alliance with Andric...

I step into the room beyond, taking in more details this time. There's a large bed, easily double the size of the mattress at the hostel in which we stayed. The bed is piled high with the fluffy wedges Hook calls pillows. These are colorful, like the tropical fruit served at dinner. Bright greens, pinks, and oranges. The bedspread looks soft and enticing. More velvet, in a blue-green that offsets the pillows.

I want to be laid out on it, trapped beneath Hook's muscled body as he slides his cock into me. Everything ceases to matter when he holds me close and rocks himself inside me. I won't miss much about being human, but I'll miss that.

Hook takes me gently by the elbow, but instead of guiding me to the bed, he pushes me gently into a chair. There's a stubby structure next to it that looks like a reverse bench. Hook calls it a desk. I'm not sure what its purpose is. The chair is hard, the expression on Hook's face harder.

He doesn't sit. He paces a line from one wall to the other, occasionally taking sips out of a bottle. The liquid that sloshes inside is brown. There was some at dinner as well, though I didn't partake of it. The scent coming off it is strong enough to make my eyes water even more than they already are.

"What is that you're drinking?" I ask.

"Sweetland port."

"What is it?"

"Spirits."

"Is it sweet?" I ask, hoping he'll give me a taste. I do like sweets.

He offers me the bottle and the sour smell arrests my nose. He seems to enjoy it though so I tip my head back and swallow a large mouthful. And then I very nearly choke and erupt into a coughing fit as the horrid stuff burns my throat on its way to my stomach.

"Terrible!" I manage.

Hook chuckles. "Then I guess ye dinnae have spirits where ye're from?"

"No! Most certainly not!"

"Mayhap a better place where ye live, then. Spirits make men do despicable things."

"Despicable things?"

He nods. "Aye. Say things they dinnae mean. Make bets they shouldnae make. I was drunk when I lost this." He raises his mechanical hand up to the light. I prefer it when he wears his hook but he wears the faux hand when we meet someone important.

"What happened to your real hand?" I ask.

He shrugs. "Got jumped by my damn kid brother's new leader. Calls himself Pan. Little fecker fed me hand to a crocodile."

"He what?" I ask, shocked.

But Hook isn't finished. He continues on as if I haven't spoken at all. "'Twas on our journey back to the coves. We were almost clear. I was lookin' to get me brother Quinn back. Me feckin' captain at the time sold Quinn off to our enemies as he owed them a great debt. Had to keelhaul me to do it, but the captain paid his debt by sellin' Quinn to the faction across the sea. Quinn's nae forgiven me for it. Feck, *I* dinnae forgive me for it."

I stare at him, quietly aghast by this new information. I know something about being cast aside like trash. It hurt more than words could express when my father banished me. I can't imagine what it must be like for Hook, to be estranged from his brother.

"Why does your brother blame you?" I demand. "You couldn't have stopped it."

"Aye, I could've," Hook rages.

"How?"

"There had to be somethin' I could've done. Could have begged the cap'n to sell me instead. But the feckin' King of Ironcross had nae interest in me."

Hook chokes. His steps stutter, and he swings the bottle up to his lips again. It's a prolonged draft this time, and a few more seconds before he can speak again.

"An' to top the whole feckin' mess off, we pissed off a witch an' got ourselves cursed."

"Cursed? Cursed how?"

He nods and wipes his face with his sleeve. "Aye, cursed. I haven't aged a day in forty feckin' years! Cannae feckin' sire children. Cannae feckin' grow old. All I can do to escape the curse is die someday."

"So you're...?" I try to do the calculations in my head. He doesn't look much over thirty.

"Seventy-three, Popsy. I'm a right ol' bastard, I am."

"Goodness!" I say, surprised.

He nods. "I've been stuck like this. Thought that leavin' Neverland might break the curse but..." He shrugs. "'Twas nae so. I've spent twenty years on this side and yet, do ye see a single gray hair?"

No. I've spent a great deal of time looking at him and he appears to be a man in his prime. Strong and scarred, but undoubtedly beautiful. In truth, he's almost as old as the weathered King in the great hall. He could be Andric's father. Or mine.

"What happened to Quinn?" I prompt quietly when he lapses into silence and stares moodily at the wall. "Why'd your captain sell him?"

A full-body shudder rocks through Hook. He looks almost as unsteady on his feet as I feel most days.

"I tried," he whispers. "I tried to train Quinn right. I did. But the kid's rubbish with a sword. Nae verra good on ships, either, which is unfortunate when ye're drafted into King Crab's army."

"King Crab?" I echo. All I can picture is the crustacean.

Hook lets out a humorless snort and resumes pacing. "Aye. King o' the Coves where Quinn an' I grew up. Big motherfecker, with orange hair an' a mean disposition. Would put kids in the pincer."

"The pincer?"

"Aye. Big vise thing. Pop their heads off if they broke a law. Earned himself a nickname."

I'm too horrified to speak. This is not the tale I was prepared for, nor am I sure I want to hear it. But the words pour out of Hook, and I can't stem the flow.

"I was drafted into the navy when I was aboot Quinn's age. Worked as hard as I could to earn his keep an' mine. But he had to be trained. Most o' the armies are made o' kids, more often than not. Nae one really lives past forty in Neverland. I was pushin' old age by the time I got cursed. Quinn was nineteen."

"Forty? That's so... Hook, how is *forty* the life expectancy? I'm twenty-five, and I'm barely more than a child. My father is a century old and he's only just middle-aged. Humans are fragile but they're not... their lives aren't *that* short… are they?"

His eyes are distant, seeming to stare right through me. The smile is a twisted mockery of its former self. "Have ye heard o' the forever wars, Aria?"

I shake my head. He rolls a shoulder.

"I'd be surprised if ye had heard o' 'em, to be honest."

"What are they?"

He nods. "Aye, let me start from the beginning, Popsy. Neverland is counted as a principality by Fantasia, but it's just technical. Nae one wants to risk the waterfall that drains into the dimension. Feckin' difficult to go back up the thing, let me tell ye. 'Tis why most people who come to Neverland dinnae leave, an' those who are born there dinnae have any option but stay."

He sucks in a deep breath. "Before ye lot had Morningstar to contend with, there was Moon. First bloke made in our dimension, or so we're told. Sprung up from dirt or somethin'. An' then he made himself two wives. One named Star, the other named Sun. He had a bunch o' little buggers with each. But when it came time to divide up resources after the poor fecker's death, the more favored wife, Sun, claimed Moon had bequeathed all his riches to her children."

"She did?"

"Aye, an' she had a massive feckin' brood o' 'em by then."

"What did his second wife do?"

"Aye, well Star knew Sun was full o' bunk an' the two wives went to war. Star had magic in her blood, an' her line spawned monsters. Eventually, the two factions split into four. Then, four into eight, as time went on an' bloodlines got muddy. Neverland has been in a constant state o' war since the death o' the first man."

"And that's why humans don't usually survive until forty? Owing to the witches and monsters?"

"Aye, 'tis part o' it. Mostly, it's war. Constant, unendin', senseless war. There arenae even kingdoms anymore, though they like to call themselves that. 'Tis all just rocks an' the warlords that have scrabbled to the top o' the heap to defend their piles o' rocks. Ye want food or shelter, ye have to join an army. 'Tis the only thing that stops the constant anarchy. An' that's what Quinn an' I grew up in."

"What happened to Quinn after you were… whatever you said you were? Killholed?"

"Keelhauled," he corrects me. "Aye, after I were keelhauled, I killed the captain an' took over once they hauled me back onboard, but 'twas too late for Quinn."

"What became of him?"

"He was sold into a mercenary group under the King of Ironcross called the Lost Boys. I didnae see him again until Pan came for me. Spared the little fecker's life for Quinn's sake. Quinn's got a soft spot for the ginger sod."

"Ginger?"

"Aye, Peter Pan's hair. It be red."

Then he looks at me expectantly and I realize he's concluded his story. "I am so very sorry, Hook," I

138

murmur. "I had no idea you had such a… difficult and painful life."

"Aye, nae cryin' over spilt milk," he says and shakes his head with a sigh. Then he glances at me again. "Why are ye here anyway?"

I suddenly feel embarrassed. "I just… I came to see why you were so angry with me." His expression darkens. "I never meant to hurt you."

Hook shakes his head ruefully. "I know that, Popsy. 'Tis me own feckin' fault. I knew better than to think this was more than it is."

"I should have told you I intended to offer the prince my hand in marriage. It was wrong that I kept that from you."

"Wrong's been done on both sides, lass," he says, finally collapsing on the colorful bedspread. "I should've held meself back. Should never have touched ye. I knew better."

"Is that why you're angry with me?" I ask quietly, tucking my chin. "Because I didn't tell you? I thought maybe you were jealous. I was hoping…"

I swallow, and fresh tears scald my skin. Damn human form! I hate losing control of my emotions so much.

"What were ye hopin' for, Popsy?"

I can't meet his eyes when I answer. "That things between us could be like they are with Kassidy and her men," I admit. "They seem happy."

Hook laughs bitterly. "'Tis nae the sharin' I mind, lass. Have as many men as ye like. Dozens, if it makes ye happy, so long as ye still call me yer love at the end o' the day. I'm nae so greedy. But I dinnae pay allegiance to kings. Never again. An' I dinnae feck their queens. Did that once, an' it ended in a curse. So, if ye marry the prince, I cannae be with ye, Aria. Nae matter how much I might want ye. 'Tis one rule I refuse to break."

It's hard to swallow. How can I possibly reconcile duty with desire? I want Hook. If nothing else were on the line, I'd follow him to the edge of the Earth and tumble off the waterfall with him. I'm smitten already, beyond the bounds of sanity. It's almost like a reverse siren's song. He's bound me, not the other way around.

But there *is* something on the line. Two worlds— that of the land and that of the ocean. And I can't sacrifice the survival of both for him.

He slides off the bed and crosses over to me with a sigh, swiping his rough fingers across my cheeks. More tears have begun to fall.

"Ah, Popsy. It guts me every time ye cry. I dinnae mean to be cruel. What can I do?"

"Kiss me," I murmur. "I'm not anyone's queen yet."

"Is that an order, lass?" he murmurs huskily.

"The only one I'll ever give you. Love me, Hook. Please. Until..."

Until the end comes, and we are parted.

And that day will come soon.

Bastion and I can't return to the land without another enchantment. My legs will be gone soon enough. And soon enough looms over me like a nightmare. I need more time with this man who makes me feel things I've never felt before.

Hook tips my chin up and slants his mouth over mine, and I forget about horror and duty for a moment as he guides me quickly toward the bed, stripping off the layers of my clothing. I will remember this. I'll remember every second of every minute because this will be the last moment I have with Hook.

His hands are on me, inside me. The feel of his body close to mine.

My sailor. My brave captain.

My doomed love.

TWELVE
BASTION

The argument is settled by morning. Andric will accompany us, commanding a force of his thirteen best men. The Chosen one, Kassidy, and her retinue of werebears will accompany us as well.

To my intense displeasure, the princess insists Hook come along, too. I cannot put up a convincing argument to dissuade her. After all, his presence brings the total number of our able party to twenty-one. Seven, and its multiples, is considered lucky. A superstition, but one that Aria believes. How can I rob her of that belief? I don't even have a logical reason to refuse. I just simply... don't like him.

The flipside, of course, is that Hook is competent. But I don't trust him. He turned easily on the princess in the throne room, brought his anger to bear against her later in the evening. I fear bringing him along is a bad idea.

And, of course, there's the seething jealousy that accompanies the mere sight of him at her side, knowing he's touched her in ways I never have and never will. Furthermore, I can see the way she hungers for him. It's there in her eyes.

Lost in my own confusion and ignorance, I finally swallowed my pride and decided to seek counsel. In doing so, I asked Nash for an explanation of what human mating looks and sounds like. He gave me a supercilious smile and proceeded to explain what a male protuberance is used for.

And that was when my anger truly overcame me and has been my constant loyal companion ever since. The thought of the human inside Aria, nestled between her legs, as he mates her...

It's almost worse than seeing her mate mark displayed proudly on his throat.

Almost.

That one still stings. It means the human will be able to swim with us without the clumsy human apparatuses that allow them to breathe beneath the water. Aria's mark ensures the human will be able to take in air through the mark until she either makes this arrangement permanent or decides she no longer desires him.

I hope for the latter as soon as possible.

We're poised on the edge of Cassio Island once again, after taking another journey under the baking sun to get to the godforsaken jut of land. It's the most direct route to Aspamia. The humans busily slick their bodies with oils and such to slide more easily into their cumbersome suits. Most of the soldiers are men, and they've stripped down nude.

I eye Andric in particular. I've caught Aria glancing in his direction now and then. Understandable, as he's to be her King someday. Another thought which makes me shudder on the inside. Of course, I would never allude to my disquiet as it is certainly not my place.

Andric's shoulders are narrower than Hook's, his muscle leaner. He's fit enough. Attractive, in his way.

His features are gentle, his eyes guileless, his smiles easy. I think it's that, more than his appearance, that charms Aria. Andric takes new developments in stride, letting worry slide like water off a dolphin's back.

My eyes follow the lines of his body down as I behold his *cock*, as the others term it. And, naturally, I make my own internal notes. Andric's protuberance is fairly large, even flaccid as it is. I'm told these cocks grow quite long when they become rigid. I have noticed the same thing occurring to my own when I think of the princess, though it has never become entirely hard as I've heard they do.

I can't help but wonder, as I behold Andric's protuberance, if it will hurt the princess to have it shoved inside of her repeatedly? I hope not.

Andric seems kind enough. And patient. I'd hate to have to rip his spine out of his head. But if he harms the princess, I will most assuredly do so.

I finish loading the last of our supplies into Kassidy's carrier sack. It's enchanted to withstand the elements and it also holds a great deal of cargo without being difficult to manage. When I lift the damn thing, it barely feels any heavier, despite the crates shoved into its depths. It's quite marvelous, in truth. Should we survive this trek, I will ask Cassiopeia to enchant something similar for me. I could tote a whole arsenal around in a pinch.

"Princess, may I have a word?" I call to Aria over my shoulder.

Aria tears her gaze away from Hook's face after a second or two, then seems to shake herself from some quiet thought and saunters over. That she's so

144

transfixed with him at all makes my gills itch. What in the name of the deep ones does he have that I do not? We're built similarly. I'm a warrior as well, with almost as many scars. Is it the facial growth? The metal hoops he wears through his ears? I can't figure out the allure. The mate mark she's placed upon him can only account for some of the draw.

Her hips swing lazily as she approaches me. Though I am not a fan of my own legs, I have to say I find hers a little mesmerizing. I've spent many an evening staring at the curve of her waist, the demarcation line between where her scales would have started. I wonder where she would be most tender if I stroked her. Though I'm still a little fuzzy on the finer points of human mating, I do find the aesthetic pleasing. The look on Aria's face when Hook had... what had Nash called it? Fingered? Perhaps that was the word. Regardless, when Hook had brought her to climax with his fingers, the look on her face had been nothing short of rapturous. Just when I thought there was no way she could be more beautiful, there she was.

I want to bring her to such rapture myself. But such is quite unlikely. We're giving up these human bodies to return to the water in short order. In order to return to the land, we would need to have the enchantment renewed by Opeia.

Aria comes to a stop just shy of my position and offers me a sunny smile. She's been smiling more often, I've noticed. Almost always grinning when she stands near Hook. I want to beat him for that, too. Aria's smiles used to be rare things, something only

145

Opeia or I could draw from her. Now, in this barbaric land with its barbaric people, she never seems to stop smiling. I wonder, with some horror at the prospect, if she might prefer it here. She's happy. She clearly enjoys these men. What would tie her to the water, besides myself and Cassiopeia?

Her people? No. They turned their backs on her. Aria has no family but for the sea witch who loves her and me. Land is full of adventure and intrigue. Perhaps it would be selfish of me to ask her to come back to the ocean with me?

I'm going to do it, anyway. Because Aria belongs in the sea. She doesn't belong here.

"Can we speak some place more private?" I ask.

I cast a glance at the rickety tin shed I found her and the sailor in almost over a week ago.

Aria's nose wrinkles. "I'll be glad when I never have to be inside a building again, Bastion. They're so confining. Can't we speak outside?"

I almost smile. It is a little reassuring to know she doesn't love everything about the land. "All right. But let's take a walk."

"What for?" she asks.

I clear my throat. "I want to talk about your security."

Aria's eyes roll skyward, and amusement tugs at the corners of her lips. "There are nineteen others on this island, Bastion. There's nothing to worry about."

"I am not worried, Princess. Merely cautious."

It's easy, familiar banter we've had a hundred times before. And I know the thoughts going through

146

her head: *Overbearing Bastion, constantly worried over this and that and constantly overreacting.*

Someone has to be the reasonable one — the one who thinks of defending the princess, even if she doesn't see the importance in it. Aria is too often cavalier about her safety, assuming because she matters little to her father, she matters little to the rest of us, as well. I know, from hearing her mutter in her sleep during the worst of her nightmares, that she worries her title and her womb are the only value she has left.

She's wrong. Her title is the reason I bear a duty towards her, yes. But her heart is what makes me love her. It always has.

I wait until we've rounded a line of the tin structures and made it halfway around the island. If I squint, I can still make out the others on the opposite side. With their superior skill on their legs, I estimate it will only take them a minute or two to reach us, if there is danger. Long enough for me to hold whatever is attacking at bay until help arrives. Fortunately, the only danger I sense on this island is still on the other side, doffing his frock coat for a swimming costume.

I scoff. A swimming costume! As if one needs more than just his body to swim. Humans are absurd.

Aria comes to a stop with another distracting wiggle of her hips. I am genuinely curious as to what those legs would feel like wrapped around my middle and what the inside of her body would feel like. There's no time to find out, even if she were inclined, and I can't blame her for wanting to keep her protective layers on underneath the baking sun.

"So, what is it you wanted to speak to me about?" she asks, tilting her head just so. Her hair catches the sunlight and glows faintly. The luminescent sheen means she's excited, almost bordering on aroused. Is it Hook? Me? The prospect of claiming our freedom?

"Hook."

The one word is enough to steal the soft smile from her lips and replace it with a scowl. "Bastion, we've already talked about this. Hook is coming with us, and that's final."

I don't like the way she's so quick to jump to his defense. As far as I'm concerned, he doesn't deserve her good opinion.

"I'm not here to argue with you about his involvement, Princess. Poseidon knows nothing can shake you when you set your mind to something. I just wanted to make you aware of some things and express my... concerns."

She arches a brow. "And these things are?"

There's really no delicate way to put it, so I lay the truth out plainly. I cannot afford to dance around her feelings at this juncture. Not when it's her very feelings that may get her killed.

"I don't believe he's trustworthy, Princess."

The lines between her brows only deepen, her mouth turning down into an even angrier frown. I'm upsetting her, just as I knew I would. I wish that fact didn't cut at me so.

Her expression turns dark. "It doesn't matter what you believe, Bastion. *I* trust him. And you should trust me!"

"I *do,* Princess. But you've known the human far less than one lunar cycle! And, as far as I'm concerned, that means you don't *truly* know him at all!"

Her hands ball into fists at her side. She's shaking and looks unsteady on her feet. Strange wetness dews in her eyes, even as she glares at me.

"Bastion, you are being unfair, and you should be ashamed of yourself."

"I am not ashamed of myself," I counter. "I am your protector and, as such, I must be weary of anyone with which we come into contact." I take a breath. "Hook isn't a noble sailor, Aria—he's called a pirate for a reason! He plunders, he raids, he turns port cities to ash if he has to. He's a villain, and I don't understand why you refuse to see it!"

"Those are lies and I refuse to believe them, Bastion."

"They aren't lies."

She glares at me. "Even if he did things in the past, I'm sure he regrets them. Furthermore, his past doesn't reflect the man he is now. You and I have both done things we regret…"

"Aria…"

"No!" she interrupts, shaking her head. "You don't know the stories of what he's had to endure. You don't know what it was like in Neverland!"

I want to shake her. She's still so blind.

"I know you want him," I growl out slowly, trying to approach this subject from a different angle, trying to appeal to her sense of reason. "But he's a *pirate*, Aria. A soldier of fortune. A killer. And I don't want him around you, especially when it's my duty to protect you!"

"You don't have to protect me from Hook," she insists.

"That human will push a harpoon through your chest the second a better offer presents itself."

"That's not true!"

It's my turn to glare at her as anger burns within my blood. "I understand you're attached to him. I'm aware that love clouds reason."

"What in the name of Avernus do you know about love, Bastion?" she yells as she turns to face me squarely. She stands perhaps a foot from me. "You have no right to condescend to me, you… you…"

I seize her cheeks in both hands, trapping her lovely, fine-boned face between my palms. Her skin is so incredibly smooth. When I was a mere boy, newly exiled with my princess, I spent my nights in the deeps praying for safety from the grotesquerie and wondering what it might feel like to touch her this way. To run my fingers over her high, sculpted cheekbones and feel heat flush into her cheeks as it does now.

Her huge, beguiling eyes are wide, and realization enters them seconds before I press my mouth to hers. It's strange and awkward to ape the odd mouth-mating ritual the humans do, but also satisfying, in a way. Warm tingles run under my skin, the blood rushing into my face so it feels much hotter than the rest of me.

My entire body yearns for her. It's almost second nature to wrap my arms firmly around her waist and draw her flush to my chest, trapping her arms between us. They press flat against my abdomen, at the line where my tail should end. Now there's only a fine trail of hair there, leading down to the awkward protruding sex organ that hangs between my legs. Inefficient and dangerous, if you ask me. Better to keep it tucked into the body and away from harm.

I expect her to push me away with an angry sound, or perhaps strike me for daring to be so bold as to lay hands on her. She is a princess, after all. And I am nothing but her protector, her underling. But her lips only part invitingly, and I can't help myself. I flick out my tongue, tracing it along her plump lower lip, tasting her. She's lovely as a coral reef under a summer sun; she tastes of the sea and feels like paradise splayed beneath my fingers.

The protrusion between my legs swells, and without clothing to disguise it, the evidence of my arousal presses eagerly into her thigh. Again, I expect her to pull away. This is utterly inappropriate. Instead, her tongue slides against mine in a movement that's foreign but so incredibly pleasant, it draws a moan from my throat and my hips rock gently against hers. She slides her hands into my hair, twining into the locks and tugging them gently.

"Princess..." I groan against her mouth.

"Aria," she murmurs into mine. "I've told you not to call me 'princess' thousands of times, Bastion."

"But..."

"If you want to touch me, you're going to have to learn to call me by name, not my title."

"I understand," I say, voice still more groan than intelligible speech.

"Now, is this bunk about Hook truly a concern, Bastion, or just the result of your own jealousy?"

My mouth finally snaps shut and I take a few steps back from her. I can't think when our skin is touching and, frankly, I'm a little offended by the assertion. The fact that I want to beat him for touching her is secondary to my fears about his future treachery.

"I stand by what I said."

"You know I'll likely have to give myself to Prince Andric at some point as well, right?"

"It's not the same thing," I say stubbornly, willing the stupid protrusion to go soft again. It hurts to stand so near without touching her.

She lifts an imperious brow. "Oh? And why not?"

"With Andric, it's... not real, Aria. Whatever you have with him is simply political. Clinical. Perhaps loveless."

Her expression drops at that statement. "It might not always be that way," she says softly.

I shake my head. "It *will* always be that way," I insist. "None of these men love you. Not like I do."

She looks at me then and there's confusion in her eyes. No, I've never admitted as much to her before, but she should have known. It was so obvious. If only she'd opened her eyes and looked. But she never did.

"Bastion?" she starts but I interrupt.

"I've loved you since I was a boy, Aria."

"Why have you never told me this before?"

I take a deep breath. "Because the time was never right. And it's not right or fair to bring it up now, but I must. Opeia has been pushing me to tell you for years, but I couldn't."

"Why?" Her voice sounds haunted.

"I couldn't tell you when you needed your focus to be on protecting our people. I couldn't divide your loyalty. It wasn't my place, not for a lowly guard. But now..." I suck in a deep breath. "But now, we're going to face Triton. There's every chance I may die protecting you." I take another breath, and then expel it. "I wanted you to know the truth, Aria. Even if nothing ever comes of it, I want you to know I love you and I always have."

I lean in, unable to help myself, and steal another of those tingling kisses. She meets the kiss and her eyelashes flutter closed. When I spot the rest of our crew approaching, I pull away.

I stride away from her before she can formulate any kind of response. Because I can't stand the idea of her trying to tell me she feels the same way. Even if she is fond of me, even if she does love me...

I already know she loves *him* more.

THIRTEEN
ANDRIC

I've always thought I knew the sea.

I was born on a boat, thirty miles off the shore of Delorood, to a woman who was known colloquially as the next best thing to a siren. My mother taught me to swim only weeks after I learned to walk. As such, my hands know the feel of rope, canvas, and wood of the *Ashray*, my mother's ship, better than the feel of my bedsheets in the castle.

But, truly, I may as well be considered a mere hobbyist, because I've only grazed the surface of the ocean's wonders.

I can't help but stare as we paddle farther and farther outward, propelled along by the aquatic suits we've purchased from a merchant. They were Geppetto's design, originally, I believe. A brilliant man, though his predilections are warped. I wonder if he's still trying to create the perfect boy out of metals and wood — a boy to act as his son. The most recent of his creations, named Dolion, was Geppetto's best yet, but the wooden boy was still banished.

We've been going for almost half a day now and we're making great strides, though my muscles burn. We'll need to surface soon.

The journey is planned out in three jaunts. Aria estimates it will take us quite a while to reach a strategic point from which to strike, owing to the slow pace these aquatic suits enforce. We have to surface every now and again to allow the suits to replenish our air supply. We float on our backs and sleep in shifts, with at least three of us awake at a time to be on guard against sea monsters or hostile merfolk.

This journey has been, in short, incredible. Awe-inspiring. Unbelievable. And I don't want to miss a single, breathtaking moment, especially not to sleep.

We traversed the thick kelp fields hours ago, staying close enough to the surface that the heat of the sun still burned through the water to lick at our backs. It was almost peaceful, even watching small predators wind through the leaves beneath us in search of prey. None big enough to challenge us or strong enough to break through our suits.

Now, we swim deeper, where the cold is more pronounced. Not so cold as the depths, Aria assures us with a light laugh, but still colder that we're used to. We're gliding over a reef and the vegetation is so colorful, it almost hurts the eyes. Lurid reds, oranges, and yellows are splashed onto the ocean floor with abandon and the curling shapes of the plants are intriguing. I wish I had longer to study them. I can only imagine how much richer our knowledge of the ocean would be if I could commit all of this to a journal.

But this isn't the time for science or mild artistic appreciation. We have a king to overthrow, and in order to do so, we have to rest. Aria plans to send Bastion down to the trenches to retrieve still more soldiers to aid us. As many soldiers as the deeps can spare, which will lift our total from twenty-one to twenty-eight. I wish the hike in numbers brightened my outlook, but alas, the only sense of joy I can muster comes with the thought that at least these final days will be pleasant—the sea spread out before me in glorious color and my lovely siren bride gliding through the water beside me.

It's hard to keep my eyes off her for any length of time, even with the splendor of the ocean to distract me. Having regained her true form, she's just as captivating in her mermaid form as she is in her human body. She has a long, sinuous tail that's the same color as the markings on her cheeks and nose. Her hair is colorless now, the magenta having drained away the second we hit the water. Too garish I suppose, to wear in the ocean, where predators might take notice of it. Instead, the long mass shifts color as the light and surroundings change. It's like watching a beautiful mirage.

And then, there's her upper body. The slender waist, the sultry curve upward toward her slim shoulders and full breasts. She doesn't seem embarrassed that they're completely bare. She even went so far as to scoff at the suggestion from one of my men that she cover them. Not that I blamed him, as they are quite distracting.

"Cover them with what?" she asked him with a frown. He proposed shells, to which she responded, "Shells? I can't swim with shells on! Algae will give me a rash. And Hook asked me not to cut them off, so you'll just have to deal with them."

Cut them off? Just the thought makes me shudder.

She catches my expression and answers it with one of her own: a grin. I love her smiles. Tentative and unsure, as though she's not quite comfortable with relaying information through gestures and facial expressions. I gather merfolk don't use facial expressions to communicate in the same way humans do.

I envy the bond that Hook has with her. Not only for the fact that he so very clearly owns her heart, but for the physical advantages it presents, as well. He seems to have gained the same abilities as merfolk without developing the attributes of a tail and gills. He can stay submerged in the water without breathing — the only concession he has to make is a pair of goggles, so the saltwater doesn't sting his eyes. I should quite enjoy being in his position.

Aria swims closer, and the motion of her body is absolutely stunning. The motion begins in the tips of her fingers and rolls down her body, moving those lovely breasts in time, aiding her tail and pushing her several yards in one go. It's a shame we're swimming so closely together — I should rather admire her from afar, when I can see all of her at once. I can — and have — watched her move all day long.

"Is something wrong?" she asks, her voice still somehow carrying through the water. I'm not sure how she does it.

"Wrong?" I ask, through the bulbous swimming mask that looks more like an upside-down fishbowl atop my head.

"You've been quiet the entire extent of this trip. I don't think I've heard you speak since we left Bridgeport, except to give orders to your men."

She drops her voice and scans the shapes moving around us. The rest of the crew have pulled ahead, led by her second-in-command, Bastion, and the Chosen one, Kassidy.

"Are you anxious, Andric?"

"No, I'm in awe, actually," I say with a laugh. My voice comes out sounding like static, owing to the nature of Geppetto's invention. Still, we're lucky we can communicate at all; most underwater models don't have this advanced a system.

Her smile grows and she tentatively tugs one lip between her teeth. I almost groan. The kittenish look on her face never fails to make me hard. Damn my chivalry. I promised not to touch her unless she wanted it and asked for it. Thus, I suppose I've promised to maintain a distant, loveless marriage, if that's what she wants. But the truth is, I want her. The evidence of just how much presses urgently against the front of my swimming apparatus. It's fortunate the material is thick and doesn't give easily, or else she'd see the proof of my desire.

"Oh?" she asks. "In awe of what?"

"The ocean." I turn my head and take in my surroundings. "I never knew it could be like this. Such wild beauty. Untouched by man. I knew it was beautiful but..." I trail off, a smile of my own tugging up the corners of my mouth. I'm sure it must look strange through the bubble of glass that protects my head.

Aria's truly grinning now, the color in her markings brighter than I've seen it to date. She's so goddamn lovely. Someone should really capture her essence with oils on canvas. Unfortunately, I can't paint.

"I'm glad you like it," she says as she studies her surroundings, as if seeing them for the first time. "It used to be even lovelier."

"Used to?"

She nods. "Some of the reefs are suffering due to Triton's negligence. The venom a kraken releases is toxic to most of the plants here, and they're slow to recover. There's a reason krakens are meant to stay in the lowest depths."

I can't imagine this place being more stunning than it is now, but I take her word for it.

"Are you sure about this?" I ask.

She turns her attention back to me. "Sure about what?"

"Your plan to overthrow your father. Are you certain it's what you want?"

Aria's shoulders hunch forward a little, as if the reminder is a physical blow. Pain spasms across her face for an instant before she's able to hide it. She steels her expression and nods. "What I want doesn't factor into it, Andric."

"Why not?"

"My people and yours are going to continue to suffer if nothing is done."

I shrug. "Still, he's *your* father. I get along well enough with mine, yet it's still difficult to disagree with the old man. It must be far, far worse for you."

The rest of our party has paused almost a mile up ahead, casting curious glances back at us as though they wonder what we could be conversing about. We should start moving before one of the curious sorts comes back to eavesdrop, but still, I don't move. The look in those pale eyes of Aria's is haunted and the expression on her face belongs to a small girl, not the beautiful and capable woman in front of me.

"My father cast me out, Andric. He banished me over a disagreement. And I was so young. I wasn't even old enough to vote on a council yet. And he cursed me, by Poseidon's name, to die alone and afraid."

Her face twists, and I'm sure if she could shed tears, she'd have been weeping.

"I am truly sorry to hear that."

She nods. "What sort of father could ever...?" she begins, but trails off. She can't seem to find the words.

I have none to offer her, either. *Wonderful timing, Andric. Become uselessly tongue-tied when a maiden is in distress.*

I take her hand in mine and twine our fingers together as best I can through the mitt-like glove I wear. The attempt is not as comforting as it ought to be, because the fingers of the suit are heavy and cumbersome. I dislike the suit intensely, more so than I have yet. I think I'd trade all the air left in the apparatus for the opportunity to hold her close at this moment.

"Your father doesn't deserve you," I tell her gently. "And you're going to make him regret every terrible thing he ever did to you. We all are."

160

Aria's head bobs, though I'm not sure she even hears me at this point. She seems to be mulling over silent, secret thoughts to which I'm not privy.

"We should surface," she says finally, glancing up at the night sky. "Your air tanks will need to be replenished and your men will need rest."

"If you ever need to talk, I'm here for you, Princess," I tell her quietly. "You'll find when I'm not being painfully obtuse, I'm a good listener."

A laugh bubbles out of her throat, and it's incredibly pleasant to listen to. It's tempting to stay under for as long as the suit allows, watching her and listening to her until my lungs burst. I'm beginning to understand why sailors throw themselves off the sides of ships for these women, these sirens of the deep. The last moments are worth the sacrifice.

"Thank you, Andric," she says, but the emotion on her face is gone and now she's all steel once more. "But let's hurry to the surface. You're going to expire at this rate."

She wraps a long-fingered hand around my bicep and tugs me upward. We move quickly, with the strength of her tail propelling us. It's no time at all before we crest the surface of the waves. The dome of my suit slides back automatically when exposed to open air, and I suck in a cool, relieved mouthful. After so long underwater, the taste of the air in my suit has grown stale.

Aria releases me and bobs in the water nearby, watching me with a smile on her face. There's only a half-moon in the sky tonight, casting white-gold light down on us. The others begin to surface a mile off, bobbing like wine corks on the surface.

Aria opens her mouth, about to say something, but she never gets the opportunity. Because a shape appears just below her in the water, hulking and dark.

It seizes her by the tail and, before I can fully understand what's happening, she's yanked beneath the waves and lost to the inky darkness seconds later.

FOURTEEN
ARIA

My captor's grip is so tight, it nearly splits my tailfin in two when I attempt to buck out of his grasp. Bubbles stream out of my mouth, the air required for speech spiraling up toward the rapidly receding surface. Breathing air isn't necessary for my survival underwater, but it's still uncomfortable when the sea fills my mouth and water tries to choke me.

Something sharp runs along my scales, sending prickles of panic up my spine. My entire body seizes in alarm and I redouble my efforts to free myself.

But it's no good.

Arms wind around my tail and I know, with a feeling of intense panic, exactly who has me. I've never seen or felt arms so muscular on a man other than my father. And since the shape pressed into my side has one tip instead of three on his scepter, I know this isn't Triton.

"Sen," I hiss.

He smirks back at me, his broad, rough-hewn face made somehow cruder by the expression on it.

"Arianwen," he croons, "we're alone at last. Such a naughty girl, bringing so many others with her into her father's territory. Triton will be *very* displeased."

What displeases my father should really amount to fish toss to me, in the end. But my conversation with

Andric earlier brought so many of the ugly, hidden feelings I've denied for so long to a painful head. Afterwards, I wasn't sure I was ready for this mission. Could I truly drive a blade into the heart of the man who'd sired me?

But in this moment, at the realization that Sen means to drag me off to rape me with my father's tacit permission, a layer of frost settles over my tender feelings. It will hurt when the time comes, but I can keep my emotion under a layer of ice until the deed is done. And the deed most definitely needs to be done.

I turn, launching a fist into Sen's face the way I've seen humans do on land. The attack is so sudden and unexpected, it loosens his grip on me just long enough that I can squirm out of his grasp. When I dart away from him, one powerful downstroke of my tail hits him on the side of his face, hopefully dazing him for a few seconds. My knuckles sting and there's definitely a tear in my tail somewhere, but I'm alive and unmolested.

For now.

I have to get away.

If Sen is here, that means more of my father's soldiers are on their way, if they aren't attacking my friends already. Sen's the most dangerous of their number, so I have to keep him busy.

He's after me in seconds, recovering his equilibrium with a curse. He's strong and fast and the edged weapon in his hand looks absolutely lethal. A glance down at his tail reveals his glans painfully exposed.

"You traitorous bitch," Sen snarls, all good humor gone. "When I catch you, I'm going to fuck you raw. Make you scream for days before I finally give you the mercy of death."

I shudder. I'll kill myself before I let him catch me. If my only choices are rape or death, I know which one I choose.

I dive, faster and with more precision than a man of his size can ever hope to achieve, aiming for a network of caves nearby. I don't know these caves as well as some of the ones closest to the trench. My forays into the world above have been few and far between; it's usually safer for others to emerge and forage for food if there's a need. But I've found myself in enough scrapes to know where the handy hiding spots are. I've hidden in this particular network before, and from Sen, no less. My eyes are adjusted to the pitch darkness, his are not. The halls are narrow here, and there's an exit near the back. I can keep him swimming in circles for several minutes and then slip out the narrow back entrance before he knows he's been had.

It's almost disorienting to enter the caves again after weeks of light and heat. Part of me hopes to escape the dark and cold for the rest of my days. Perhaps Opeia will be strong enough, after seizing power, that she can make my legs permanent? I could return to the sea in one of Andric's boats? He surely has enough affection for me to grant me a boon. We may never love each other, but I think there's enough affection between us to guarantee kindness.

And there's always Hook, right? Perhaps we could work something out? Some type of agreement?

But even as I delve into the frigid blackness, waves pelt against me. There's one complication that keeps me from deciding to live the rest of my days (if I have any left after this) on land, and it comes in the form of my oldest friend and ever-loyal protector.

Bastion.

The mute frustration and bouts of temper make sense now. Bastion has been in love with me for years, as he admitted. No wonder he's been cold with me since we came here! First he dealt with my fascination with Hook and now Andric. I must be the most callous woman in all of Fantasia to have been blind to Bastion for so long. I'll admit I've always found him to be the most attractive of the mermen, but...

Gods, it's all so complicated! I can't think of what the future will bring. I won't *have* a future if I don't leave Sen trapped in these caves.

I make my way along the walls by feel, noting as I do that they're no longer just craggy stone, the way I remember them. Stringy plant life has taken root in the deep stone cracks that run the length of the place. Any plant life has to be hardy to keep alive at these depths. I just wish they weren't impeding my progress such as they are. It's hard to tell one direction from the other in the gloom.

My heart hammers hard against my ribs when I hear Sen enter the caves behind me.

Calm down. You'll find your way out. The exit should be around...

I grope in the darkness, almost certain I've found the right place. The curve here is almost ninety-degrees, cut sharp as glass. I've bruised my ribs on it several times over the years. Sure enough, thick stone jabs into me now as I reach for the rip, ready to wriggle my tail out the narrow exit...

I find the pockmarked surface of a boulder where my exit should be.

For a second, I'm too stunned to summon much beyond mild confusion.

This can't be right! I've been in these caves a number of times. This is the exit point! Has something fallen on it or...?

Then the ugly truth hits me with the force of a charging bull shark.

The exit has been blocked. By Sen.

I've played straight into his hands.

My insides feel like they're withering to nothing as I turn, too late, to find him already behind me.

He lets out a soft note, unusually melodic for a merman of his size, and the caves are suddenly alight. Bioluminescent plant life clings to every spare crack, casting neon splashes of color throughout the caves. It's so reminiscent of Opeia's tunnels, it leaves me muddled for a fraction of a second. Warm familiarity battles with the pressing terror of the coming violence. Ultimately, terror wins out and I back futilely against the boulder, pushing against it with all my might. It doesn't budge.

Sen lets out a rolling chuckle and the sound is so filthy, I feel my glans try to draw up and into myself. Anything to get further away from this disgusting creature. I can't believe my father's thuggish yes-man has managed to dupe me so thoroughly.

"I have to say, I didn't expect you to be daft enough to try this again," Sen says, running his blade idly along the wall.

The rasp raises gooseflesh along every inch of my skin. The blade gouges a furrow into the walls, and will push through my flesh as easily as the thick butter spread I encountered in the world above.

I try to summon magic into my palm. I've never been exceptional at witchery, like Aunt Opeia. I'm a warrior, like Bastion, but even in that regard, I'm nothing special. My only real talent seems to be staying alive, and even that looks like it's about to fail me.

The corridor is barely big enough for someone of Sen's proportions to squeeze through; there's no way I'm going to be able to get past him. I can't flee, and he's so damn big that fighting him will be useless. The second he gets me in position, I'm literally and metaphorically fucked.

My only plan is conceived in despair and nurtured by fear. I have to keep Sen busy, but I'm unwilling to just lay down and play cold fish while he fucks me. So I'll fight, if only to retrieve the only thing I really want. I need his blade. One well-placed thrust upward, and I think I can reach his heart or, failing that, my own.

Sen continues to glide forward, the arrogant, lascivious smirk on his face making my stomach turn. He continues his little monologue as if I'm hanging on every word that dribbles out of his gob.

"Triton almost had my tail flayed when I lost you in the caves," he says. "So, I prepared this nice setup."

He pauses for a moment and looks me up and down. "I like you like that, backed up against the rock face." He runs a hand through his hair, swapping color for color as he does. "Shall I make my hair yellow, like your pathetic little lickspittle, Bastion? Or do you prefer dark, like those pathetic humans who've been mooning over you as you made your way past our borders?"

I dislike both colors intensely. I don't want to be thinking about any of the men I love while Sen draws ever nearer, his glans protruding grotesquely toward me.

The others have no idea I'm here. And that thought causes me to panic because all I have right now is myself. And that's a fight I won't win.

I coil my body tight and prepare to launch myself at Sen in my last futile gambit to fight him and get away.

I don't get a chance to spring away, before Sen opens his mouth to speak again, but he jerks forward instead, his eyes going wide. At the same time, dark, oily blood gouts from his throat, and I stare dumbly at the metal hook that protrudes from his neck. Sen tries to jerk his head down to look at what's speared him, but he can't force his chin down more than a half-inch before it knocks into the metal. A shocked gurgle gets trapped in his throat, but that's the only sound he can make.

With a harsh grunt, someone yanks the metal *through* Sen's neck. It comes loose after the second labored tug, taking a gobbet of flesh the size of an orange from his throat. More dark blood billows into

169

the water, rolling toward the ceiling of the cave like a putrid cloud. Sen's hands clutch at his throat, trying in vain to staunch the flow.

I can see it in Sen's eyes when he realizes he's a dead man. He draws himself up to his full height, summoning every ounce of spite his frame has to offer, and then spins, trailing more thick blood through the water as he shoves the tip of his blade through his attacker.

It hits one of the large mechanical suits the humans wear. With horror, I realize the human inside is Andric. My breathless shriek of denial is the last thing Sen hears as his eyes close and he loses the battle against the hook in his neck. But I'm no longer concerned with him. Instead, I bat his sagging body out of my way with one powerful stroke of my tail as I swim over to Andric.

Bubbles stream out of the suit, every precious one of them stealing the air Andric needs to survive. I have to do something — and quickly, before he suffocates to death. I tear at the hole Sen made in the metal for a futile second or two, trying in vain to rend it apart. The materials are too sturdy, even with my siren's constitution to aid me.

"Hatches," Andric pants, expending more of his precious air. His face is screwed up in pain, but he's not screaming. Maybe we've gotten lucky and Sen hasn't stuck him somewhere vital.

"What did you say, Andric?" I ask, confused and growing more and more panicked.

"The... suit. It has hatches... Comes apart in pieces. You have to undo... the hatches. They look like... little wheels."

I scan the suit and see what he means. At regular intervals, the suit has small, barely noticeable hatches that might be mistaken, from a distance, for those human contraptions called buttons. There are a series of them around his headpiece. I seize on the first and lock eyes with Andric.

"I need to take this off," I tell him soberly. "I need the suit off in order to heal you."

"I'll drown," he pants.

"You won't."

"How?"

I shake my head. "I have a plan, but it'll be risky." I pause for a moment as I search his eyes with my own. "Do you trust me, Andric?"

He doesn't even blink before answering. "Yes."

"Good."

Then, I began unscrewing the first hatch.

FIFTEEN
ANDRIC

My lungs burn with the effort of holding in the last of my air. One lungful of the wintery black water and I'm a dead man.

I have to trust that Aria has a plan, but damn, it's difficult with the pressure building hard and fast between my eyes. The skin of my chest feels stretched tight like cloth on a loom and I fear I'll tear myself apart at this rate. Aria is unfastening the hatches as quickly as her shaking fingers will allow, but I'm afraid it's not going to be enough. I think I understand her idea, in principle. The suit is heavy, and it slows me down. She's faster than I am, even without it, and unencumbered, she can drag me to the surface.

What I don't have time or energy to point out is that re-pressurizing the suit would be the safest course. We're probably past that now though, even if she could grasp the science of the suit within the next ten seconds.

Whatever the case, it won't be enough. I've expended the last of my air instructing her where the hatches are located. Even if she tears me free of the suit in the next thirty seconds, it won't be enough to save me. I will have swallowed half the sea by the time she hauls my limp body to the surface.

Finally, she undoes the last hatch on my helmet. Icy water sloshes into my suit at once, waterlogging me further. My limbs feel like they've been frozen stiff, and I have to shut my eyes against the oncoming sea water. My face stings as the salt rubs in a million cuts I didn't know I'd sustained.

It's going to hurt like Avernus when the sea water finally reaches the gash in my side. The hulking merman that cornered Aria tried his best to carve my flank off. Even if I can somehow stop the bleeding and find a healer in the next minute or two, the wound will scar badly. Not that I'd care—I'd much rather be alive.

Aria's fingers wind into my hair and she jerks my neck to the side. A thrill of mixed anticipation and dread pulses through me. It's almost like those old wives' tales that my nursemaids used to tell me about the monsters at the edge of the Enchanted Forests—the blood drinkers. I half expect Aria to show her teeth and take a bite. Instead, she buries her face in my neck and presses a searing kiss to my throat.

The heat of her mouth shouldn't register at this depth, in this deluge of cold, but for almost half a minute it's all I can feel. The soft, generous fullness of her lips pressed against me. Everywhere our skin touches, I warm until I feel somewhat human again. My limbs unlock and I'm able to move them awkwardly around her shoulders, holding her to me.

The ache of my chest eases a little and I wonder if this is the end. It's a good way to go, all things considered. Rescuing and being kissed by a fair maiden who is meant to be my wife, before I drift off into that infinite night. Black spots, somehow thicker and more ominous than the water around us, begin to burst in my vision and I slump sideways, barely catching myself on a rock shelf.

"Breathe, Andric," Aria murmurs against my throat. "Breathe, or you're going to pass out."

At my searching, incredulous look, she rolls her pale eyes skyward with a small smile. "Do you trust me or not?"

I shudder, brace myself, and then suck in a deep breath through my nose, expecting the salt to burn all the way down. It doesn't.

Relief is instantaneous, my body flooding with elation so potent, it saps the pain of every injury I've sustained. I feel a little punch drunk, basking in this new glorious knowledge.

I don't know how it's possible, but I can breathe underwater!

Then the reason why dawns on me: Aria has marked me as her own, pressing her claim into my flesh the same as she'd done to Hook. Forget the rings, ceremony, and empty words of a marriage ceremony — Aria has marked me as hers in a real, tangible way I never dared hope for. Before I can stop myself, I've freed a hand from its clumsy mechanical prison and cupped her face, drawing her as close as I can manage with the rest of the suit in the way.

Our lips come together in a sweet, almost longing kiss. It feels so bloody good when our lips touch. Is this what it's like for mated mercouples? Is this the reason Hook can't keep his hands off her for more than a few minutes? I'd thought it was just his nature, being a pirate and a notorious scoundrel. But if this is what it's like to be mated to a siren, I will never cast aspersions on him again. How could someone *not* want to touch her, to feel her, to possess her?

Aria is the first to draw back, though I can tell she's as unhappy by the loss of our contact as I am. I'm already straining toward her again. She stops me, placing a gentle hand on the exterior of my suit. I still beneath her touch, though I could press the issue.

"You're injured," she reminds me gently. "The only reason your wound isn't incapacitating you with pain is this cold. We need to treat you now, before we surface again."

"How?" I ask with a frown.

Aria pulls her lip between her teeth. It's always been damn distracting but now, with her claim on my skin, the need to touch her is nearly overwhelming.

"I'll need to sear the wound closed."

"Sear it?"

She nods. "I know how. Aunt Opeia showed me a spell that works on battlefield amputations, but it will… hurt. I can keep your mind occupied while I do it, though. Turn the pain into... something else."

"Okay."

"How opposed are you to illusions?"

I want to retort that I'm a prince and a warrior and that pain is not something I fear. But sometimes we do things not for the sake of our own pride, but to spare others pain in our stead. If I grit my teeth through the coming spellwork and fail to hold in my screams, I'll worry Aria. She's still a tender soul, even after all that's been done to her. So, I swallow my pride and give her a lazy grin instead.

"I'm happy to be subject to whatever illusions you wish to show me, Aria."

Relief shows plain on her face for an instant. Then, the illusions begin.

In an instant, she's her human self again, bare as she was that night on the cliffs. Still a thing of incredible beauty, though this time she appears less fragile. Her eyes are half-lidded, the set of her mouth almost sultry as she advances on me.

"Take the suit off," she purrs, leaning in so our lips are a fraction of an inch from touching. Her mouth slides like silk over mine when she speaks, and she tugs on one of the hatches for emphasis.

That's all it takes. The gentle prompting sets me in motion, twisting each of the hatches violently until the suit falls to pieces at my feet. I kick it away so she has room to step closer, to put her body to mine. There's still the wetsuit to contend with, but it can be removed quickly.

Aria smiles approvingly and hooks one calf around mine, pressing all her long, lean frame into me. It's like fireworks exploding everywhere we touch. I try to turn and catch her lips when she presses them to my cheek and then to the corner of my jaw. She laughs then, a rich sound that belongs to a more lascivious creature than the unassuming Aria.

I know it's an illusion, yet it doesn't feel like one—it's difficult to convince my brain that she's simply weaving an artificial web about me, playing with my senses. It's near impossible to argue with my mind, which tells me there's a very warm, very willing woman pressed to my front, rubbing herself, cat-like, against my thigh. I'm already hard, and she's barely touched me.

She continues her slow exploration with her mouth, yanking the fastenings of the wetsuit off in her haste to bare more of my skin. She trails hot kisses and hard nips of her teeth down one pectoral, down the line of my abdomen, and then further down until she reaches my straining cock.

"Do you want me to touch you here?" she asks with a knowing smile.

"Yes," I croak.

Gods, taking the illusion is probably the best choice I've ever made. Even knowing this isn't truly happening, it's still so… amazing.

Aria makes a little humming noise in the back of her throat and then slowly draws my length out into the open. I almost expect the thing to draw back from the cold but, as before, anywhere she touches me feels warm. No, not just warm—*burning*. Burning with the need to be inside her.

She studies the thick head of my cock for an appreciative second before flicking out her delicate pink tongue to taste it. Then, she guides the length of me as far inside her mouth as I can go.

I almost cum then and there.

The electric sensation of her mouth on me for even an instant sends my need into overdrive. She's going to kill me, she's going to suck my lifeforce right out of my cock—and I'm not going to regret a damn second of it.

I don't know how she manages to convey her amusement around a mouthful of cock, but I get the impression she's grinning up at me. Then she wraps her lips around me, sucking hard, traveling the length of me twice before she lets up the pressure to twirl that magnificent tongue around the head. Her mouth may be the single most glorious thing I've ever felt, but I want more.

"Stop," I pant. "I don't want to cum yet, Aria, I want..."

She draws her head back, her lips slightly swollen and distractingly shiny from her efforts. She smirks at me. "More?" she guesses.

"Yes."

"What exactly is it you want?"

"You. Your body. I want to feel the inside of you."

She smiles lasciviously. "How do you want me? Below you? On top of you? Do you want to take me from behind?"

Gods, the thought of her riding me has my balls tightening in anticipation. "On top. Please."

She moves on top of me, as agile as a lemur, and anchors herself around my neck, her long legs locking around my waist with vise-like strength. I couldn't shake her even if I wanted to. Not that I want her anywhere else, at the moment. I'll cut off a finger before I let her go now. I push my face into her hair, bucking upward into the heat that lay between her legs, sheathing myself inside that sweet, hot channel in one languid stroke.

She shudders, stills for a moment, and then lets out a soft moan that tickles my ear. "Fuck me," she groans. "Oh, Andric, please..."

Hard to argue with a request like that.

I thrust into her again, guiding her hips up and off my cock before slamming myself home again. She meets me stroke for stroke, quickly finding her rhythm. She traces her pleasure into my back, arching into every thrust with a soft cry. Her eyes flutter closed, head lolling back as I fill her, guiding her toward climax. I only get a second's warning before her hips buck. Then, she's squeezing me tight, her body going taut and tipping me over the edge with her as well.

When I come down from the high, I realize, with a sense of loss, that Aria is no longer in my arms. She's standing a few feet away, wholly siren once more. She watches me and her hand traces soft circles into a point on her tail.

I become aware of a throbbing ache in my side. When I glance down, I find a neat semicircle of my flesh just gone, the edges blackened like a braised steak. It hurts less than I think it ought to, but every few breaths or so, the pain snakes a tendril up my side and reminds me I am, in fact, injured.

"Thank you," I murmur, still panting. "That was... something."

Her breathing comes quicker. "I felt it too, just so you know. It was a... meeting of the minds, so to speak."

"A meeting of the minds?"

She nods. "I felt you just as fully as you felt me."

"Any possibility of an encore?" I ask, only half-teasing. If being inside her was that incredible in my head...

Her grin is positively impish for a moment. "Someday soon, I hope." She pauses, and her expression drops slightly. "If we are victorious against my father."

It's a sobering reminder that there's still a mission to complete and a tyrant to depose. But there's a possibility of *someday* waiting for me if we win.

"Good enough for me."

SIXTEEN
ARIA

"Gods, grant me patience," I mutter as I swim away from our gathered forces.

The rest of Sen's guard had been dealt with by Bastion, Hook, and the others, while Andric and I handled the threat of the general, himself. Though we were successful in fending off this attack, I'm wary of such a small defeat overly bolstering our bravado.

We've been given at least a few days reprieve, and we've used the time to strengthen our numbers, camping outside the trenches for a day and a half while the humans rest and the remainder of us arm ourselves for the coming war.

With what's looming on the horizon, one would think men could let go of trivial things, like their dislike for one another and their petty differences. Apparently not.

Bastion scented Andric's release the moment we returned to the surface and hasn't spoken to me since. His cold silence allowed Hook to very quickly deduce what had happened as well, and Hook started a silent protest too. The only friendly conversation I've had, besides Kassidy, is with Andric, who serves as a reminder of why the other two men in my life are presenting me with a glacial silence.

"Men," I grumble.

"I hear you." Kassidy's voice comes out slightly muffled due to the glass dome on her head, but she doesn't seem to have difficulty keeping pace with me as we swim away from our encampment. "And they say *we're* moody."

She and her bears seem to need less rest than most the others, and so have been assigned to guard me, since Bastion can't be bothered to do it himself at the moment. At this point, I'm not sure if he's more liable to strike me or just fuck me into a coral bed. I'd take either, at this point. At least it would be a change from the stoicism on his face and the constant silence of his tongue.

"I resent that remark," Nash cuts in, the potency of his growling voice lost behind the layer of glass that covers his head.

Kassidy rolls her eyes as she looks over at him with an affectionate smile. "Seriously, Nash? I'm not sure whether you're the worst offender or if Sorren takes the prize."

"Wow." Nash covers his heart, as if she's offended him deeply.

She laughs, shaking her head. "I love all of you, but dealing with your moods can be exhausting at times."

"Our moods?" he continues.

"Yes." She nods. "Your moods were the worst in the beginning, owing to your jealousy, I guess." Then she sighs, fogging up the glass of her helmet. "But I think Aria may have it even worse. At least you three had blood in common and were willing to share me.

The men vying for her attention are nothing more than greedy bastards!"

"No, it's just Bastion who's that way," I sigh.

Kassidy considers me for a second before making a shooing gesture at the three bears trailing us less than gracefully in their suits.

"The three of you can go now," she says.

"We are not leaving you," Leith says stubbornly. "Either of you."

"Agreed," Sorren seconds with a nod.

Kassidy's huff of frustration is audible even from a distance. "I need to talk to Aria about *girl stuff...*" Her face twists momentarily in horror, and the words come out layered in the same sort of tone one might use to say, 'I need to talk to Aria about a reeking pile of shit.' But then she collects herself and continues, "And that doesn't include three very masculine and headstrong and nosy bears!"

Leith's laugh is a warm, touchable sound and his face lights up with a grin so utterly charming, it could part a mortal woman's legs in an instant. "I don't think there's anyone less suited to giving feminine advice than you, Goldilocks," he says, eyes twinkling with mirth.

"Oh, fuck you, Leith."

"Soon," he says, his tone making it a sensual promise. "But only after we've saved the world once again, shall we?"

Despite her irritation with the three of them, Kassidy shivers and her eyes glaze over for just a moment, focused on some erotic scenario he's painted for her. I've never been more envious of her and her situation. Eventually, she makes another impatient shooing motion.

"Go, you brutes, before I come over there and kick every single one of your furry asses!"

They begin to retreat, but not before Nash jabs a finger at her in warning. "Stay in sight, reprobate. I'm not fucking losing you to a shark."

"Not enough meat for a shark to bother," I say, looking Kassidy over with a smirk.

She spears me with a glare next, then turns the withering stare on each of her laughing men in turn. "Fuck all of you," she mutters.

Then she seizes my hand and tugs me away from the men. She doesn't stop moving for another five minutes, until we're floating lazily near the base of a rock formation half a mile from the trenches. She looks intensely uncomfortable for a second, as if she's not used to this sort of thing. And knowing that she's spent her life as a thief and a 'reprobate,' as Nash calls her, I imagine such is exactly the case.

"So... Bastion?" she starts awkwardly. "He's the problem?"

I shake my head, nervously smoothing my hands down the planes of my stomach. In all honesty, I'm little better at this sort of communication. For years, I've had no one but Aunt Opeia to confide in. It's not the same as having a female friend to swap secrets with—if that's even what Kassidy and I can be classified as. I suppose she's the closest I'm going to get to an unbiased observer.

Hopefully, someday, I can count her as a friend. I wonder if she considers me the same?

184

"No," I admit with a sigh. "All three of them present problems. Hook's willing to share with Bastion and even Andric, so long as I don't marry the prince."

Kassidy gives me an expectant look, as if she doesn't understand why Hook wouldn't want me to marry Prince Andric and is waiting me to explain, but I shake my head.

"It's... really not my story to tell. But I understand why Hook's reluctant. Andric understands this marriage between us would be political and he knows he'll have to share me with at least one merman so I can have children to inherit my throne. Bastion understands we need the alliance with Delorood and knows I'll probably have to invite Andric into my bed at some point to solidify the pact."

Kassidy screws her face up in concentration. "So, if I'm getting this right... Bastion approves of Andric but not Hook. Hook approves of both your other admirers, but for some reason doesn't want you to marry, and Andric is the only unselfish one of the lot?"

I knuckle my eyes, trying to scrub the fatigue from them. Kassidy is right. These men really *are* exhausting.

"I suppose I'm the selfish one," I mutter.

"How do you figure?"

I shrug. "I care for all of them and I want all of them, but it's not my place to feel the way I do. I should do right by at least one of them and allow the others to be free to find themselves women who might make them happy."

"Which man would you pick for yourself then?"

I shrug again. I've asked myself this question repeatedly and still haven't come up with an answer. "I need Andric to unite our two kingdoms. He's the most important connection. Bastion is my oldest and dearest friend and I love him deeply. And I know him the best, of course… I think we could be happy together." I grow quiet as my mind turns to thoughts of Hook. "And Hook… if I have to let someone go, he's the logical choice, I suppose."

Kassidy shakes her head. "But he's a fucking gorgeous pirate with a dark past and a roguish smile — and he's a good man, beneath that rough exterior."

"I know," I reply dreamily.

"And you're absolutely in love with him?" Kassidy guesses with a wicked grin.

"Yes, I am," I admit, frowning. It would be so much simpler if my heart didn't get involved in these sorts of things. If marriage and sex were simply unemotional.

"So, what's the problem?" Kassidy asks.

"It's selfish to ask Hook to stay," I mumble. "He has rules about being with married women. And if I marry Andric, I'm asking Hook to compromise his morals for me. I'm not worth that."

Kassidy jabs a finger at me, her face contorted into an expression of anger. She's quite frightening, actually.

"What is it with you gorgeous, come-hither types?" she demands, shaking her head. "'Cause, I swear, you sound just like Neva."

"Who?"

"Neva. One of the other Chosen Ten. I met her recently and I guess she's become… a friend of mine. Anyway, it's really fucking annoying when the average girl on the street has to compare herself to women like you and Neva. Never mind the fact that you have to go and throw your own humility into the mix!"

I have no idea what she's going on about but she seems insistent, so I just let her continue.

"You don't get to choose whether or not you're worth it, Princess!"

"I don't?"

"No! That's up to Hook and it's up to Bastion and it's up to Andric."

"Oh."

"I'm a thief, so take it from me, Aria: Worth is in the eye of the beholder. Trust me when I say that those men think a great deal of you, and they obviously think you're worth it. So, you tell them what you want and what it takes to be with you. And if they can't handle that, then fuck them. Or don't. Up to you."

She makes it sound so simple, as if it's just about asking and getting what I want. But I know better— maybe it was easy with her bears, but the three men in my life aren't the same.

I scrub my face once more.

"Now isn't the time to be sorting out the particulars of my tangled love life," I say finally. "Now's the time for decisive action."

"Well, that's true," Kassidy agrees with a clipped nod.

The more I think about it, the more I decide I'll shelve all this romantic angst and focus instead on the blossoming battle ahead of us. That's where my thoughts should be, at any rate. "If it's okay with you, I'll sleep at the edge of the camp with you and your men, so I don't antagonize Hook, Andric, and Bastion further. And in the morning, we'll—"

A scream cuts the air and I go silent mid-babble, whipping around to find the source of the sound. It's coming from our camp, but I'm too far away to be able to tell exactly who or what made it.

I'm off like a loosed arrow, churning the water furiously in an attempt to reach camp faster. If any of my men have been hurt because I've been sulking on the periphery, I'll never forgive myself.

When I arrive, I'm dumbfounded and don't even know in which direction to look.

Chaos reigns.

Our provisions are scattered, people fleeing in every direction. And at first, it's difficult to tell who's who in the writhing mass of shapes that converges on the camp. We're being attacked by creatures I don't recognize. They're long, almost serpentine, but lack scales. At first, I judge the mass to be some sort of miniaturized and misshapen kraken, but that's not it. Whatever the shadow figures are, they're loose, moving freely of one another. It isn't until I see one of their dorsal fins light up with sullen red-orange light that I'm able to realize what they are.

Eels.

But like no eels I've ever seen before. Most species tend to be six feet in length, maximum. Even the truly massive ones that swim in the grotesquerie only reach a length of about ten feet. Somehow, each individual eel in this throng is easily two times longer than the largest eel I've ever seen, some with a length three times that! They drive forward, faster than my eye can track, and I watch in horror as one descends on one of Opeia's men, wrapping its muscular length around the man twice before squeezing tight.

The man's eyes bulge and he thrashes wildly, trying to escape the creature's grip. But instead of going for his throat as I expect, the eel's fins begin to glow fire-red once more. The man lets out an otherworldly shriek, struggling in vain as enormous blisters begin to form anywhere the eel touches him. I can feel the heat emanating from my position a half-mile away. The water is beginning to ripple, threatening to boil as the eels continue to descend on my people.

The blisters spread like a pox, quickly enveloping the soldier's entire body in angry red boils. His eyes—already fixed wide in fear and staring at me, pleading for some sort of rescue—begin to seep out of their sockets, liquefied by the extreme temperature.

I can only stare in horror, perched on the periphery like useless flotsam.

What *are* these things? What in the name of Avernus can I do to stop them? I can barely stand the temperature from where I float limply. I'm forced to stand by, watching, as the black shapes converge on our fighting force and decimate it. I see ten of our men at arms fall within the first minute of the attack, some burned to death by the eels directly and others bursting out of their suits like soup from a bag, the heat swiftly liquefying them inside the contraptions.

I have to do something.

But what? What the *fuck* can I do to these things? I've never seen them before. My tail feels like limp seaweed, my arms useless hunks of coral at my side. All my training flies out of my head and I'm just left with... terror. Pure, unfettered terror. For myself, for my human friends, and for my men.

Gods, my men.

Where are they? I know Hook and Andric don't need the suits, so maybe they've been swift enough to escape the killing field. But Bastion? Is he one of the charred skeletons that litter the rim of the trench? Were my last words to him cruel? Has he died without knowing how much I truly care for him?

The eels' frenzy seems to be winding down and they scatter, finally putting feet of space between their bodies so I can truly appreciate how massive they are. On average, they're twenty feet long, with the biggest of the bunch topping out closer to fifty.

"Fuck," I whisper.

One of the big ones turns its great slimy head in my direction, as if I've called to it personally. One luminous yellow eye bores into me, its animal gaze brimming with malice. It hares away from the group, crossing ten yards in mere seconds. I'm not going to move out of the way in time. It's going to get those muscled coils around me and that will be the ignoble end of Princess Arianwen, exiled daughter of Triton.

She died while acting the part of a useless stump, too frightened to aid her friends.

I'm so scared, I can't even think, can't act. Instead, I just remain in place, staring at the hideous thing as it approaches me. I squeeze my eyes shut, preparing for the pain.

And then, strong arms wind around my waist, yanking me backward then up, and up, and up, toward the surface.

I crane my neck to see who has me, my heart leaping into my mouth when I see Bastion's familiar, hauntingly beautiful profile. I try to croak his name, but I think it comes out as more of a song.

He's alive! Oh, thank the Gods, he's still alive!

He tucks me in tight to his body.

"Hold on tight, Princess," he warns me. "This is going to get rough."

SEVENTEEN
BASTION

My heart thunders, battering my ribcage with sledgehammer blows. I know what I need to do to stop its panicked racing: I need to be still and breathe. But there's no time for that. No time for anything but escape.

Aria's upper body goes limp in my arms the second she realizes I have her, and I'm grateful. She's stronger than her lithe form would suggest, and it helps that she doesn't fight me as I attempt to rescue us both. I can't deal with that *and* guide us to safety.

I get a surer grip on her, sliding one hand to brace beneath her breasts so I don't impede her movement. She begins moving her tail in time with my own, propelling us through the water double time. We're outdistancing most of the survivors.

Gods, survivors.

I knew going into this battle that we'd have casualties. In a coup like the one Opeia suggested, such is inevitable. But our soldiers weren't supposed to die like *this*, swarmed and torn apart like they'd been set upon by a shoal of piranhas. Where's the dignity in a death like that? It's senseless, tragic violence. Worse still, I have no fucking idea where these eels came from or how they've come to adopt such a monstrous form, and I'd thought I'd seen everything fighting for the grotesquerie.

Clearly, I was wrong. Unimaginably so.

"Stay with me!" I call over my shoulder to the others attempting to flee the death promised by the gargantuan eels below. "Link arms and hold on when you catch up!"

I see only six of our number still living, besides the princess and I. Kassidy and her three bears, Andric — now suitless and far more mobile, thanks to Aria's mate mark — and Hook, trailing behind. As I watch, he takes a swing at the nearest eel, sinking the tip of his hooked hand in deep, parting the eel's head from the rest of its body in one savage yank. As much as I hate the bastard, I'll admit he's not completely useless.

Hook seizes the headless body and hurls it into the path of another oncoming eel. The limp creature slams into its fellow, slowing it for just an instant so that Hook can catch up with the rest of us.

There's only one way out that I can think of, and it's just as dangerous, if not more so, than facing the eels. But at least I know what to expect in the direction we're facing. I'll take the monsters I know over the ones I don't every time.

I dive for the trench.

We're two miles up from Opeia's main holdings, but I know this terrain well enough to navigate my way through. It's best we don't drag the new threat of these monstrous eels to her door, so I turn the opposite direction.

"Where are we going?" Aria bleats, coming alive in my arms again when we plunge into the dark.

I push pulsing golden color into my hair once more, exuding as much light as I can so the others will have an easier time following me. Aria cottons on to what I'm doing and pushes that lovely magenta color into her own hair, in an attempt to do the same. The humans will need the light with which to navigate the darkness of our destination, even if we'll draw undue attention to ourselves. The neon color will attract every predator within a mile radius but, again, I know what lives in these depths. I don't know what the eels are or who sent them or how powerful they truly are.

Of course, I've seen what they've done to their prey — boiled them. That's a fate I don't wish to meet.

"The eels run hot, so I believe the cold should slow them," I huff, dragging her down as fast as I can. We're covering an incredible distance. I've never pushed my body this hard before, and I can feel the exhaustion beginning to claim me. I can't keep this speed up for much longer. "And I think we can lose them in the gyre."

Aria bucks once in shock, successfully escaping my hold. I don't let her go far, locking firmly onto her wrist and keeping us moving downward. A quick glance up shows the remainder of our party has entered the trenches now. They aren't far behind us. I'm relieved to see the suits have some sort of lighting system of their own. Magic or mundane, I can't tell. I only hope the brightness of the suits will allow the users to see for long enough to reach our destination.

"We can't go down there!" Aria snaps. "Bastion, that's suicide!"

The gyre that runs beneath Opeia's kingdom is a swift and deadly current that runs about eight meters wide and loops around the trenches, spitting whatever's inside it out and around the trench nearest Triton's castle. From there, we'd have only an hour's journey to reach the back entrance of the castle. We could sneak in and make our way to the throne room and the glass case that holds Poseidon's trident. Without Sen and his guards to alert Triton that we've breached his perimeter, this plan could work.

The reason I didn't suggest it on the surface? It's the most imbecilic course we could possibly take. If the pressure or cold doesn't kill the remaining humans, the grotesquerie might. Many of its smaller members ride the current, kept away from Aspamia only by the scepter Triton wields. We have no such advantage. We could easily be eaten by a goblin shark or batted from the steam by a kraken's tentacle, only to be shoved into its maw.

But we have no other choice. Either die by eel or trust our luck in the gyre. "It's a risk we must take, Princess," I counter.

"Bastion, we won't survive."

"What else can we do?" I demand. "Stay above the reefs? The eels are too fast and too powerful to evade for long. They'll burn every one of us to a crisp."

"Maybe we could outswim them."

I shake my head. "You saw what they did to our men," I insist. "Until we understand how and what those eels truly are, I'd rather face the monsters I know how to defeat."

Without a good counter-argument, Aria falls silent. Her eyes are still huge in her face and most of the color has fled her cheeks, leaving them ashy gray instead of luminous silver. Her green markings stand out prominently under the magenta halo of her hair.

If we don't survive this and my last image is of her lovely face, I will die contented.

But I won't allow myself to ponder such morose thoughts just yet. We still have to try, and try we will.

We pause just long enough that Aria's able to link arms with one of the humans. It's Hook, I realize with a scowl. Of course, the fucker manages to reach her first. Just like always. I'm truly beginning to loathe him. Aria hooks her arm securely around his, clinging to us both like we're a tether to life itself. It does warm me just a little to note that she clings just as tightly to me as she does to him.

Kassidy has a hold on Leith, who clings to one of his cousins. Andric brings up the rear, clutching with white knuckles onto the quiet, pensive bear. I believe his name is Sorren.

"What's the bloody plan, mate?" Hook asks as he turns to face me. He's shivering already, which is not a good sign. The deep is about to get much colder.

I can't see them yet, but I feel the approach of the smallest members of the grotesquerie, drawn to the light of our hair and the lights of the suits like the lure of an angler. We don't have much time.

"Three miles down, there's a gyre that will take us through the trenches and deposit us near Triton's castle."

"Verra well, then," Hook says and glances down.

"It's not as simple as that," I start, grabbing his attention once more. "The problem is the gyre's surrounded by members of the grotesquerie. Sharks, anglers, mundane but still deadly eels, and more. And then, there's the possibility of running into krakens. I wouldn't normally propose we do such a dangerous thing, but..."

I glance pointedly toward the distant light above. The eels have paused at the edge of the trench, swarming like insects above us. Hook looks pale beneath the bronzed cast of his skin.

"Aye, the eels are a problem, mate. An' ye think this gyre will be any better?"

"It's better than the only other option facing us— and that's them," I say, gesturing at the swarming black shadows of monster eels.

"Aye, I'd rather take me chances with the gyre," Hook agrees.

I nod. "We can't give up now. Opeia can't hold the grotesquerie inside the trenches for much longer. Triton has to be defeated, and Kassidy is the best chance we have to put Aria or Opeia on the throne. Traveling the reefs isn't an option, clearly, so..."

"So, we risk it all for a chance to live?" Leith finishes grimly. "Sounds familiar."

He shares a secret smile with Kassidy and his cousins. I'll ask the meaning behind that dry remark later. *If* there is a later.

"It's your choice," I say simply to Aria, before glancing up once more at the light above us.

"What is yer belief?" Hook asks, and I'm surprised he's asking for my opinion.

"I'd take my chance with a kraken. At least the poison's quick and relatively painless, if the brutes don't snap your spine first."

Hook frowns.

"A ringing endorsement if I've ever heard one," Kassidy drawls. "But Bastion's right. I don't see what choice we have, and traveling the gyre may get us that much closer to our goal."

"Then it's decided," I say with a clipped nod. "Everyone enter the gyre and try to stay behind us. If you aren't able just meet at the back entrance to Triton's castle, but stay hidden."

Aria faces me and nods, giving me an encouraging smile. "Lead the way, Bastion."

I pump my tail, dragging Aria behind me and, with her, the line of humans and shifters. It reminds me oddly of a human game I saw on the surface, one in which a child strung together a series of small toy animals, linking them by their arms and tails until they appeared as a long string. I'm not certain what the point of the game was.

We descend quickly.

I'm correct in my assessment. There are hundreds of anglers waiting below, weaving this way and that so their lures look like bobbing fireflies. The humans behind us suck in shocked breaths as the cold begins to penetrate even their thick suits. Andric and Hook, without their suits, will fare even worse, but we can't stop to cater to their comfort. The only way we'll escape this nightmare is if we do things quickly.

Shrieks sound around us as the anglers rush us from all sides. One particularly large female sinks her teeth into my elbow and I'm helpless to bat her away, lest I lose my grip on Aria. Thankfully, Aria has the presence of mind to send a bolt of yellow-green energy at the thing, sending it spiraling away into the darkness. Some of the teeth are still lodged in the crook of my arm, but there's no time to pull them free. It's probably best I don't in any case—my blood would attract the goblin sharks.

The magic Aria just performed is a trick Opeia taught her, but not one she's particularly adept at. Aria's magic is better suited to healing and illusions; she doesn't have the energy to produce many bolts of light energy.

More shadows loom in the dark and I push myself as fast as I can, Aria doing the same behind me. The pressure of the dive is beginning to make my temples throb and I fear I might end up disgorging my last meal. Adrenaline shoots violently into my veins when the bellow of an aggressive, territorial male kraken vibrates the air around us.

Fuck, fuck, fuck.

It's a big one, I can tell by the timbre of the cry. It's got a mate tucked away somewhere, and possibly an infant or two along with her.

"Bastion," Aria almost squeaks, the quiver in her voice spearing me more effectively than any harpoon.

She's frightened. Gods, I don't know the last time I've seen her frightened. Upset, angry, indignant, and mutinous, but never afraid.

Not my Aria.

"I've got you, Princess," I say, using her grip on my arm to draw her even closer.

Fuck it. I might as well take the opportunity, because there's a high probability we're all going to die soon. I turn, pausing my stroke for an instant so I can

199

cup her face with my free hand and press my lips to hers.

Her lips are warm.

So incredibly warm, it feels like a brand against my mouth. I don't draw away, though. I want to savor this feeling. I want to take the taste of her with me into the beyond if I perish in the next few minutes.

With a gasp, she wrenches herself free of me. "Not now, Bastion," she says. "Once we survive this." Then, she turns and paddles urgently toward the gyre below. It's very near now — its roar is almost louder than the kraken's, at this proximity.

It's impossible to miss, a streak of byzantine purple against the pitch dark of the deep. There are more shapes inside it, being whipped quickly out of sight. I draw in a deep breath and hurl myself inside, dragging the others in after me.

The instant the current snags my body, I'm jerked forward with incredible speed, tumbled end over end like dice in a cup. Just up ahead, the tentacle of the male kraken shears through the current before us, the beast's roar rattling my bones.

Closing my eyes, I brace for impact.

EIGHTEEN
ARIA

The kraken's tentacle misses its mark, just barely, and doesn't crack our skulls open like velvety turtle eggs. Instead, the scything tentacle comes down hard between Hook and me. I release my hold on him the second I realize what's happening, pushing him away in an effort to save his arm from being pulverized. I'm not sure if I succeed, because the next instant, the current whips me away from him.

Releasing Hook — and the rest of our party — significantly reduces our weight, flinging Bastion and me with still greater velocity along the turbulent gyre. I can only hope Hook hasn't just had his arm severed. I can't stand to be the reason he loses another limb. If I ever meet the mysterious Pan who mutilated him, I'll hold him beneath the waves until he's good and waterlogged before I let him breathe again. And then I'll kill him.

If I live, that is. That's the tricky bit.

Most of the creatures within the gyre are moving alongside us, as helpless to control their motion as we are. There are some exceptionally strong swimmers, though, like the bluntnose shark up ahead. Though Bastion tries to avoid it, we go careening toward the speeding shark and smack right into it. Broadside, thankfully. If we'd made contact with its many rows of teeth, that would have been the end of us both. As it is, the contact still scrapes my arms raw and sends blood fountaining into the water. The shark adjusts its course as it picks up the scent, fathomless black eyes fixed eagerly on new prey.

Worse, it nearly knocks me loose from Bastion's grip. I cling onto him tenaciously, wrapping myself so tightly around him, I almost become a second skin. His arms wind even more securely around my body, anchoring me to him. I don't think I've ever been more grateful for my steadfast and patient friend and guard than I am now. I don't see how it took me so long and so many near-death experiences to appreciate him.

He's been unswervingly loyal to me, even through the apparent betrayals of his trust with Hook and Andric. Though nothing was ever agreed upon in our childhood, I've always somehow known Bastion was mine. My shield, my confidant, my friend… and maybe, someday, my lover? And that's when all the white lies I've told myself tumble to the forefront, revealing the naked truth.

I love Bastion.

I've always loved him, but I took him for granted because he was always there. But, yes, I love him, and I believe that love rivals the love I feel for Hook. And I love Bastion more than I love Andric, though the gentle prince continues to grow on me. My affection for him is still blooming.

But Bastion? He's deeply rooted within me, as crucial to me as an arm or a leg. I know he'd willingly step in front of one of the monsters we've faced, above and below, to save my life because he loves me just as deeply.

I hope it never, ever comes to that.

I keep my eyes trained over Bastion's shoulder, tracking the bluntnose as it continues to spiral through the gyre after us. There's no sign of the others and I realize they must be far behind us.

The gyre moves quickly and should spit us out within the next few minutes. But will we all survive that long? I'm loath to dim my hair, in case the others are still able to see it and, in seeing it, follow it, but I don't have much choice. I'm drawing every predator in the area to our position.

"Princess," Bastion starts. "If we don't make it out of this... I want you to know..."

He extinguishes the light of his hair, as well.

Darkness slides over my eyes and I blink against the sudden lack of light as I draw myself as close to him as I can possibly manage. So close I can feel his heartbeat against my breasts. My nipples tingle invitingly as they drag across his chest, the contours of his body cut finely. Gods, I wish to have more time with him.

I feel so incredibly stupid that it took this — moments before our possible death — for me to understand just how much this incredible man means to me.

But, better late than never.

"I know, Bastion," I say. "I love you, too."

He looks at me in shock. "You do?"

I nod. "I always have."

Bastion isn't given the chance to respond because the gyre roars loudly around us and we cling to each other as tightly as we can to avoid being separated and lost. After another few seconds, it's over. We're catapulted violently out of the stream and into a soft mound of... something. I'm almost afraid to see what we've landed on. If it's the head of a kraken, we're truly fucked.

Open your eyes, Aria, I instruct myself sternly. *How can you expect to face Triton if you can't even face what's in front of you?*

Sometimes, I hate it when I'm right.

I force myself to direct my gaze downward and inspect what I'm lying on and regret it almost instantly.

It *is* a kraken. A very young, very dead one. The mottled colors indicate late stages of decay. We're lucky the skin held up under our impact, or we'd be wading through its putrefying insides. The rest of the mound is composed of more dead bodies, mostly small members of the grotesquerie who were unfortunate enough to be swept into the gyre and thrashed to death.

I look around myself and realize we're nowhere near the rear entrance to my father's castle. The gyre has booted us out either early or late, I'm not sure which. Now it will simply be a matter of finding our way back to the castle, where we will hopefully meet the others.

"Aria," Bastion says as he pulls away from me and inspects me, "are you hurt?"

"No," I say as I look back up at him and smile with relief.

"What you said," he starts.

I nod. "I meant it."

"Then... you love me, too?" He seems confused, almost as though he doesn't believe he heard me correctly.

It's then that I realize how important this moment is — to both of us. Granted, we need to get moving so we can meet the others at the castle entrance, but I decide to take another few moments to make sure Bastion understands what he means to me. Especially in case either one of us, or both of us, don't survive...

"Mark me, Bastion."

He hesitates for a few seconds but then obediently drops his head and presses his lips to my throat. Magic pulses from his mouth into my skin, searing into me with a sensation so pleasant, my back arches of its own accord and my hair lights involuntarily.

I will have to choose between Andric and Hook at some point. I know that. Only one of them can bear my mark forever. And I already know what my answer is, what my actions will be. If we survive this quest, I'll release Andric. We're to be tied in marriage, and that will be enough. If I can somehow convince Hook to stay with me, if such is even possible, I want him to bear my mark as my mate.

Meanwhile, Bastion has marked me as irrevocably his. His chosen. His mate. And I'll bear his mark proudly. We'll all be tied to each other, in some way or another. The thought makes joy bubble through my veins, even as I wonder if Hook will ever agree to be with me... knowing I'll have to marry Andric.

"Up," Bastion orders, getting a grip on my underarms and hauling me toward the distant lights of the surface before I can argue. "We have to find our way back to the castle."

After we breach the trench, I feel myself crumble. I'm exhausted, physically and emotionally. But every foot we ascend toward the surface thaws my frozen limbs and injects life into my body. I don't think I've ever been more grateful to be near the surface than I am now.

It's not until we come to a stop that I realize I'm still shaking. Violent tremors run from the crown of my head to my tailfins. I can't stop, and I don't recognize the sound that comes out of my mouth. It sounds like a cry.

Bastion adjusts his grip on me and presses me into his chest. It's a lot like how Hook holds me when water leaks out of my eyes, which feels strange in this body. Merfolk aren't usually this close to each other without mating taking place.

"I'm here, Aria," Bastion soothes, running one rough hand down the curve of my spine like he's stroking a dolphin's back. "Calm down, Aria. I'm here. It's all right."

"Nothing is all right!" I shriek as the realization hits me that no one has followed us out of the gyre and that we're far away from where we're supposed to be. I keep looking back into the pitch blackness, for some sign of their glowing suits, but I don't see… anything. "They could all be dead."

"Or the gyre spit them out where it was supposed to," Bastion argues with a shrug. "Maybe we simply missed the opening, leading to the castle?"

I barely hear his response and it certainly doesn't penetrate. I can only wonder what's happened to the rest of them—if the spiraling corkscrew of water has killed them, or perhaps the shark or some equally unsavory creature.

"I'm leading you all into a killing field," I say with a shake of my head as the realization of what's happening weighs down on me. "There's no way I can defeat Triton. Even with Kassidy on our side, it's fucking hopeless! If Kassidy is even still alive," I finish in a softer voice as I continue to scan the periphery.

"You can defeat your father, and you will," Bastion says, hands coming to rest on my biceps so he can still my shaking body. "I believe that."

"I'm not a sea witch like Opeia. I couldn't protect myself when my father cast me out years ago. I couldn't even fend off Sen. If Andric hadn't killed him, I'd have been raped and then Sen would have killed me. I'm not as good a fighter as you, Bastion. And I'm nowhere near as strong as you are."

"I see greatness in you, Aria. I remember your first lessons with Opeia. You have power—power that you're too frightened to wield, because you're afraid it's going to turn you into *him*. But you are not your father! You never will be. You have too much heart."

"It's all a moot point, anyway," I say in despair.

"The others will emerge where they were supposed to," he says softly. "And we'll face down your father together. And we will be victorious."

"What if they're dead?" I ask as I continue to stare into the void. What if the kraken crushed Hook? What if the bluntnose got them?

Bastion seizes my face in both hands again and kisses me. It was pleasant when he did it on shore. It's somehow... *more pleasant* now. I can't place my finger on the difference at first. He feels similar, though there's an added thrill of having his heavy, muscular tail brushing along the length of mine. It's something I never thought to experience like this. We don't mate with our mouths, the way humans do. Occasionally, a depraved strumpet hanging around the coves will offer to lick a man's glans with her tongue, but good sirens don't and most mermen don't ask.

The kiss is better because Bastion finally seems certain. On land, he'd been almost reverential in his dealings with me, a man in the presence of a goddess. Now, with his mate mark seared into my flesh, he finally seems willing to push aside propriety and *take what is rightfully his.* And honestly? I've never found him more attractive.

"They survived, Aria," he says.

I shake my head. "You don't know that."

"They're strong and they're able, and I know the gyre didn't defeat them. Right before it spat us out, I could see all of them."

I gasp as he grips me, rubbing my breasts against his chest. I'm unusually aware of them these days. Perhaps I'm beginning to understand why humans find them so appealing. Face to face with a partner, the way the humans do it, they become quite sensitive.

"I love you, Aria," Bastion says when he pulls away from me, holding me at arm's length "For so long as the seas beat the shores, that will be my only truth."

If I were human, that statement would make me weep. Gods, I'm the most myopic mermaid alive if I've missed the adoration he's plainly held for me for so long.

"And I love you," I tell him, though it probably rings false, coming at this eleventh hour.

The smile that graces his face at those words is like dawn breaking over the horizon. Too beautiful for words. It breaks something in me. Then I'm throwing myself into his arms again, kissing him with all the vigor my exhausted body can muster. I want him, want to have him before the soreness and weariness steal my desire. We don't have long and, for all I know, we may be the only ones left to face Triton. This could very well prove to be a suicide mission.

"Mate with me," I murmur against his mouth when I draw away again.

His eyes widen, just a fraction. "Princess..."

"Call me Aria, please," I say as I lift a hand to stroke the mark on my neck. It tingles pleasantly on contact. "I'm wearing your mark, Bastion. I'm your mate. You can call me by my name."

"Aria," he says, choking out my name with difficulty. "I... I would never dare to presume..."

"It's not presumption. I'm asking. I want to be with you, to experience... love with you."

"The others are waiting for us," he argues.

"I know but we sacrifice a few more minutes for the chance to... know one another this way." I pause for a moment. "We might not ever be given the chance again," I finish, hoping I don't sound too morose.

He's so close, his groan vibrates my front, sending electric sensation zinging through my nipples. It's enough to draw a small, echoing groan from me, as well.

"Gods, Aria, *of course* I want to experience mating with you. It's all I've wanted since I've been old enough to understand what I was feeling."

"Then why are you hesitating?"

"Because I know you love Hook. I still don't trust him, but I'm not blind. I know you want to be with him. And you have to be with Andric if we all survive this. There's no room for me, Aria."

"There's room if I say there is," I chide him, sliding my fingers into his hair.

It lights up at once, diffusing golden light into the water around us. Not as noticeable here as it was in the deeps, but it's still beautiful. His eyes flutter closed, and he lets out a soft moan.

"Andric will be my king," I murmur. "I wish it were different but that's the nature of our situation. Hook is my mate, because I chose him, and I'm yours. But there's a good chance Hook chooses not to stay, Bastion."

"What do you mean?"

"He doesn't want me to marry Andric and I might not be able to change his mind. Regardless, I love you and I love Hook. Both can be true at the same time."

"And Andric?"

"Is brave, kind, and selfless, and I'm sure someday I'll feel the same way for him."

"Then you can never be just mine?"

I shake my head and feel guilt to the depths of my soul. But I have to be honest. I have to tell him the truth. "I'm sorry, but I can't just be yours, Bastion."

He lets out a gusty sigh and the bubbles stir my hair in a pleasant, ticklish rush.

"The truth is that I know that. I've known since we stepped foot on land and I realized Hook existed." He's quiet for a moment. "And… I can live with it. I can share you, if *they* can share you."

"You can?"

He nods. "I'm sorry for being selfish. Can you forgive me?"

"Only if you can forgive me for the same." I grin up at him coyly.

His eyes gleam with something primal and triumphant, and my glans begins to throb in response. I'm sure he can scent my desire. Gods, I can't believe this is really happening. Finally.

"I wanted to try human rutting," he admits, tracing his thumb along my bottom lip. "You seemed to enjoy it when Hook pressed into you. And human protuberances are different than…"

He gestures vaguely down at himself. I take a good look and am a little shocked. His glans is larger than most males I've seen, almost disproportionate in relation to his body size. Sen's was only average, even though he was massive. His friends' glans were even smaller. But Bastion's has contours that are smooth and inviting. I have the brief, taboo urge to trace it with my tongue, the way I had with Andric's cock in his vision.

Thoughts of Andric give me an idea as I reach for Bastion, running my fingers along the rounded nub. Gods, but he's *huge.* I didn't know male glans could get this large. Will he even be able to part my slit?

Bastion shudders violently beneath my touch, his glans pulsing against my fingers. He's warm and slick and I curiously trail my fingers through that secretion. No seed yet, but it's still fascinating.

"There's a way we could do both," I murmur again, swirling my finger around the nub. His body bucks, tail lashing almost violently against mine.

"How?"

"Illusion spell," I answer as I look up at him. "Do you want it?"

"Yes," he groans.

Then his mouth is on mine, his fingers threading into my hair and stroking with such incredible precision, my back arches and my body threatens to spasm into a violent orgasm already. He's clearly done this before. I wonder which of Opeia's handmaids he's been fucking over the years to be so good. Irrational jealousy sears through my veins, chasing away some of the ecstasy of his touch.

I regret the feeling almost immediately. After all, I've been focused anywhere but on Bastion. He's as much as admitted he never planned to tell me of his true feelings. If our circumstances had remained unchanged, he'd likely have fucked a few children into the maid and carried on, keeping his feelings from me for the rest of our days. I can't fault him for having a lover before me. Or many.

And what if he wants a lover after me? It's wrong of me to tell him no. After all, I'm planning to take all three of my men. But my instinctive reaction is to try to hide him away so no other woman can touch him. Bastion is mine; I won't let another have him.

Bastion scrapes the nails of one hand over my scalp and brings the other up to weigh one of my breasts in his hands, the way Hook often does. He pinches the nipple to a taut peak and then twists it gently. The slight pulse of pain tips me over the edge and he swallows the scream of pure pleasure when I buck into him. He grins against my mouth, pure, masculine confidence etched into that smile.

He's so sexy when he's domineering like this. If we survive this mission, I want to see this side of Bastion more. Much more.

"Illusion spell, Aria," he reminds me.

Right. Yes.

I press my fingers into his biceps, focusing the meager amount of magic I possess into him. I've been told I have more magic, and perhaps he's right. I've never truly applied myself to the arcane arts Opeia tried to teach me. I've seen what absolute power has done to Triton and I never want to be like him. It's probably why I've avoided having sex for so long, why I've shrugged off magicks that weren't entirely essential to my survival and tried to remain as honest with myself and others as possible.

Bastion is right. I don't want to be anything like my father.

But this spell is harmless, meant to ease the sick or dying into death with minimal discomfort. Our dead so rarely see final rest. It's too perilous to haul them to the surface for a Shepherd or Shepherdess to guide them to the other side. Most of our dead reside in Opeia's home, restless souls appeased only by the illusions we provide for them. Illusions of a better life, where Triton doesn't rule.

I intend to make that dream a reality, if enough of us survive to carry out the plan. For now, I want Bastion. I want the feel of him pressing against me, the illusion of him deep inside me.

The reef around us disappears, fading away into the illusion of Cassio Island, with its pristine white shore. It's far away from the metal buildings with their array of death-dealing implements. In the vision, Bastion's body hovers over mine, long, lean and nude.

I take a moment to appreciate just how beautiful he is in this form. Though his protuberance — or cock, as Hook calls it — is strange looking, I already know it provides great pleasure. There's a sort of artful beauty to the way the male human body is constructed. Bastion's hipbones are cut at a strong angle, his thighs are sturdy, his skin smooth. He lays thick and heavy between my legs.

I smile and roll my hips just a little, pushing against him in both reality and illusion. His cock throbs against me and he groans, tangling his hand in my hair once more, rocking his hips into me. This isn't the ideal position if we're going to join in real life, but for now, the sensation of his hands in my hair is enough to coax me toward another orgasm.

My hips jerk up in surprise when he slides a finger into me. Not so strange in the human form, as Hook has done it often enough. But in my siren form? Never. Even I don't often touch myself there.

Bastion's fingers curl inside my slit, stroke along my walls, and explore me. It's enough to make me arch into him with a moan as a climax rips through me. He hasn't even put his glans against me yet and I'm already so dizzy with pleasure, I can barely keep the illusion up.

This is incredible.

I can't wait to feel him pressed against me, spilling his seed inside me.

"Bastion..." I pant. "Oh, Gods..."

"You're so beautiful, Princess..." Bastion growls against my throat, slipping back into the formal address out of habit. I don't correct him. At this moment, I don't care what he calls me.

"Please. Inside me, Bastion, please..."

And then, both in illusion and reality, he flips me, spinning me in the sand so I'm on my knees. And in reality, who knows? I'm probably pressed into a rock or flattened beneath his bulk. Perhaps he's tied me in the kelp and plans to ride me until we buckle from exhaustion.

I shiver. Gods, if he isn't doing that at the moment, he *should*. If we make it out alive, I'm going to command it.

It's mere seconds before he's there, back bowed over mine, his sex pushing against me. My mouth opens, but no sound comes out. The illusion of his cock filling me steals my breath and the reality of his glans on me has my entire tail tingling. He's so *big*. I'm not sure I can take it. I arch my back and moan, trying to adjust to the new sensation. It jostles my breasts, which are so damn sensitive. I might just explode from the sensation of the water on them. I knew they weren't just for nursing young, but no one told me they were so sensitive during copulation — that a man touching them could only aid my pleasure.

Bastion palms one yet again, lavishing attention on it even as he begins to move. When he thrusts into me, I think I might weep. It's so *good*. How have I gone all my life without having this? How idiotic am I, to have overlooked him? We could have been doing this for years.

"If we make it out alive, you are fucking me every day," I pant, struggling hard to vocalize past the pleasure. It's interspersed by a few moans.

Bastion's rolling chuckle causes me to clench tight. It's a thick, velvety sound. Bastion's laughs are rare; my poor, solemn friend and guard has had little to be joyful about in the years since we left Aspamia. Even the few chuckles I've coaxed out of him aren't like this. He's unguarded for the first time in years and it makes me want to kiss him. Hard to do, in the position we're in, and even if we could, I wouldn't want him breaking pace because, Gods, this is delicious.

"I will worship your quim every day, if we survive, my Queen. Don't you doubt it."

He drives into me as vigorously as he can, kissing me, stroking my hair, tweaking my nipples all in quick succession until I cum again in a blinding wave of ecstasy, screaming so loudly I fear everyone will hear it all the way to Triton's castle.

Finally, Bastion sags as well, spilling himself deep inside me. The illusion flickers and dies, letting reality creep back in increments. I'm half-bent over a stone, posed like one of those sirens in the Drowning Cove, as if I'm trying to coyly lure in a sailor. Bastion's weight is still behind me, his tail curled around mine.

He kisses my throat softly, tenderly, worshiping my flesh, just as he promised. "Are you with me, Aria?" he murmurs against the shell of my ear.

An aftershock of pleasure riots through me but I nod, too overcome to search out words. I feel rather than see his smile.

"Good. Rest for a moment and then we need to be off. We have friends to find and two kingdoms to save."

He's right. Things aren't over, and we're not safe. There's every chance this mission will get us killed. And if I have to take a memory into the great oceans beyond, this is the one I'd like to live in.

I straighten, test my tail a few times. I'm pleasantly sore. He's big. That will take getting used to.

"Let's go."

NINETEEN
ARIA

It takes longer than I feel it should to find our way back to the castle. Dangerous as the journey through the gyre was, it brought us that much closer to our goal. The only thing between us and the rear entrance to the castle is Andromeda's garden — and that's a more daunting challenge than one might think.

Hidden among the more benign species of kelp, waterwheel, and coral is a number of enormous *caro comedenti*. They're the only species of sea anemone I've ever seen that devours not only other plants, but fish and even merpeople, as well. They aren't large enough to eat a full-grown siren or human, but they can take out a large enough chunk to cause blood to billow into the water, drawing any of Andromeda's pet sharks to the spot in an instant.

I'm weary, I'm sore from the vigorous fucking with Bastion, and I feel more than a little ashamed of myself for losing my head and throwing myself at him. Yes, I love him. And I always have — of that, I have no questions nor confusion. And I don't regret what happened. But ye Gods, the timing! Just more of Aria's selfishness coming to the fore and making itself known.

We find the rest of our party about a mile up the southern garden wall, sheltering in a forest of giant kelp. I smile a little to myself, knowing Triton would

throw an absolute fit if he knew where they were. This
is the rumored sacred resting place of Eudore, one of
the nereid and a supposed cousin of mine, many,
many generations removed. It's the reason this location
hasn't been uprooted like everything else in my
father's kingdom has been. Triton has always been
more superstitious than me (a feat, to be sure) and he
won't risk Eudore's wrath, even from beyond the
grave.

There's probably some irony in this, but I'm too
weary to parse it out at the moment.

As soon as they see us, Hook approaches first,
arms outstretched to seize me. He's perhaps thirty feet
closer to us than the others and I wonder if he was out
scouting, searching for us while the others huddled
together to remain safe.

"Aria! Are ye well?"

I can feel Bastion's displeasure at seeing Hook
and, from the corner of my eye, I notice his posture
turning erect as he holds himself upright, squaring his
shoulders. This constant competition between the two
of them is going to need to stop at some point. Though
that point isn't now, because we all have bigger
subjects on which to focus our attention.

I don't answer because my own attention is,
instead, on his body. He's not moving swiftly, and I
hold him at arm's length so I can examine him
thoroughly. What I see makes my stomach twist and
my eyes itch with the desire to cry.

He has deep bruises on one side of his body. If the
pattern weren't so regular and recognizable, I'd have
said he got on the wrong side of an octopus. As it is, I

know what's happened to him. The swipe of the kraken's tentacle, which had been meant for me, hit Hook instead. His ungainly lurch toward me comes from the fact that his leg appears to be broken.

And the worst part? None of his injuries or the pain seem to bother him much. Even though he's more mottled than a sea hare, he just shrugs off my hands as I try to palpate his wounds, to understand the extent of his injuries. He folds himself into my arms, squeezing me as tightly as he can.

"Thank the Gods," he says, voice thick and strained like he too wants to weep. "I was afraid we might have lost ye, Popsy."

"Hook, you're hurt," I whimper, though the sentiment seems woefully inadequate and unhelpful.

Hook rolls one shoulder in a shrug. "Aye, but I've suffered, worse an' by a fecker much smaller than that beastie. I'll be fine."

He is *not* fine. He's got at least one broken bone and who knows what else. He needs a healer. He can't make it through Andromeda's gardens in this lowly state, let alone take on the castle guard or Triton. He'll be the first of our team to be killed and I won't allow that to happen.

No, Hook means way too much to me. I would do everything in my power to ensure his safety.

My eyes rove over the rest of our ragtag group as they swim closer to us and my panic rises to choke me. All the fears that plagued me prior to the incredible sexual liaison I shared with Bastion are now lapping at the edges of my thoughts again. Even though we lost most of Andric's and Opeia's recruits, I'm beyond

220

relieved to see our core group still alive. Also, I can't ascertain the possible damage done to any of them owing to their suits, which cover them completely.

"Aria, where the fuck have you two been?" Kassidy asks, her eyes wide with fear and... anger?

"We were thrown out on a different side of the gyre," I explain as I face her and feel myself instantly color with embarrassment as I remember exactly what went on between Bastion and myself — while the rest of them were probably scared to death that the two of us had been eaten by something. I face Kassidy and then her husbands. "Are you all unwounded?"

Kassidy nods, answering for the four of them.

It's when I turn my attention to my future husband that my stomach drops again. Andric is equally as bruised as Hook, with a cut under his right eye and purple and blue already marring his handsome face. But as he moves in the water, I notice he appears otherwise unhurt.

Thank the Gods.

There are only seven of us left and anxiety claws like a beast at my back door, ready to gouge out my sanity if I allow it. We're outnumbered and outmanned, and almost a third of our fighting force is injured. Not to mention the fact that we are all exhausted after having narrowly escaped a perilous journey to arrive here.

"What happened while you were in the gyre?" is all I can think to say.

It's Kassidy who jumps in, glowering at Bastion and I as if she knows what we've been up to. I tuck my chin and stare very deliberately at my tail. She's got every right to be angry with me, but I can't take condemnation and disgust on top of my own feelings of guilt and anger with myself. Thankfully, her voice comes out tart, not furious.

"We were thrashed harder than a borrowed mule and several things tried to eat us. We were spat out about a mile north of here and we swam as best we could until we spotted the castle. Hook and Andric had it worst, since they're human and they weren't wearing suits."

I feel even worse about the sex between Bastion and me now.

Kassidy continues. "We can't go against Triton with a good portion of our fighting force incapacitated like this. Those eels decimated our forces. We can't face any more enemies unless we're all in better shape."

"Yes," I agree with a quick nod as I face Hook again and, more pointedly, his leg.

"What are ye proposin' exactly, Popsy?" Hook asks wearily. "Because we dinnae have time to rest, an' Triton knows we're comin'."

"It doesn't change the fact that Kassidy is right — we're all exhausted and some of you are injured," I point out.

Hook faces me and shakes his head. "Give Triton time an' he'll amass a feckin' army to fight us off next time. Or mayhap he'll just send more eels."

"Anything he sends after us, we won't be able to fight off," I say.

"There is nary a way we surfaced in this area without bein' seen, an' that gives us aboot ten hours to get our loot an' get out or this whole thing will be for naught. Every life we lost will be naethin' but a senseless casualty. I dinnae know about ye, lass, but I cannae abide that."

It's hard to tell owing to the restrictive suit, but I think Kassidy's shoulders tense and her face seems to grow even paler in the ghostly green light of the kelp forest.

Normally, I adore the surface. When I was a child, the rippling tide through the seagrass could lull me to sleep in minutes. Now, even the gentle swaying motion of the kelp around us makes me jump, as if eels might slither their way through the broad leaves any second.

Still, despite Kassidy's pallor, her eyes are green flames in her lovely face, spitting fury at Hook.

"I don't see you jumping in with anything useful other than a whole bunch of whining, you scallywag." She takes a breath. Hook's eyes go wide, but he doesn't say anything and merely crosses his arms against his chest, frowning at her. And at me.

"All your talk doesn't change the fact that we can't go against Triton like this," she continues. "Look at us! We wouldn't last a minute."

"She's right," Nash says, and Sorren nods.

"If we leave an' come back, we will have lost the advantage of surprise," Hook insists.

"And Hook has a point, as well," I say.

"You could draw the lifeforce from Aria and Bastion, Kassidy," Leith says, speaking up for the first time. "In order to heal Hook and Andric."

"But then Aria and Bastion won't be as strong," she argues, but I can see by the expression on her face that she's seriously weighing his idea.

"If merfolk have anything in common with shifters," Nash starts, "they'll replenish their strength quickly."

I nod eagerly, lunging away from Hook in an almost drunken motion, arms outstretched toward Kassidy. "Nash is correct," I say. "Merpeople are known for our quick healing ability."

Yes, yes, yes!

If there's a way I can help my men, I'll do it in a heartbeat.

Kassidy stops me mid-lunge, holding me at bay with one bulky metal-suited arm. Her expression appears torn between amusement and consternation. "Bridle your seahorses, Princess. If we do this, I think I should start with Bastion first."

"Why?" I ask, not following her logic.

"Because, and don't take this the wrong way, but you're a woman."

"What is that supposed to mean?" I demand, certainly taking it the wrong way.

Kassidy shakes her head. "There are two reasons."

"What are they?" I press.

"You're physically not as strong nor as large as the men," she says with a stern expression. Before I can interject, she continues, "I'm not saying you're weak or anything, but you're smaller than the men. Just like I am. And that means your internal reservoir is likely to be smaller, too. Not a hard and fast rule, but for Hook's injuries, I want to try to draw on Bastion's strength first. And that brings me to my second point, which is even more important than the first."

"Which is?" I ask.

"None of us can afford to lose strength right now, but you, Aria, can afford it least of all. You need to live through what's coming so you can rule this territory once I've gotten that damned sea fork for you, got it?"

I nod meekly, too grateful for her presence and her willingness to heal my men to put up more than token resistance. I obligingly backstroke a few paces to allow her a direct line to Bastion.

I expect him to object. He's made it no secret he distrusts and dislikes Hook. Healing Hook must chafe at Bastion. But, to his credit, he doesn't say anything, just gives me one sidelong glance. He bobs his head a fraction of an inch in assent and closes his eyes.

I turn back to Kassidy. When she acts, there's no fanfare. The exchange is barely noticeable, and if I weren't hanging on her every motion, there's a chance I wouldn't even catch on that she's doing anything at all. She doesn't even touch Bastion, simply faces him and closes her eyes. It looks like a soft haze of heat emanates off her, roiling through the water, a very weak echo of what the eels did. The reminder makes me shudder. I still don't know what the eels truly are, and that ignorance chills me. What madness has my father cooked up now?

I glance at Bastion and notice he grimaces at the loss of his power, the silver sheen of his skin dimming as Kassidy siphons off his life force to feed it into Hook. Even knowing Bastion will replace the lost energy and strength quickly with food and rest, I hate witnessing his pain. I hate it that I've brought them all to this point.

I'm an arrogant, presumptuous little girl to think I can tangle with my father, and I've never realized that more than now. Triton is Poseidon's favorite son, nearing godhood himself. And what am I? A study in failure. Too weak to fight my father when I was a girl. Too frightened to fight him all the rest of my life, until there was no other choice. If we fail now, I've as good as condemned my kingdom to death. No, condemned all of *Fantasia* to death. The humans are right. Without supply lines, the war is over before it's even begun. It's as good as wrapping a garrote around the nation's throat and looking on as it meets a flailing, gasping end.

The stream of Bastion's life force hits Hook mid-chest and he flails for a second before recovering himself.

I let out a shaky, relieved exhale as the power sinks into him. It's apparent from the first few seconds of contact that whatever Kassidy's doing is working. The navy-black bruises decorating Hook's face dull to a yellow brown. The color still bothers me, but it isn't quite as alarming as the midnight shade they were a few seconds ago. Most astonishing of all, Hook's broken leg fuses together within the first minute, coming together with a soft pop. Hook tests it warily and lets out a soft chuckle when it moves without difficulty.

"Well, would ye look at that!"

"How are you feeling?" I ask.

He looks at me and grins broadly. "Sore, but happy to be alive."

Hook gives Bastion a look edged with concern. Bastion may not like Hook, but the feeling clearly isn't mutual. I can't read anything but sincerity in his dark, beguiling gaze.

"Ye've done right by me, mate," Hook says to Bastion, "an' I will be forever grateful."

Bastion doesn't say anything, just nods.

I turn to face him. "How do you feel, Bastion?" I ask, moving closer to him. He holds me back with an outstretched arm, clearly afraid that if I touch him, my own life force will be leached from me through him.

"Like I've done a circuit of the trenches at top speed," Bastion admits after a moment. "But I've fought for longer with worse damage. I'll be fine."

Kassidy drops her hands and opens her eyes, and the mist of her magic disappears in the water. She turns to face me.

"All right, Princess," she says impatiently, waving me forward. "Your turn next."

"I don't believe the princess should undergo this," Bastion says.

I turn to face him. "I have to. And I want to. It's the least I can do."

"I can't heal Andric without her power," Kassidy explains.

"Please be understanding, Bastion," I say.

He remains quiet but his jaw is tight.

"It won't take much of her strength," Kassidy continues. "Andric isn't in as bad shape as Hook was."

Bastion just nods once, and I take a few strokes through the water until I'm closer to Andric. Up close, the cut beneath his eye looks worse. Guilt batters me again.

Thoughtless, insensitive Aria, staying away to fuck Bastion while the others were this badly hurt. If we had arrived sooner...

Kassidy wastes no time. With one lazy flick of her fingers, it begins. It feels like an undertow, tugging and pulling at my tailfins, the pressure threatening to drag me out to deeper waters. Kassidy skims across the top of my already depleted energy and my vision swims alarmingly. I'm afraid I might pass out, and then...

Something in me bursts like a rotted sea cucumber.

It's like a tsunami. Energy swells inside me, roiling and frothing like sea foam. Every cell of my body is battered, left tumbling in the wash of power. The amount is almost as crushing and cold as the deeps and I let out a breathless sound of fright.

Kassidy echoes the sound, though louder and punctuated by a fervent, "Fuck!"

She drags just a fraction of the new power from me along with the stale top layer she'd already skimmed and shoved into Andric. His back arches, his eyes roll up into his head, and every injury he had disappears in the time it takes to blink. Still, he continues to shake.

"Fuck," Kassidy repeats. "It's too much."

But she still isn't finished. She turns away from Andric and faces the others in our entourage. She moves her outstretched arms to each of them, in turn, and the energy moves like a wave, hitting each of the

228

men, ending with Hook. The last of his bruises slough off like filth after a good washing. Then the rest of the energy travels through the kelp forest, stirring the plants around like wind through a giant's hair.

Kassidy whirls on me as she drops her hands and inhales deeply, opening her eyes in shock and surprise once they focus on me.

"Why the fuck didn't you tell us?" she demands, jabbing a metal finger into my sternum.

"Tell you what?" I respond, shocked by the outraged expression on her face. "And stop shouting, or we'll be heard!"

Kassidy lowers her voice, but she doesn't wrench that furious gaze from my face. "You're Chosen. Why the fuck didn't you tell us?"

My tail twitches once in shock and I put distance between us quickly, shaking my head. "Chosen?" I repeat, shaking my head. "I'm not. You're… confused."

"Oh, come the fuck on, Princess," Kassidy says, shaking her head and continuing to glare at me. "That's bullshit and we both know it."

"One of the Chosen?" Andric repeats as he looks at me.

"Chosen?" Hook echoes.

I just stare at Kassidy, nonplussed. "I don't know what you're talking about." I wonder, silently, if the magic she's just performed has somehow addled her mind? I hope not, because we need her. She's instrumental to this mission.

"Explain, Kassidy?" Leith says.

"I reached for your power," Kassidy continues, not sparing a glance for anyone else. Her eyes are riveted on mine. "There was a lot of stagnancy and rot at the top, when I first dialed into the flow of your power, but underneath that was a fucking ocean."

"What do ye mean?" Hook asks.

"I mean, I almost drowned myself trying to call on Aria's power," Kassidy responds. "For fuck's sake, you can't *not* know you have that much power? You had to know on some level you're Chosen?"

"I can't be," I argue feebly. I just… I just don't understand how that can be.

In the deeps where no light pierces, a hero lies, and rises to do battle, blotting out the fire of the skies," Sorren muses with a strange smile on his face. "Hmmm. I wonder why we didn't see it sooner…"

"Because any spare second ye lot are feckin' like rabbits?" Hook mumbles. "I've seen ye together. Nary much on yer minds but gettin' alone. 'Twas damn distractin' when we were on the Jolly Roger."

"That's not it," Leith argues, shaking his head. "Someone still should have seen this! All of Fantasia has been on the lookout for the Chosen Ten for well over a decade."

"Makes you wonder why we're all coming out of the woodwork now, within weeks of each other," Kassidy grumbles. "First Neva, then me, and now Aria."

I continue to shake my head. "How do you even know —" I start, but Kassidy cuts me off.

"Maybe the powers need time to steep or something? I mean, most of us would have been really young when the last war was raging. Maybe it's fate's way of preserving our dignity?"

"What do ye mean, lass?" Hook asks.

She faces him with a shrug. "I mean, shove ten toddlers in front of Morningstar and he'd have laughed in our faces before smashing us flat."

"Stop!" I cry out, at last, flinging my hands up defensively. I can't stand to hear them prattle on about this when none of it is true! I'm not a Chosen and I never have been. "I'm not what you think I am. There's no way I'm—"

"You are," Kassidy insists. "Trust me, I know. I didn't think it was possible, either, when it happened to me. But you have a truly staggering amount of power, Aria. I felt it. I've never felt power like that in anyone else before. There's no other explanation for it."

I cross my arms under my breasts, the way I've seen human women do when agitated. It mounds my cleavage and I catch Andric, Hook, and Bastion staring before they wrench their gazes away, frowning at each other.

"Aria, think about it," Kassidy continues. "Just push aside your disbelief for the moment and try to understand how it might possibly be true."

I nod as I take a deep breath of ocean water and try to rationalize how she could possibly be onto something. "My grandfather, Poseidon, is a *god*," I say in a small voice. "Maybe you're right and there's untapped potential within me, owing to that? My father did his level best to make me scared of my own shadow from the time I was a small girl, let alone my own power." The more I think about it, the less sense it makes, and I shake my head. "If there's anyone that prophecy Sorren mentioned refers to, it's my aunt, Cassiopeia. She's incredibly powerful — probably as powerful as my father. The only difference being that he has many more merpeople under his authority. Regardless, though, Opeia is far, far more powerful than I am."

"Then why can't she wield the trident?" Kassidy counters. "If she's Chosen, why didn't she manage to stymie Morningstar during the first war? Your aunt fought with us, you know. Accompanied our fleets into battle. But she never, not even once, held a candle to Morningstar's power." Kassidy grows quiet for a moment or two, her mouth turning into a tight, white line. "It's *you*, Aria. It's always been you."

It can't be true. It just can't be. Because if Kassidy's correct and I am Chosen, it means I've wasted my life in the deeps, cowering in fear of my father. I can't accept that. I can't stand the thought of all the wasted years that I could have spent with Bastion. The years I could have known Hook and Andric.

Worse still, if Kassidy is correct, then that means I have the power to challenge Triton on my own — it means I dragged twenty-one hapless souls into the ocean to meet painful ends and it was completely and utterly *pointless.*

"It doesn't matter," Andric interjects before Kassidy can gear up for another argument. I'm backing away from all of them, as if physical distance can make the assertion disappear.

Kassidy's brow thrusts up and disappears into the messy golden sprawl of her hair. The stuff is so thick, it mostly fills the dome of her suit.

"What?" she demands as she turns to face him.

"I said it doesn't matter, in the end, does it?" Andric repeats. "Chosen or not, we still have to go up against Triton. The only thing this really changes is whether or not Aria will be able to help in the final battle. But either way we look at it, we need to fight *him*. That's non-negotiable. We *have* to defeat Triton, whether it's you wielding the trident, Kassidy, or it's Aria."

I'm so grateful for Andric's intervention, I could kiss him. Because he's right. I don't kiss him, because I've already filled my quota for inappropriately timed physical intimacy for the day. I do offer him a grateful smile, though, which he returns.

I'm so glad I gave him a mate mark. With it, I can feel my energy like a distant echo within both him and Hook. It's a balm to know they're both whole and healthy. More than that, I can almost catch the tenor of their emotions through it.

Hook's are all sharp, as fierce and potent as the man himself. Relief, hope, and happiness vie for prominence. He's a spiraling, tumbling force of nature like the gyre on which we rode here. Andric's emotions are quieter, but no less powerful. Inevitable, like the push and pull of the tides. He stares at me, brimming with quiet awe and something so tender, it makes my heart ache.

Love, or maybe something close to it? I don't understand, because it seems too soon. Bastion has had time to fall in love with me because we've known one another for years, since our childhood, and we've been inseparable ever since. But Hook and Andric? We've only been together a short while. What is it that compels them to feel this way about me? I've done little to earn it.

Kassidy finally tears her frustrated gaze from mine and nods sharply.

"You're right, Andric. We've got ten hours. Probably closer to nine and three quarters, now."

"What's our plan now?" Hook asks her.

She shrugs. Then, they all turn to me in an eerie, almost synchronized motion. "The gardens," I say finally. "It will be dangerous, but the gardens will be mostly unguarded and they provide direct entrance to the back of the castle."

"That's fucking moronic of Triton," Sorren snorts. "What king leaves his back entrance unguarded? Maybe this will be easier than we anticipated."

"Less so than you think," I say with a chilly smile. "Because the garden is full of *caro comedenti.*"

"What the bloody hell is that?" Hook demands.

I turn to face him and swallow hard. "Flesh-eating plants. If we make it past Triton's *house plants* alive, I'll be more optimistic. They're deadly and they're persistent."

"Any way to get past them, Popsy?" Hook asks.

My lips twitch again. "Yes, but you won't like it."

Kassidy huffs another frustrated breath. "Do we ever like what comes out of your mouth? Spill, Princess. What's the trick?"

So, I tell them.

TWENTY
ANDRIC

If we make it out of this alive, I'll never eat another ocean creature again. If Aria's aversion weren't reason enough, what's currently facing me is enough to curb my desire, possibly forever.

In preparation for our entry into Andromeda's garden, Aria encouraged us to first make a stop at a small lagoon, where she revealed a pit of enormous, lazing sea slugs. Enormous as in man-size! After each of us revealed our absolute disinterest in even touching the unsightly things, we proceeded to *roll* on top of the largest male, coating ourselves in mucus. Perhaps a bit redundant for those in suits, but none were exempt. Better to be slimy than underprepared and dead.

Apparently, this layer, if thick enough, would counteract the digestive juices of the flesh-eating plants within the garden. However, the mucus doesn't last long, so we must be quick. Even knowing the importance of protecting ourselves with the slimy and sticky stuff, I'm still disgusted by the coating that clings to my skin.

It's quite revolting.

"Will this stuff ever come off?" I ask, trying to restrain the nausea that churns my stomach. Even the strong ocean current that whips through Triton's palatial grounds doesn't seem to affect the mucus at all. It continues to stick to us.

"With dedicated scrubbing or exposure to fire," Aria answers. "Don't be so eager to scrape it off, though. That stuff is extremely valuable. Extract of *limax mare aeternae* can sell for up to a thousand gold coins per ounce."

I almost choke on my tongue. "What?"

She nods with a secret smile as we approach the edge of the kelp forest. When we emerge, we'll be forced to make the silent, eerie journey down the rolling sands and into Andromeda's deadly gardens. Perhaps I'm being a touch cowardly, but all I want to do is stay at the edge of this shady, peaceful forest and watch Aria until exhaustion claims me. I could do it, too. According to Aria, the mark makes it possible for me to stay beneath the waves indefinitely with no ill-effects. In fact, the longer I live beneath the water with her, the more likely I am to fully transition to a merman — in fifty or so years. And Aria would have to complete the mark, as well. As it is now, neither Hook's nor my mate marks have been finished. Not that I'm sure I would want to transition into a merman; I'm quite happy living my life on land.

Only Hook and I have the mate-mark advantage. So, I steal the moment, using this new tidbit, to distract myself from the very real possibility of death that may await us in Triton's halls.

"They may not look like much, but they're probably the most valuable treasure Triton owns, besides the trident itself," Aria continues as she looks upon the slugs with a fond expression. "They're called the eternal sea slug for a reason."

"And what is that reason?" I ask.

"They're not quite of this world, so all their secretions have special properties. Applied topically, the mucus can extend life for many years. And injected or swallowed, it can put someone into a death-like sleep."

"Death sleep?" I echo. "I thought that only happened in stories. Like what happened to Princess Briar Rose."

"Precisely," Aria says, turning her attention from the rather ugly sea slugs to me. "The dark fae, Maura Lechance, was the last person to come to Triton with entreaties for the extract. I suspect Maura slipped some extract to the poor babe long ago."

"And that is why the princess has been asleep all these years?"

She nods.

"Do you think she will wake?" I continue.

Aria rolls her thin shoulders in a distracting manner. It thrusts her breasts out noticeably, making my eyes follow the long, lean line of her body. Gods, I wish she had legs at the moment. Nothing would brace me for this battle more than knowing we'd made love once before I face my potential death. Then I could leave this world a contented man.

"It depends. Usually, certain criteria have to be met in order for the effects of the slug mucus to be reversed. It depends on the slug it was taken from."

"Which slug did Maura Lechance take the mucus from?"

"*I* took it from the slug for Maura," Aria corrects me and shrugs. "If I remember correctly, I think it was from Garrin." She pauses. "He's a romantic."

"A sea slug?" I ask, sounding incredulous. "Romantic?"

"Yes, very," Aria says with a frown as she turns to face me again. "He was very polite when I asked for his mucus and he was very pleased to know it would be going to a good cause, such as preserving the princess."

"So, going back to our original conversation," I say as I try to grasp a few things. "These slugs have names?"

Hook joins us. "An' ye... talk to them as if they're people?" he repeats dubiously.

"Well, of course!" she answers. "You can't very well not respond when someone or something addresses you, now can you?"

Hook frowns and appears wholly confused. I don't blame him. "I didnae see any mouths upon them, Popsy."

"How else do you think they speak!" Aria says, as if the rest of us are inane for questioning her. Then she cocks her head to the side. "Well, they can also communicate mind-to-mind, but they *do* have mouths. They *eat* trespassers and thieves."

"They eat people?" I press.

Aria laughs. "Yes, but don't worry, I vouched for all of you." Then she pauses, facing the ugly things again.

Kassidy seems as concerned about the slugs eating us as I am, though it's hard to tell through her suit. I'm secretly glad to be rid of the damn thing. It's incredibly uncomfortable to wear, not as maneuverable as it needs to be, and days on days of breathing in stale, metallic air is enough to drive anyone half-mad.

On the other hand, if we're attacked by flesh-eating plant life or fire eels, it does offer momentary protection. So perhaps it's an even trade.

We all hesitate on the precipice of the garden, even Aria. Lush and lovely as it is, there's a sense of menace, knowing that among the colorful coral and specially-bred multi-hued kelp and the abundance of sea flowers, there's a threat lurking. It must have been a minefield for Aria as a child.

Was she even allowed to play? I've never met Triton, but his reputation leaves me with the impression of a granite-faced taskmaster. I have to wonder what sort of life Aria lived here before her exile. Has she ever once known what it's like to feel true, childlike joy?

I look automatically to her, scanning her expression as I've done repeatedly since we found ourselves in this situation.

She's a warrior, and hopefully a queen by the time we're through here. I should like to see nothing more than for Aria to take her father's throne. But all of that is secondary. I look at her because she's just too beautiful and vulnerable for words. And her vulnerability is a peculiar one. It's not necessarily weakness, but... pain, so naked and raw on her face, it triggers every instinct I have to protect her, even if she doesn't need my protection.

"Aria?" I prompt gently. "Are we ready to go?"

239

She shakes herself, eyes icing over with determination, steel bracing the delicate curve of her spine. She nods once. "I think I remember the path."

She arcs forward, as smooth and graceful as a dolphin. I lag behind her for a few seconds, even as the rest of our number trail behind me. She's truly a sight to behold, here in her element, the sun glinting off her scales even through the slimy coating we've been forced to don. The realization that she's covered in slug trail and yet I still find her stunning makes me smile thinly to myself as I paddle after her. I've fallen fast and hard, haven't I? Still rhapsodizing about her while she's covered in the slimiest, smelliest muck I've ever had the misfortune to come across.

She leaves a shiny trail of mucus droplets behind her in the water, like a trail of breadcrumbs to follow. Disgusting, but effective.

Hook swims up just behind her, almost as graceful as she is. He's a born sailor, more comfortable on deck or in the water than he will ever be on land. He was born for this. Born for her.

Not for the first time, a pang of doubt hits me. Aria likes me. At least, I have to assume she does because we've gotten along well enough and she's placed her mark on me. She doesn't seem to do that on a whim. But what do we have beyond that? It's clear she adores Hook and, even if she's not aware of it, Bastion adores her. And she obviously values him; they move together in a sort of synchronicity I've never seen outside of long-married couples. Hook matches her on land and sea, and she has Bastion as her warrior consort. What am I, but a title with a person attached to it?

I don't have long to dwell on my uncertainty. Up ahead, one of the bears strays slightly off of the trail Aria has left in the water. Almost at once, something large, slim, and red darts out from behind a screen of undulating yellow kelp, striking quickly like a frog's tongue. The bear is quick, even in his clunky aquatic suit, and does a clumsy roll through the water and out of the way.

A closer look at the frond that reached out to him shows the surface is dotted with tiny barbs, similar to those on the exotic plants in Wonderland. There they referred to it as a fly trap. Unbelievably, the fly trap was one of the least-threatening specimens in the Red Queen's garden. The carnivorous white flowers scared me far more.

Between this garden of man-eating plants and our journey through the gyre, this still isn't the most frightening thing I've seen in my life. But it's certainly disquieting to watch the frond grope the air where the bear had been. It shoots out a stream of green droplets that glitter like poisoned gems in the water until the sea dilutes them to the point of uselessness.

"Fuck," Nash rumbles as Kassidy berates him for steering off course. Even trying to be quiet, the brute is loud. "That was too close. You sure this slime will hold?"

"It should," Aria responds in a whisper. "But don't get hit more than once, if you can help it."

That's easier said than done. In the next few minutes, we're forced to dodge several more of the wickedly pointed barbs, shuffling like skittish crabs along the winding trail that Aria weaves through the foliage. One very fraught encounter brings the acid in contact with my slimed skin.

"Dammit!" I say as I wave my hand, trying to divorce myself from the nasty stuff. The glittering droplet burns halfway through the mucus on my arm before fizzing out like a spark. It's several seconds before I'm able to swallow against the hammering of my heart that seems to have become lodged somewhere in my esophagus.

At seeing me snagged by the hideous plant, Aria stiffens, her eyes impossibly huge in her delicate face and her pallor almost ashy. The naked fear on her face cuts me. The last time I've seen her with this sort of expression, she was facing down a massive merman easily double her height and triple her girth.

"Andric," she calls as loudly as she dares. "Andric, are you…"

"Fine," I say, cutting her off as I shake my head, not wanting anyone to panic unnecessarily.

I make a dismissive shooing gesture, urging her forward, trying to marshal my own expression into something comforting. I'm not sure I succeed because she continues to stare at me with concern in her eyes. Yes, she certainly cares for me. I'm just not certain about the depths of her feelings.

But that is a question that will have to remain unanswered because we reach a sweeping ramp that leads down into the gardens.

Aria pauses as her eyes sweep over me once more, concern still evident in their depths. It's easy to forget

that underneath all that truly impressive muscle and
stunning beauty, she's still a woman in the bloom of
youth. In some ways, the most inexperienced of us all.

"Go," I urge quietly.

It costs her something to turn away from me—I
can see as much in the expression she wears. She has to
divorce her concern, a weighty sacrifice revealed in the
set of her shoulders and the proud bearing in her face
just before her profile disappears from view. It touches
me that she cares. Perhaps, someday, she'll feel for me
what I'm beginning to feel for her. It's that bloom of
hope I use to quell my rising panic. We've made it past
the first obstacle that is Andromeda's garden.

Now, to penetrate the castle's defenses.

The first corridor we enter is so breathtaking, the
majority of our party draws in a shocked inhale.
Bastion looks a tad wistful, and while I can't read
Aria's expression from my angle, I assume it must be
similar.

The hall is composed almost entirely of cut and
polished peridotite. The verdant color is a shining
assault to the eyes. Somehow, after the flowing motion
and frenzied activity of the gyre and gardens, the fixed
immobility of the stone seems a little sinister. Probably
my own nerves talking. And even through the tense
coil in my stomach, I can appreciate the beauty of this
place.

A wave-like pattern has been cut into the stone,
the whorls and eddies studded with sapphire,
turquoise, and aquamarine. Where it meets the floor,
the wave pattern shifts in color, composed of smooth,

colored marble. Plum, green, and white run together in abstract swirls that convey a sense of grace.

And this is just an *access corridor*. I can't imagine what sort of obscene displays of wealth await us in the bedchambers and the throne room.

I cut my gaze very briefly to Kassidy, who looks like she's a few minutes away from filling her glass dome with drool. Her jaw swings open slightly, her emerald eyes wide, overall looking as though she's been concussed.

Leith nudges her in the ribs and, though the gesture was meant to be a light tap, it makes her stagger a step.

"Kassidy," he murmurs, his voice almost too low to be heard between his glass face shield and the gentle swoosh of the water through the corridor.

"Sorry," she mumbles, shaking her head as though to knock the sense back into herself. "I think I'm having an orgasm. Fuck me. This place is..."

"Incredible," Hook finishes. When I turn, I see his expression is almost a mirror of hers—awestruck and full of ready avarice. And now I remember why he's called a pirate. The man knows his treasure.

Perhaps his obsession with Aria from the outset should have clued me in to the fact she's a gem. More than a gem. She's the entire treasure.

"We can't dally," Aria reprimands us all lightly. "The trident is in the throne room. We're going to have to create a diversion to draw away enough of my father's guards to make an incursion possible. I'll take Bastion and Hook toward the east wing and disturb my mother's old chambers. Doing so ought to anger my father enough to come deal with me personally. That will give Kassidy enough time to get the trident."

"Not a chance," Kassidy hisses back, shaking her head. "In case you've forgotten, you're one of the Chosen."

"I haven't accepted that as fact," Aria responds grimly. "And even if I am Chosen, what does that have to do with anything?"

"Um, I'm pretty damn sure you can pick up the trident yourself, Princess," Kassidy responds.

"And if I can't?" Aria snaps. "Then I'm stuck holding the useless fork while my father cuts through my friends and lovers. I won't risk it. You have been proven to be Chosen, Kassidy. You need to wield the trident."

Kassidy's jaw flexes stubbornly, and she glares back at Aria. Leith is forced to step between the pair of quarreling women.

"This is pointless, Kassidy. Even if you're right about Aria, it doesn't change the fact that she needs to face her father on her terms. You know a thing or two about disappointing fathers. If you had a chance to go back, would you have ended things differently?"

Kassidy's shoulders slump and she gives Leith a sullen look. "I'd kill my father myself, instead of letting my brothers do it," she mumbles. Then she frowns. "Well-played, Leith. I'm so getting you back for that when we reach Delorood."

Hunger stirs in Leith's eyes when he stares down at her and his voice comes out with a husky note of promise when he speaks. "Looking forward to it, Goldilocks."

Kassidy can't contain a shiver at his words and poorly hides a smirk before glancing at the other two. They're staring back at her with equal hunger. Three guesses what they'll be up to if we survive the next few hours. I doubt they'll even wait until Delorood— they'll probably find a nice unoccupied shack on Cassio Island and bed down there for a day or three. I can't blame them. If we do survive, I plan to demand a thorough tour of the castle from the new queen and see if I can coax her into christening every room with me.

One can wish.

We start down the corridor, the human or near-human members of our party walking across the marble floors out of habit. We've spent so much time in the open water, being attacked from all sides, there's something comforting about settling our feet on something solid. The marble is cool beneath my bare feet. Unlike Hook, I didn't come prepared—I never anticipated swimming without my apparatus. Thus, I'm only wearing a skintight suit that barely keeps the cold away.

And that's why I notice the muck on the ground first. Most of the party have their eyes focused ahead or behind, watching for intruders. Kassidy's attention is split between her lustful appreciation of her men, with a fair dash of lust directed at our lavish surroundings. I don't think it's truly malicious on her part, just ingrained during her many years as a Guild thief. I was raised in luxury and even I'm having trouble refocusing my attention.

I jerk my foot back instinctively, catching myself before I can groan in disgust as the muck coats the bottom of it. It's a light golden color, which is the only reason I don't immediately assume it's shit. That, and I don't think even the most classless boor would be able to shit on these floors.

My reaction draws the nearest bear's eyes to me, and he follows my gaze down to the floor with a frown.

"What's that?" Sorren asks.

I shrug. "I wish I knew." Or, perhaps I don't.

He pauses, hunkers down and swipes two metal-clad fingers through the goop. I almost tell him not to, given that most things beneath the sea seem easily able to disintegrate the suits. Nothing catastrophic happens, though. Sorren just frowns down at the stuff as he studies it.

"It's organic matter of some sort."

"Right you are," a voice drawls.

And from around the corner steps a tall, well-built man.

No... that description doesn't do him justice. He's a golden-skinned man with flaming yellow and orange hair and eyes blazing with white-gold bursts. He appears around the corner as if he's the sun punching through the clouds on a winter day. He radiates such immense light and heat that the rounded corridor abruptly feels like the stem of a pipe. His presence stabs at my eyes and I can't look at him for more than a second or two. The water boils off him, so he's standing in a bubble of open air that hovers a foot around his person.

I know who I'm looking at, and it's enough to stomp out any sliver of hope of survival I might have held. He visited our kingdom just once, to negotiate terms of preemptive surrender with my father. His visit was the very thing that had convinced me we needed to side with the Guild.

"Lar," I breathe.

The brother of the god, Sol. The second most powerful god of light Fantasia has ever had the displeasure to know.

The light of Lar's smile reflects painfully off every stone in the hall. For a few seconds, I think the black shapes that dance in my vision are the beginnings of blindness. Then, they resolve themselves, and I wish it were something so benign.

Thirty more enormous eels swarm around him, like flickering, deadly shadows conjured by his light. He kicks something toward us and I see, my stomach sinking down to my toes, that it's a crate of Ambrosia. The one Kassidy had assumed lost. Triton's men must have found it, and now Lar knows what we've been up to. Which means Morningstar will know as soon as he emerges. There will be no mercy for us now.

We win, here and now, or we die.

Lar lovingly traces a finger along the back of a nearby eel and its fins flare an angry red-orange in response.

"You're responsible for those... abominations?" Aria spits at him.

Lar turns to face her with a wicked grin. "I consider them my offspring. Eels specially engineered to attack and kill anyone who opposes Triton."

"They're as revolting as you are," Aria responds.

"Feast, my pets," Lar purrs. "Leave the princess' head for Andromeda. I think Triton's wife would like to mount it to her bedroom wall."

The eels seethe like living darkness down the corridor toward us. We have only seconds to react, so I do the only thing I can. I lunge forward, seizing Hook's arm at the same time he grabs Aria's. Then I yank hard, pulling them both out of the way of Lar and the eels, even as Aria takes the lead and drags us away at inhuman speed.

Kassidy and the bears will have to fend for themselves.

TWENTY-ONE
HOOK

Never thought I'd find myself grateful to the little shite who cut off my hand. My time as an immortal pirate and irredeemable scallywag has prepared me for much, but not losing a limb. And especially not this... fucking *insanity* I've been embroiled in since meeting my lovely princess.

But I find myself grateful for Pan and the fucking crocodile as Andric and I are forced to face down the eels coming for Aria. The tissues around the stump are mostly numb, which is a good thing because it means I won't feel pain from the metal hook, which means the reinforced fae-spelled thing is the best weapon I have against the eels. Can't burn my hand on a weapon, the way Andric does.

Angry blisters pop up along his skin anywhere he touches his sword, but the stubborn prince doesn't drop it. Lad's courageous and damn tough. Not bad, for a Prince. I suppose Aria could do worse for a husband.

No time to wade through the stew of unpleasant emotions that thought brings up.

The mucus keeps the worst of the heat off my skin, and even so, I feel like a lobster stuffed into a boiling pot. We streaked away in one direction while Kassidy, Bastion, and the bears went another. The eels are so fast, I would not believe it were I not seeing it with my own eyes.

But Aria is equally so. She outdoes herself, dragging us along at her top speed, and yet the eels are still only a foot behind us—and are gaining incrementally every time we're forced to take a corner or ascend a chute leading up a level in the castle. For one or two bewildered seconds, I didn't understood why there were no stairs. But, of course, no feet. So stairs are unnecessary.

I lunge, sticking the nearest of the eels with the curved point of my hook. It's more difficult than it should be to wound the fuckers. Their skin is like rubber, thick and hard to penetrate, even with a blade. But when the point does sink in, I wrench the hook across its throat, tearing through the fat and sinew until its stubby head hangs limply off the side of its neck. The red-orange glow of its fins dies and it floats limply down toward the marble floor.

Andric and I have killed a pair each, but that still leaves eleven of the things pursuing us. Our surroundings flash by, not so pretty now that the murals and gem-lined walls reflect the scene of terror back to us in nightmarish shades of red and gold.

"Where are we going?" Andric pants, volume stolen by the effort it takes to hold onto his burning sword. Blisters cover his hands.

I'm not sure even one of Tenebris' vaunted healing potions could heal the damage done to him. The poor lad's going to have scarring for the rest of his life. We come out of this alive and I'll christen him with his own Neverland moniker. Call him Scar, mayhap.

Doubt he'll appreciate the title for the honor it is, but he's earned something for saving Aria twice now. For being there when I wasn't...

"Throne room," Aria says after a moment. The strain is beginning to sound in her tone. She can't maintain this speed forever.

"Are you sure?" Andric asks.

She nods. "We have nothing to lose. If Kassidy's wrong about the trident, we die. If we stay here, we die."

Inescapable logic, in my book.

Lar turns the corner just as we begin to slow, preparing to ascend to a higher level. The gardens brought us in at a sub-level, and we have at least another story to climb before we reach the throne room. It's that change in velocity that saves our lives.

A beam of white light lances from Lar's finger, thin as fishing line, but more deadly than a cannonball. It streaks through the water, missing us by mere inches, and blows a hole the size of long nine in the marble pillar we just passed. The stone flies apart, spitting debris all over the fine floors. A chunk the size of an apple hits one of the eels and knocks it senseless, sending the thing pooling on the ground like black ribbon. Another strikes me in the thigh so hard, it steals my breath. A soft cry to my right tells me Andric was hit, as well. Poor fucker. I'll never complain about him to Aria again.

Aria pauses only long enough to allow some of the debris to settle before she's off again, streaking upward in a spiral toward the distant light above, holding each of us by the arm.

I spy a vaulted ceiling and more of the same grand architecture that pervades the castle. This must be the throne room. The pillars here shine like opal, casting patches of shimmering, multi-hued light around the room. What appears to be a delicate, trailing tentacle of gold wraps around the top of the pillar like ivy. As we ascend, I see the rest of the creature's body is constructed of gold, the many tentacles of a kraken statue winding around most of the supporting beams. Clearly, the artist has never seen one of the beasties up close. This thing is delicate and appears quite harmless.

Real krakens are anything but.

We've just cleared the chute when something grabs the front of my swimming costume and yanks me hard enough that my arm almost pops from its socket. I'm forced to release Aria's hand before she's dragged sideways with me and slammed into a pillar. The force of the impact to my head leaves my vision pulsing white for a moment. My body staunchly refuses to register the pain for the first few seconds, and when it finally does catch up with the inevitable, the agony bleeds in slowly.

A long-fingered hand wraps around my throat, smothering the blackened mate mark that allows me to breathe. I seize, thrashing uselessly around the implacable grip my attacker has on my arm.

"Hello, sailor," a woman's voice croons into my ear. "Remember me?"

Ah, fuck.

I *do* remember this voice. So many people have tried to end me, the names and faces tend to blur

together. Only a few truly stand out—the Lost Boys,
Agatha, the Unseelie King, Septimus, and this bitch.
Andromeda.

I suppose some would consider her fair. She's
objectively bonny, with the same silvery sheen to her
skin that Aria sports. She's also got an upturned nose
and a full mouth, but that's where the similarities end.
This woman's hair shines a white-blonde, the way it
had when she tried to lure me into the cove all those
years ago. Her eyes are the flat black of rubbery eel
skin. That struck me, too, when I saw her the first time.

"Let him go, Andromeda!" Aria shrieks in the
distance.

I have to wrench my neck to peer around my
captor's head. Aria has been hauled across the throne
room. The place is cavernous, easily double or triple
the size of the great hall in Andric's castle. The floors
are made of more polished stone, this time some sort of
volcanic glass. Three more sirens are clustered around
Aria, each pinning some part of her. The smallest of
them jabs a knife at her throat and I thrash harder
when dark blood beads on her skin. Andric is in a
similar position, with two sirens holding him down.

Andromeda turns her head slightly to give Aria a
triumphant smile.

"Thieving little bitch," she says, voice layered with
sweet poison. "This one should have been mine years
ago. Isn't that right, my handsome sailor?"

With a smirk, she trails a finger along my jaw,
then darts a pink tongue out to lick along the line of
stubble down to my neck. I shudder when the fine
edge of her teeth tests my shoulder. When I'm inside

Aria and she bites like this, it's thrilling. I never want to feel this woman's anything on me ever again. Not when this is so clearly a show put on for Aria's detriment.

I can't say any of this out loud, of course. I can't even draw in a breath past her hand that covers the mark. I'm going to drown at this bitch's hands years after I thought I escaped her.

"Enough," a voice booms.

The one word is so loud, I feel its vibrations deep in my bones. The pitch is deep and resonant, and it triggers instinctive terror, like the roll of thunder or the rushing of a million rocks as they pelt down the side of a mountain. When I turn my head, I find the body matches the volume.

The shape on the throne is truly monstrous—twice as tall and broad as any of Kassidy's bears, the entire wide expanse of him layered in ready muscle. His head is completely bald, his face as craggy as a cliff, lacking any of the beauty Aria possesses. It's as if he was hewn directly from stone and is capable of just as much pity.

Triton. It has to be.

Andromeda's grip on my throat loosens just a fraction, but she doesn't release me.

"Triton, my love..." she begins, dripping sugary falseness.

"The mortals are mine to punish or absolve, Andromeda," he tells her, eyes narrowing.

It's jarring to realize they're the same color as Aria's—the same exquisite blue. They shift to me next and I stiffen under their pitiless scrutiny,

unconsciously trying to move away from the eerie
magnetism of them. Power crackles off Triton in
waves. I haven't felt anything so potent since I was
nearly killed by the Unseelie King.

Triton is a demigod, a semi-divine being with
enough power to exert at least some control over the
sea and all the beasties in it. Enough power to pry
open my throat and scour my insides with salt and
boiling water.

"You," he says finally, flicking a finger in my
direction. "You're called Hook, correct?"

The water between my body and Andromeda's
shifts, and she's shoved off me though I don't do the
shoving. The second her hand is off the mark, I suck in
as much air as it will allow, hoarding every precious
molecule of oxygen like it might be my last.

"Aye," I say at last. "What's it to ye, mate?"

I don't like it that Triton knows my name. True,
it's not as though I've gone out of my way to avoid
being known. In the early days of my cursed
immortality, I sought infamy, hunting for danger and
courting poor company. It was the encounter with
Septimus that truly set me on a new course. I'll never
see eye to eye with Pan and his ilk, and I'll still bend
rules to get the job done, but I don't fuck around with
evil any longer.

But perhaps Triton doesn't know that.

The beginnings of a plan begin to take shape in my
mind. My eyes flick very briefly around the room, now
that breathing is no longer a chore. There's a seating
area behind the pillars where subjects likely gather
when Triton holds court, and several smaller thrones

are scattered in the shadowy alcove behind him.
Shelves full of treasures ascend in rows to the vaulted
ceiling. And beyond that, at the zenith of the room,
whirls a fantastically complex orrery, its delicate
moving parts done up in a metal that doesn't tarnish.
The spinning spheres within are represented by
gemstones as big as my head. Topaz for Venus, a
sapphire for the Earth, a ruby for Mars, and so on and
so forth, with diamonds reflecting the light from above
like stars.

A month ago, I'd have traded my remaining hand
for a chance to loot this place — to collect even one of
the stones and steal away, setting my crew up for life,
then sail the sea until the world ended. Now? All I
want is to escape this room with Aria and Andric alive.

I spy the trident in its glass case spinning at the
center of the artificial universe. I need to get that
blasted thing to Aria, and there's only one way to do
so.

I have to hurt her. Fuck it all.

"I'm surprised to see you've thrown in with my
cunt of a daughter," Triton continues, eyes barely
flicking to Aria when he says the words. Hate echoes
through them. The vulgar word causes my remaining
hand to ball into a fist, ready to slam into the anvil-like
side of Triton's jaw. It'll probably break my hand but
fuck, it'd be worth it.

I push the desire down with a vengeance. I have to
make this work. "Who says I have?"

Aria's sharp intake of breath spears me, and I can't
bring myself to look at her face. If I see the anguish

257

carried in that one small sound playing out in her expression, I'll never be able to do this.

One of Triton's brows juts upward. They're thick and as enormous as the rest of him. "You bear her mark."

"Aye, but I didnae ask for it, mate."

"Then how did you come to get it?"

"One o' yer beasties batted me ship into the sea. Woke up with this thing on me neck an' the lass rubbin' on me leg like a bitch in heat."

"Hook!" My name comes out of Aria's mouth on a sob. Gods, I can't do this... what if she believes my words? What if she doesn't realize what I'm doing?

She's never going to forgive me.

Triton's smile is shark-like, and his laugh shakes me down to my bones. "Is that so?"

"Aye, 'tis true. Needed her to get off the damn island an' thought I might get some loot so I could rebuild the *Jolly Roger.*"

"Your ship?"

"Aye, me ship. Yer feckin' monsters destroyed it."

He nods, a smirk hiding on his lips. "Apologies."

"Ye have any idea how difficult it is to get fae craftsmanship now that the crazy feckers have wiped out the Seelie?"

"And you thought robbing my palace would endear you to me?" Triton asks.

"Wasnae aboot ye. Just lookin' for treasure, an' a good fuck to boot. Happy to take a pardon an' an escape now, though."

"I will kill you," Andric seethes as he glares at me. "You say another fucking word about Aria, and I swear to all the Gods I'll…"

There's no warning, no fanfare, no speech, the way villains do things in the stories.

Triton simply turns slightly in his chair and raises a length of jewel-encrusted stone as long as my forearm and points the tip at Andric. In the same second, Andric recoils as though he's been struck hard in the stomach and part of his flank simply *disappears.*

Blood billows into the water like a plume of scarlet smoke and Aria screams.

I'm frozen solid, staring in horror at the wounded prince. I've seen my share of battlefield injuries; the lad's got minutes left to live. Probably less. Fuck!

Triton lowers the scepter and turns his implacable gaze back to me, those cold eyes fixing once more on my face even as a cruel smile alights on his lips.

"Sorry for the interruption, pirate. You were saying?"

It takes me several crucial seconds to collect myself. I can't tear my eyes off Andric for long. The sirens holding him have let his body drop, trailing blood as he sinks toward the obsidian floor.

"Right. I was sayin' I dinnae have a problem with ye, King Triton. Nor any o' yer brood."

"I have no argument with you, pirate," Triton says.

"Aye, then keep the daft bint alive long enough for me to use her mark to get to the surface an' I'll never set foot in yer kingdom again. Just want a pardon an' yer promise."

"Only if you give yours first, pirate," Triton says. "You will never return here?"

"I swear it."

He shakes his head. "Swear it to me by your blood."

As if blood means anything to this fucker. "I swear it to ye on me ol' dad's departed soul. If ye oblige me, I will leave here an' never return."

Triton considers me for a few more minutes before nodding to Andromeda. She approaches again, shoulders slumped and her full mouth set into a childlike pout that spoils her fair face. She's like a petulant child. Her hands wander over my backside, squeezing it once out of Triton's sight as she escorts me up to the throne.

"You will kneel at my feet and swear again, pirate. And you will kiss the scepter and then perhaps I'll allow you your freedom."

Aria's screams are interspersed with sobs and cries of Andric's name. I'm going to be sick all over the obsidian floors. Fuck, fuck, fuck. That wasn't supposed to happen. Is the princeling still living? He should be screaming in agony with a wound like that. Has he already expired, or is he deep in shock?

I kneel at Triton's feet when prompted, back stiffening when he leans over me with that scepter. He can blow my head off so easily. I'm tensed and ready for a killing blow, though every second I pray I get through this alive. Aria's last memory of me should not be one of a cowardly escape attempt.

"Ye know," I say conversationally, lifting my head as he begins to lean over me, "Ye're nae too bright, ye bleedin' bastard."

He blinks, fat brows squeezing together in confusion.

"Me father was a fecker, a lot like yerself," I tell him in a stage whisper. "Want an oath from me? 'Tis me brother I swear by."

And then I lunge up from my crouched position, scoring his face with my hook, turning those enormous, inhuman eyes into a ruin of blood and slurry.

Triton roars.

Andromeda lunges for me.

And I dive for Andric at the very second Kassidy and the others spill into the room, bringing light, thunderous sound, and the remaining eels with them.

Andromeda misses me by inches and I lodge a fist just beneath her impressive bustline, putting as much power as I can behind the punch. I hear something crack and the siren gives a breathless shriek that claws at every nerve in my skull. My muscles lock and I freeze solid, wasting more of my dwindling supply of seconds before the cry cuts off and I'm able to move again.

I reach Andric's side just as the two sides clash above me. The fine cloud of blood—now alarmingly large—drifts lazily around Andric, and I can taste it on my tongue as I kneel by his side. It sinks into my clothing and will probably stain it. Good. I deserve to bear the stain of his death if this doesn't work. Summoning the last of my strength, I use my bloodied hook to scrape a layer of the slime off my skin, recalling Aria's earlier words.

"Applied topically, the mucus can extend life for many years. And injected or swallowed, it can put someone into a death-sleep."

"Dinnae die on me, mate," I growl before shoving the wad of the vile stuff into his mouth.

To my relief, he swallows thickly after a few seconds. Then, he goes utterly still, eyes fixed. For a horrible second, I think I'm too late. But then he blinks several more times, and his chest rises and falls, taking in air through Aria's mate mark.

Thank the fucking Gods.

Blinding white light strikes the pillar nearest me. I barely have time to look up before a chunk the size of a croquet ball bashes me in the side of the head and my vision dims, the roaring in my ears dulls, and I barely feel it when my head hits the floor.

TWENTY-TWO
ARIA

When Hook's head hits the ground with a crack and he settles limply beside Andric, I lose control of myself and scream as wild anger burns through me, combined with grief and worry the likes of which I've never experienced before.

I can't lose them. I can't lose either one of them. Not like this.

I scream loud and long, and with such intensity, it makes the water in the throne room froth in agitation. Andromeda's surprised wail sounds like a whistled tune in comparison.

Every creature in the throne room comes to a stop. Every single one of them. My sisters, my stepmother, my newly arrived allies, and even Triton are fixed in place for a suspended moment. The swarming eels halt in place, their flaming colors strobing wildly in response to the sound. Even Lar's eyes fly open wide. He's the only one in motion.

He raises another finger and sends a jet of light streaking toward my father, before he sees my father's shredded and useless eyes.

"Attack her, you blind fucking fool!" Lar yells out at him. "She's…"

My father raises his scepter and looses a bolt of power that sizzles through the water and sends Lar through a supporting wall and into the antechamber beyond. Then, he spins around, faster than the human eye can track, and unleashes another bolt in my direction.

A scream sounds in my throat, though the fury raging inside me is far from satisfied. I dart upward as fast as my battered body will take me, feeling the burn in every single muscle. I keep myself moving forward through sheer, unadulterated contrariness.

The orrery has begun moving again, the spheres whirling round and round the center with metronomic precision. The light catches every stone as they pass the moon roof. It's just as beautiful as I remember.

When I was a girl, I would sneak past the guards at night to lay on the cold obsidian floor of the throne room and stare up at the orrery. My mother had been something of an astronomer, and she'd had it commissioned before her death. At times, it felt like the orrery was all I had left of her. I'd stare up at the beauty of the dance of false stars and think of her.

And it's thoughts of her now that push past my final resistance. Triton has taken everything from me, one way or the other. My mother, my home, my people, my birthright—and he would take the men I love if he's able.

I can't let that happen.

I reach the strut of the first sphere just as Triton releases another bolt. It collides with the mammoth topaz gem of the orrery and the stone flies apart in an incredible explosion, sending pieces of fractured gem and metal hurtling down toward the distant floor. It shreds many of the eels just below me into ribbons, leaving the few remaining in no shape to continue their pursuit. Another blast, and Neptune's gem erupts as well. Triton is firing blindly, but correctly assuming I'm above him, questing for the trident. Probability says he'll hit me soon.

I push my shoulder against the boulder-like shape of the ruby that symbolizes Mars, trying to heave it off its titanium ring. It takes me three tries, even drawing on the power reserves that I've been told I possess. I've always been too afraid to dip my toes into that particular reservoir, certain a monster lurks beneath. Now, I'm counting on that monster to end something far worse.

Finally, the ruby rolls free of the ring.

I spin, using my tail to bat the massive rock, with as much strength as I can muster, toward the box at the center of the orrery.

As I suspected, the damn thing is enchanted. The ruby sails past the wards and begins to shrink as layers of it flake off and disintegrate like tissue in water. Still, the momentum carries it forward. It's about the size of my fist when it hits the glass, but it's enough. The glass shatters, sending more deadly rain down to the floor. The trident floats free in the air. I reach my magic toward it and pull.

Now is the time of reckoning. If I'm not able to wield the trident, I will die and so will all the people I care about.

Please, let me be one of the Chosen, I whisper to myself. *Let me hold the trident!*

The trident spins once in midair, handle down, and streaks toward my outstretched hand. The metal warms on contact with my fingers and a sensation of intense joy settles over me, though it's the last thing in the world I want to feel.

It worked! I can't ponder what this means or the reasons why I'm floating here, able to hold the trident in my hands. I still have too much to do…

The power of the trident is immense and thrums in time with my blood, pulsing that feeling of absolute rightness through the rest of me.

I fear nothing, the power hums into my ear. *I am a goddess. All mortals will bow before the might of the sea.*

The thought is so alien, though the voice sounds like my own, that I nearly drop the trident. This thing is… aware. And evil? No… not evil exactly. But primordial. Arrogant. Beyond reason and capable of great destruction if wielded by the wrong person. It needs a strong and a level-headed master to curb that power.

How can I possibly be worthy of bearing it?

I don't know but at the moment, I'm the only one capable of wielding it.

Triton aims his scepter upwards again and sends a current of power at me that blows twenty feet of the roof off.

It's then that I see Bastion as he just manages to dive and seize Andric and Hook, moving them before the section of stone flattens them. Kassidy and her men quickly take the two injured men off Bastion's hands and I barely hear him shout over the groaning of the ceiling. Triton's strikes threaten to bring the ceiling down on all of us.

"Get them to Bridgeport!" Bastion yells and he's right. It's the only place I can think of that where they'll be safe.

"Aria needs our help!" Kassidy replies hotly.

"What am I, three-day old chum?" Bastion shoots back. "I've got her. Go, before either one dies!"

I'm glad someone is thinking, because I'm far beyond the reach of reason at this point.

Finally, Kassidy seizes one of Hook's limp arms and one of her bear husbands, though I can't tell which at this distance, takes Hook easily into his arms and scissor kicks as hard and fast as he can out of the hole Triton blew into the ceiling. Another follows, bearing Andric, who's still trailing blood. Gods, I hope they don't attract any sharks.

Bastion brings a blade to bear. With its jewel encrusted scabbard, it looks at home in the formerly lavish interior of the throne room. I know it belongs to Hook, because I've seen it laid out among his things. I don't think he'll begrudge Bastion the use of it now.

"Get Andromeda, Piper, and the rest to safety, Bastion," I say as he swims beside me.

"Fuck no," he snaps back, glaring at the side of my face. "I'm not leaving you."

I lean in, being careful of the trident and press a brief but fervent kiss to his lips. "Please," I beg. "I need you safe and my sisters don't deserve to die."

"They abandoned you."

"Everyone abandoned me, Bastion. Everyone but you. And that's why I need you to leave. I love you. If you die, I can't..."

Grief strangles the end of my sentence and I trail off, a silent wail battering the inside of my chest. At the beginning of this day, I had three men… three men I loved — and if things continue the way they have been, I'm unlikely to have any by the time Triton is done with me.

Looking stricken, Bastion swallows hard a few times to keep himself from arguing, then finally nods.

"Don't you dare fucking die on me, Aria," he whispers. "Not when we've just begun."

"I promise I won't. Now go."

With a sound of frustration, he whirls and dives once more, narrowly avoiding another blast from Triton's scepter. My father tries to use sound to guide him but it's a tricky thing in water, not quite as easy to locate as sound is on land. The blast blows apart his throne and shatters more of his treasures on the shelves behind it. Andromeda shrieks in fear as a weighted scale impacts her with incredible speed.

Bastion exchanges a few words with her I can't hear, but they must be persuasive because, the next instant, she disappears down the hall with him, trailed by my sisters. A knot of fear in my chest loosens when I'm sure they're gone.

"Where are you!" Triton roars when his most recent attack fails to hit me.

"I wield the trident, Father. I can end this here and now."

He bares his needle-teeth in a snarl. "You? The trident would never accept you as a master, you mewling little bitch. Even self-righteous Cassiopeia couldn't claim it."

"Last chance, Father. Surrender to me now and I'll trap you beneath the ice caps in the far north. Fight me, and you die."

In answer, he thrusts the scepter up toward me, a furious spiral of foaming water at its tip as a whirlpool begins and spreads rapidly outward. It's a favorite trick of his to use against hated foes—draw them near and crush their skulls between his massive hands until their brains slop out like sea slugs to the floor.

I twirl the trident into its ready position, tines pointed toward the rapidly expanding whirlpool. Glass, gemstones, stone, and various shattered treasures are caught in the current and spin like pottery on a wheel, but I'm not drawn in. The trident is like an anchor, keeping me firmly locked where I am.

The metal begins to glow silver-blue, the power of the ocean threatening to crush me flat as I loose one bolt—just a single bolt, the same size and intensity as one of Lar's light beams, cast into the center of that swirling storm. It's carried down through the water like a funnel straight to Triton and impacts a second later, splitting his stone scepter down the middle before the power touches his flesh.

Triton bursts.

Simply explodes into bits of blood, bone, and silvery skin, leaving no pieces larger than a fingernail.

The storm ceases, every object settling lazily in the wake of the attack. Lar appears then, watching the debris and pieces of his ally settle to the floor in front of me with a look of quiet horror dawning across his lucent face. I adjust my grip on the trident, aiming for him next.

Kill the intruder, the voice of the trident agrees. *The heavens have no place in the sea.*

Maybe I could have killed Lar. Maybe I couldn't have. I'll never know, because he flees the second I move toward him, streaking away as fast as his namesake. He's gone in mere moments. I'm left standing alone among the wreckage of the throne room, with nothing but debris and corpses for company.

The sea is placid.

I am not.

The sense of alien calm the trident imbued within me during the battle seeps away, and a wail escapes my mouth. I want to be on land so I can release the flood of salty water that builds behind my eyes. I need the catharsis of tears. Instead, I sink to the ground, tail folding beneath me as I'm hammered by grief.

I won.

But I also lost.

Lost Hook, lost Andric.

It's not worth it. No victory is worth their lives.

Gentle hands take me by the shoulders and pull me up. I barely have the strength to look up, and my eyes are slow to focus when I do.

Bastion's hands settle into my hair, petting me softly until the edge of pleasure pushes back the tide of sorrow that beats against me. His eyes are soft, full of understanding.

"You're alive," I whisper.

"Yes," he says with a soft smile.

"It hurts," I gasp. It's not an adequate explanation, but I'm beyond words. I can't explain the complexity of the feeling. "Bastion, it hurts."

"I know, Aria. I've got you."

Then his strong arms close around my shoulders and slide beneath my tail, pulling me up from the floor like I'm a mere fingerling.

I nestle my head into his shoulder, trying to ignore the death and destruction surrounding me.

TWENTY-THREE
BASTION
Two Days Later

Aria is nearly catatonic for the next two days.

She barely reacted when she was pulled ashore, except to shiver from the cold. A storm front swept in, backwash from the level of power she called upon to defeat Triton. Fortunate for us, though, because it curbed the amount of energy Lar could draw upon as he fled. Reports say he still blazed a path of destruction along the shore of Delorood, leaving most fishing boats razed to ash and at least fifteen dead before he left the country's borders.

Opeia had to guide Aria briefly to reinforce the spell that contains the grotesquerie. Then she cast the enchantment to give Aria legs again, legs so she could go to Andric and Hook to ensure they were being properly cared for. I was given legs again as well, to keep watch over Aria.

Hook pulled through, opening his eyes the evening after we arrived on land. He's got one hell of a knot on his head and the physicians say he's almost certainly sustained a concussion. He doesn't move quickly, light bothers him, and he rests often, but he's alive.

Andric is another matter, however.

Hook's quick thinking saved the prince's life, in a way. The mucus Andric ingested will keep him at the point of death until he can be healed. But there's no telling when that will be. Regardless, he can't serve as king to Aria's queen now.

After Andric's condition was discovered by his father and kingdom, it looked like we might take the blame for the state of affairs we found ourselves in, but cooler heads eventually prevailed. Andric's father wrestled a promise from Aria, one she was only too willing to keep.

Andric's body had to be kept safe, and all indicators led the king's counsel to believe Delorood would continue to be targeted now that the sea had been conquered by our side.

Furthermore, Bridgeport's strategic position meant it would be a prime target when Morningstar eventually broke from his prison. So, Andric couldn't remain in his kingdom. Aria promised to take him safely away as soon as Hook was well enough to travel.

Now, Opeia is regent in the sea, until Aria returns from her voyage, at which time Aria will take her father's throne and rule the ocean as she was meant to do.

As regards the prince, Aria plans to entrust his body to the only authority the people of Delorood trust besides their own rulers.

Huntsmen.

The four houses still loyal to the Order of Aves have agreed to keep Andric's body safe in their stronghold until a solution can be found. Good for Andric and Aria. Awful for me, because I'm to stay here.

Aria catches me scowling out at the water, though I've been trying to hide my displeasure from her all evening. I lean against the railing that runs the length of the bow of Hook's new vessel, the *Siren's Song,* which he named for Aria. It's newly built, the process expedited by Opeia and Aria, who funded the operation with the spheres from the orrery that survived Triton's attack.

Broken down, the boulder-sized hunks of silver and gold meant to symbolize the sun and moon will keep Delorood's economy funded for years, and that doesn't include the surviving gems of the same size. The cost for Hook's ship was a mere drop in the bucket. It hadn't even made the counsel blink to hire a sorceress to enchant it to fly, as per Hook's request.

"You're angry with me," Aria murmurs, coming to stand beside me, leaning her weight against the rail as well.

"Concerned," I correct her. "This is dangerous, Aria. I don't like sending you away from Delorood. Not now."

Not since we've heard tales that the seals holding Morningstar back are degrading further. Lar got out, and it's rumored Sol may be out, as well. The seals are thin, and I need to be at Aria's side if Morningstar breaks through.

"I'll have the trident and Kassidy will be with me. Two Chosen against Lar? I don't think he'll risk it."

"You'll be far from your seat of power. You should let me make the trip to see the Huntsmen with Hook."

She smooths the front of my coat. The thing is royal blue and trimmed with white and green, like the nation's flag, designed to be worn by the King of Delorood. It's meant to be Andric's, not mine. I'm no king. But apparently everyone thought it a fucking brilliant idea to make me regent on land while Opeia is regent in the sea.

Months or years trapped in this human shell, only seeing Aria during scheduled visits? The idea makes me shudder. But I'll do it. For her, and for Andric. The prince proved himself and he deserves to come back to an intact people. Aria trusts me; I'll have to trust that she knows what she's doing.

"I'll protect her, mate," Hook says quietly from his position behind the wheel.

I flick a glance at him over my shoulder. He's paler than usual, still not entirely returned to himself. His healing will be a long road. I wish I could find it in myself to dislike him, as I used to, but I can't. I'm too grateful to him. He saved Andric. I'll owe Hook for that for so long as I live, because it's the only thing that gives my princess peace of mind.

"You'd better, fucking scallywag," I mutter.

"I swear it by me brother, Quinn. I'll bring Aria back safely. May a crocodile eat the rest o' me if I fail."

A smile ghosts across my face. "I'll hold you and the crocodile to it."

"Stop brooding, Bastion," Aria coaxes, fisting her hand more firmly in the lapel of my coat. "Come to the cabin with us."

My cock stirs at her words. Aria has been promising for days that, on the eve of the journey,

275

she'll treat Hook and me to a night we won't forget. It's bittersweet, as Andric isn't capable of joining us like she would have wanted, but I can't deny I've been looking forward to it. It's wrong, but the thought of having her human body in more than illusion has been occupying my dreams for longer than I care to admit.

I cast another glance at Hook, who grins at me, making an "after you" gesture toward Aria. She's so fucking beautiful in one of the gowns human women wear. This one is pale gold and flickers like candlelight as she moves, the fabric whispering along her pale calves. Odd that I missed her long legs so much.

"Kings before scallywags, mate," he says with a knowing look.

He knows what I want to do, and he'll let me. The fucking deviant. I can't help another smile. Aria answers it with a soft, sad one of her own.

"Give me a proper goodbye, Bastion. Make me feel it tomorrow morning."

I seize her waist, drawing her into my chest as my mouth comes down to cover hers in a kiss that could scorch the sails above us to cinders.

"As my queen commands."

EPILOGUE
ARIA

Kassidy's reunion with her brothers looks more akin to a brawl than an actual greeting. I've only ever had sisters and have never been close to any of them, so I can't say if this is normal or not.

She hits the first of the two broadside and almost tackles him to the ground before he catches himself, planting his back foot to recover, and swings her around to dangle over the side of the dock.

"Some Chosen you are," he mocks with a grin. "Still telegraphing your lunges, little sister? I should drop you in the harbor."

"Don't you fucking dare, Titus!" Kassidy growls, baring her teeth in a kitten-like snarl of defiance. But beneath the threat, there's a hint of laughter. "I'll drag you down with me!"

Titus is handsome and purely masculine. He's both stocky and broad and stands perhaps just under six feet. The bulk makes him look a little disproportionate, though it does have its own sort of charm when you get used to it. His hair is ash brown with just a streak of red sweeping through it to break up the dark color. It's probably shoulder-length when down, but he has it tied in a messy bun at the nape of his neck.

A long-suffering sigh draws my attention to the second brother. He's easy to miss when standing near

Titus. He tends to keep utterly still, only moving when he has to, and as slender as the sword for which Kassidy tells us he's named. Well over six feet tall, he towers above both Titus and Kassidy, though it's not a difficult feat with the latter.

His hair is snowy white, but there's not a single line on his handsome face. While he barely looks older than twenty, I know he has to be twice that in order to have fought in the last war. Like Titus, there's a stripe of unnatural color running through his waist-length braid, a startling blue this time.

"Titus, put her down before we start attracting attention," Sabre chastises quietly. "This tradeoff is going to be difficult enough as it is."

He's right, of course. People are already staring at our ship, though we've tried to be as inconspicuous as possible. Flying the royal flag of another nation will tend to do that. Heaven help us if they find out what cargo we're giving the huntsmen. It seems fundamentally wrong to fold Andric up like a quilt and shove him into a crate to be shipped away, but we can't risk exposing him. It will be too easy for some bandit to steal his body and extort Delorood if they have any inkling what the huntsmen are here for.

It's with much difficulty that I agreed to hand Andric over to the huntsman. Andric truly owns a piece of my heart, ever since he proved his courage and his love for me, I realized what an incredible man he is. Actually, that's not true—I'd always known what Andric was made of, even if I didn't want to reveal as much to myself.

But, the truth is I love him. I love him just as much as I love Hook and Bastion. And I love the three so much, I completed the unfinished mate marks on each one of them. And it was an easier conversation than I'd thought it would be.

Maybe it was owing to the intense drama that had unfolded in my childhood palace, but both Bastion and Hook had dropped their differences and they'd both agreed to share me. I'd already known such would be the case with Andric so I wasn't concerned that he wasn't able to partake of the conversation.

It had come as a surprise that Hook had decided to stay with me, after his decision never to bed another queen again. Perhaps it was his fondness for Andric that caused his change of heart? I'm not sure, as Hook never did say and he doesn't appear eager to discuss his reasons.

And that is fine by me—Hook's reasons can remain his alone. I'm just beyond joyful to be able to call him my own, as well as Bastion and Andric.

I'm pulled out of my reverie as I watch Titus swing Kassidy back over the deck as he drops her with a good-natured laugh. She punches him hard in the bicep, which only makes him laugh harder. Kassidy's men watch all of this all with amusement, and I with bemusement.

What a strange family.

Hook and I unload Andric ourselves, guiding the long packing crate toward the back of the huntsmen's waiting carriage. It seems wrong for anyone else to do it, even Kassidy or her bears. Andric is my lover and, Hook can grudgingly admit, his friend.

This is our burden.

I kiss the wooden exterior before the carriage is sealed up. It's all I can do under the circumstances, and it falls woefully short. And although Andric's alive, I can't help but feel I've failed him.

"Guard him well for us, Sabre," Kassidy says, smile slipping when things have been settled.

"We cannot," Sabre says after a moment of hesitation. "That responsibility will fall to Bishop, I'm afraid. We have a mission elsewhere."

He lifts his hand to show Kassidy a signet ring. On it is the image of a small bird in flight, and the symbol glows blue-white. The ring is active, meaning there's a hunt afoot.

Kassidy blinks once in shock.

"Who is it?"

"A Gryphus huntsman bound for Ascor."

"Why Ascor?" she asks.

Sabre nods. "He's been sent to kill Princess Carmine before her wedding."

The Happily Never After Series
To Be Continued in…
ROSE
NOW AVAILABLE!

Other Series by H.P. Mallory

Paranormal Women's Fiction Series:
Haven Hollow
Midlife Spirits
Midlife Mermaid

Paranormal Shifter Series:
Arctic Wolves

Paranormal Romance Series:
Underworld
Lily Harper
Dulcie O'Neil
Lucy Westenra

Paranormal Adventure Series:
Dungeon Raider
Chasing Demons

Detective SciFi Romance Series:
The Alaskan Detective

Academy Romance Series:
Ever Dark Academy

Reverse Harem Series:
Happily Never After
My Five Kings

Get FREE E-Books!

It's as easy as:

1. Go to my website: www.hpmallory.com
2. Sign up in the pop-up box or on the link at the top of the home page
3. Check your email!

About the Author:

Plum Pascal (also writing as HP Mallory) is a New York Times and USA Today Bestselling author who started as a self-published author.

She lives in Southern California with her son and a cranky cat, where she's at work on her next book.

Printed in Great Britain
by Amazon